One Wicked Wish

A Scandal in Mayfair Book 1

ANNA CAMPBELL

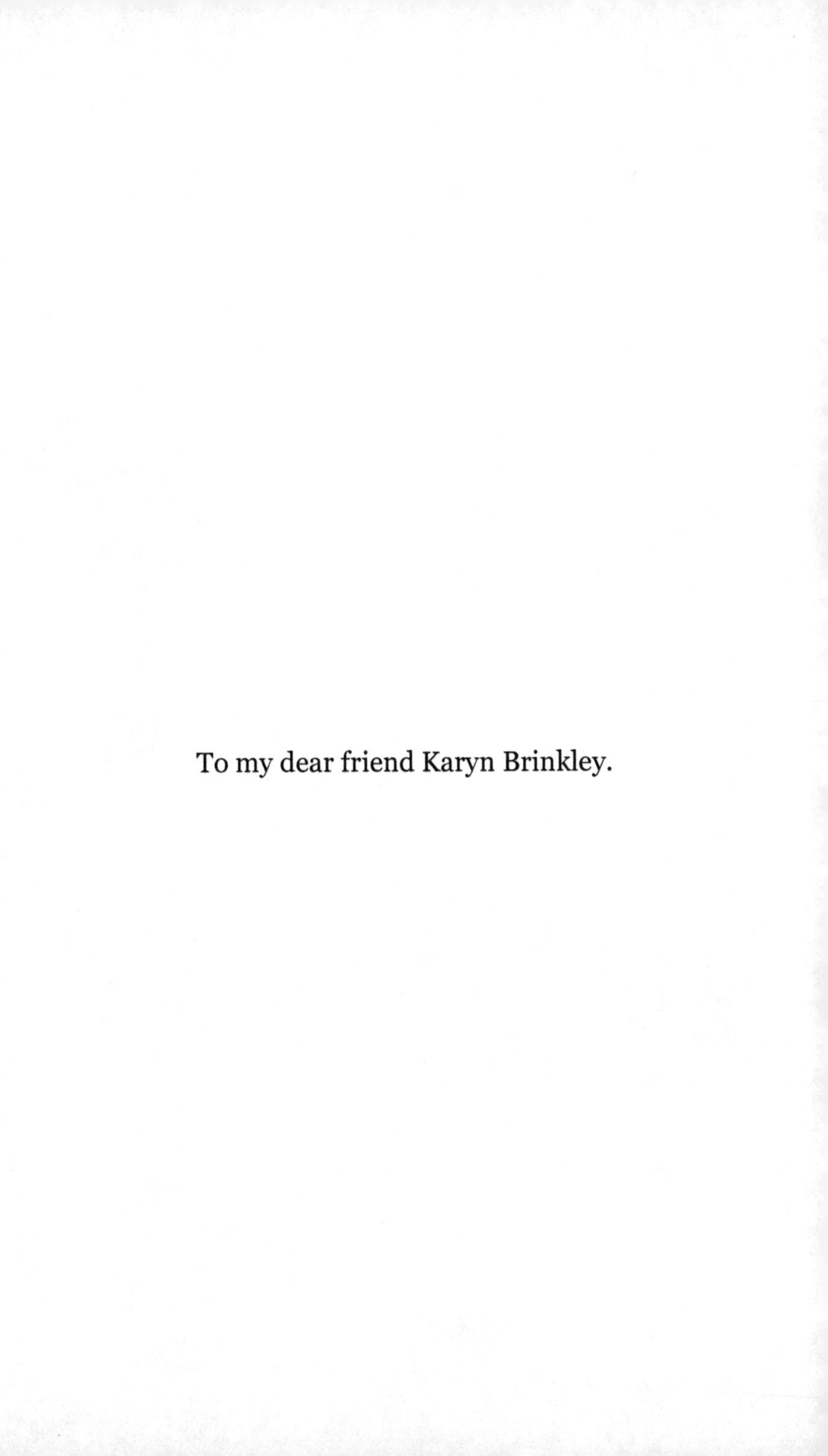

To my dear friend Karyn Brinkley.

CHAPTER ONE

Comerford House, Lorimer Square, Mayfair, London, April 1816

As she slipped through the dark garden, Stella Faulkner pulled her paisley shawl tighter around her shoulders. Like most of her clothes, including the teal gown she wore, the shawl was a hand-me-down from her cousin, Lady Imogen Ridley.

Tonight she didn't much care that the shawl's pink pattern made her complexion look like mud, she was just grateful for the warmth. The calendar might say it was spring. The temperature proclaimed that winter lingered past its welcome.

If her cousin was so determined to rush headlong to ruin, why the deuce couldn't she pick a warmer night to do it in? However cold it was, Stella had to stop her. It was her duty as a chaperone, not to mention that she was sincerely fond for Imogen. She was worried sick about the mess the girl was getting into.

Music and the rise and fall of talk and laughter drifted from the house behind her. Lord and Lady Lumsden hosted one of the most popular balls of the season, so the place was packed with London's great and good.

Not long ago, Stella had hovered on the edge of that glittering crowd, although nobody in their right mind would call her great. And if anyone knew of her past, they'd struggle to think of her as good either.

All the mansions lining Lorimer Square were blessed with large gardens. More in optimism than expectation, Lady Lumsden had placed torches along the paths, in case her guests wished to take the air. The garden remained unfrequented because the air, sadly, was freezing.

Stella shivered again and pulled the shawl even closer. Should her cousin indeed be outside, she'd be turning blue to match her fashionable silk ball gown. If the little minx must elope in April, why the devil didn't she have the nous to leave by daylight and wearing suitable clothes?

Although a daring moonlit flit from a ball would appeal to the girl, Stella supposed. Most harebrained romantic schemes did, plague take the silly chit.

In this distant corner of the garden, torches were fewer and farther between. Stella's vision had adjusted to the dimness, and the full moon helped. Ahead loomed a dark construction that could only be the gazebo she sought. She marched up to it, climbed the half-dozen wooden steps and set foot inside, expecting to surprise the two lovers clasped in each other's arms.

To her dismay, the building was empty.

Tiny flickering lamps in the ancient Roman style lit the small wooden summerhouse. But the glow from the niches didn't reach very far. Stella assumed that was the point. Never in her life had she seen a place more designed for assignation. There was even a brazier filled with hot coals in the middle of the floor, so any adventurous lovers didn't get frostbite.

So where was Imogen? Was Stella too late to stop her from making a terrible mistake? Surely not. It was only a few minutes since she'd seen her cousin disappear from the ballroom, and the letter that Stella had discovered on the girl's dressing table asked her beau to meet her at the gazebo in the Lumsdens' garden at eleven.

All day, Stella had tried to get her cousin on her own so she could talk some sense into her. But Imogen had proven elusive, spending the afternoon with her friend Lily Bilson and arriving at the ball with the Bilsons' party.

With rising apprehension, Stella glanced around the building. What in blazes could she do now?

She supposed if her cousin had already run off, she must tell her uncle, but if she did, the fat would well and truly hit the fire. Was there any chance that Imogen was yet to arrive? Was it worth waiting? Stella would much rather convince the girl in private that running away with a rake was unwise than report her to her surly father.

Her cousin was clever, if inclined to follow her impulses and rue her rashness later. But if one caught her in time, she'd listen to good advice. Sometimes.

Or was Imogen already on her way to Gretna? In that case, perhaps Stella should go back inside and find Imogen's brother Eliot. He might have some idea how to quash a scandal, and he was renowned for his even temper.

At least Eliot wouldn't tear strips off Stella for failing in her duties. He knew his sister was no saint.

Whereas her father had far too rosy a picture of his daughter's docility.

Extending her gloved hands over the brazier and breathing in its scented smoke, Stella struggled to decide whether to betray her cousin or look for her somewhere else. With every second, telling her uncle became the obvious choice.

Then someone would have to chase after Imogen, which meant endless ructions and her cousin's reputation in tatters. Not to mention Stella hauled over the coals because she'd allowed this to happen.

"You're not who I expected to see," a drawling baritone said from the shadows. "At least at first."

Stella started and backed up a few steps on shaky legs. Her eyes darted around the dark space.

A point of red flared from the window seat beneath one of the latticed windows. Whoever shared the space was smoking a cheroot. If the brazier wasn't filled with perfumed pastilles, she'd have smelled the tobacco.

"Show yourself," she said sharply, although a queasy feeling in her stomach told her that she knew who this was.

A long-suffering sigh was the response. She had no difficulty in picturing the superior expression on the man's high-bred face.

A black shape unfolded from the seat and rose with a languid ease that was an insult in itself. Stella could make out enough of the man now to confirm that she was right about his identity.

So she felt no surprise when he stepped into the light. Or what light there was, which wasn't much. "Lord Halston."

Her perfunctory curtsy made his long, expressive mouth curl in sardonic appreciation. "Very polite."

"I've been taught to respect my betters," she said grimly, and knew that neither of them would describe him in those terms.

The earl was tall and lean, and his every movement expressed lazy grace. He was dressed in black, although his white shirt and neckcloth formed pale patches in the gloom.

In this light, his saturnine face was all angles and hollows. But she didn't need illumination to recall those sculpted features and the hooded green eyes that seemed to notice everything. After two weeks of observing him across crowded ballrooms, she was well aware that his indolent air was deceptive.

"I'm awaiting your fair cousin."

Stella was so flustered to find herself alone with Lord Halston that only now did the true significance of his solitude strike her. She released a gasp of relief. Imogen hadn't turned up for the rendezvous. "I'm looking for her, too."

"If you find her, pray tell her that it's bad form to invite a gentleman to a tryst, then fail to appear."

Imogen must have come to her senses before she did anything silly. Thank God. "A pity that she disappointed you," Stella said with a hint of irony.

As he fixed that unreadable gaze on her, the hand holding the cheroot made a dismissive gesture. A black silk sling supported his left arm. For the last few weeks, London had buzzed with tattle about Halston's latest mistress shooting him, after he handed out her marching orders.

"I wouldn't exactly say I'm disappointed. I'm sure you can amuse me perfectly well in your cousin's place. In fact, I might even say I'm delighted with how events have turned out."

Just like that, threat bristled in the air. Nerves pinged in Stella's midriff, as she drew herself up to her full height and glared at him. She was a tall woman, but to her regret, she didn't measure up to Lord Halston, who was well over six feet.

"I doubt it, my lord." Her voice was almost as cold as the air. "How will your reputation as a rake survive, if people find out that you wasted your masculine wiles on me? There's not much cachet in flirting with a middle-aged governess of no attractions and no distinction."

"How wrong you are. Anyway I'm amused already." His low chuckle sent another wave of unease washing through her. This time, her shiver had nothing to do with the perishing cold. "But I'm touched to discover that you have my welfare at heart."

He stopped as if expecting a reply, but wisdom kept her silent. She needed to bring this discussion to an end, but not just yet. Before she left, she had to discover how far things had progressed between Halston and her cousin.

When she didn't speak, he went on. "Nor would I precisely say that flirtation is my goal." He paused again, which gave her time to worry about what he meant. "Or not flirtation for its own sake, at any rate."

"You wanted to seduce my cousin?"

"Not at all. I want to seduce you."

Dear God, that was unexpected. Every hair on her skin lifted, and fear coiled in her stomach. Fear, and a reluctant fascination. Because she'd noticed him and wanted him, however out of reach he was. He was so dark and dangerous and forbidden. How could she resist?

Through her astonishment, she realized that he couldn't mean it, so she returned a light answer. "It's too cold to contemplate sin."

"It's never too cold to contemplate sin. Although I didn't mean that I planned to jump on you this minute."

"Well, that's a mercy."

Her dry tone made him laugh. "Not to mention that these wooden seats would be damned hard on the knees."

He was incorrigible. She didn't for a moment believe that Halston had any serious designs on her virtue, although some imp inside her enjoyed the back and forth between them. "I'm not worthy of your attention, my lord."

"But then you're not seeing with my eyes," he responded with a smoothness that stirred her disquiet. She knew that this was a game, but he sounded like he meant what he said.

Lord Halston raised the cheroot, drew on it one last time, then dropped it to the marble floor. As he extinguished the stub with one elegant foot, Stella studied him. Was he so lost to morality that in her cousin's absence, any female would do instead? Even a lowly governess?

She decided that must be the case. If only that knowledge made her despise him, but she was no angel herself. The shameful truth was that she'd noticed Lord Halston's louche attractions from the moment she saw him at her first London ball.

How could she not? He prowled through the ton like Satan seeking congenial company to drag down to hell with him. Those sensual features promised endless pleasure to the lucky woman he chose to steal away.

Nonetheless Stella was no fool. She knew which side her bread was buttered on. A dalliance with Lord Halston, however enticing, was a diversion she couldn't afford.

To her regret.

"Yet you came out here to meet my cousin. I didn't even know you were acquainted with her."

One of the greatest shocks in finding that letter was learning that Imogen had linked up with this reprobate. Stella had never seen them dance together. She'd never even seen them speak.

In general, Halston didn't show much interest in debutantes. Stella recognized Imogen's many qualities, but something inside her insisted that an innocent like her cousin wasn't Halston's usual quarry.

Although perhaps, given the interest he expressed in Stella, he wasn't as discriminating as she'd assumed. She didn't know him beyond what she'd seen. She'd never spoken to him before.

Almost every night since she'd arrived in London, Stella had attended a ball, but not as a guest seeking an evening's pleasure. She'd been relegated to sit against the wall and observe the gaiety. Such was the role of a companion.

She reminded herself once more that Halston could be nothing to her, other than a face to fit to her overheated fantasies when she lay in bed at night. In his presence, memories of those sultry dreams made her stomach pitch with secret embarrassment.

Which still didn't explain when he and Imogen had found the opportunity to cook up an elopement.

"I don't know your cousin," he said calmly. He stopped as if he considered further. "I mean, I know who she is. She's pretty and an heiress and accounted one of the catches of the season. But we've never been introduced."

For pity's sake, what was going on? None of this made sense. And in the meantime, Stella was turning into an icicle. She shifted closer to the brazier, even if that meant shifting closer to the libertine lord. "So what are you doing here?"

"She wrote me a note, asking me to meet her in the gazebo in the Lumsdens' garden at eleven."

"And you came? Are you hoping to get your hands on her fortune? I imagine your habits are expensive."

"You don't pull your punches, do you?" To her surprise, that sounded like praise.

Stella stamped down a traitorous spurt of pleasure. "I hadn't heard of you being in Queer Street."

He gave a short laugh. "To Hades with you, this is none of your damned business, but as they stand, the Maddox coffers are adequate to my needs."

She was glad that in this light, he wouldn't see her chagrin. He was right. It was the height of bad manners to discuss a man's financial affairs. "I'm sorry."

"No, you're not."

No, she wasn't. Not really.

Stella frowned and spoke before she recalled that she was a staid poor relation and not this man's social equal. "If Imogen's a complete stranger, why in the name of all that's holy are you planning to elope with her?"

"Elope?" He'd come close enough to the brazier for her to make out his expression. For the first time, genuine surprise wiped the mocking amusement from his face. "Why in hell would I elope with your cousin?"

It seemed that Imogen had been busy with more than just her correspondence. At last, Stella understood what happened here. She should have twigged that some scheme was afoot when she found that indiscreet, unfinished letter addressed to Halston and left out in the open.

She cursed herself for not being awake to her cousin's antics. Most of the time she was. But the mention of Lord Halston had turned her usually reliable brain to porridge. Much as his presence now threatened to do.

Her cousin hated London and wanted to go home. Not only that, but her father had already chosen a suitable suitor in John Jerrold, Baron Chippenham. A power broker in parliament with prosperous estates in Cheshire. From the first, Imogen had made it clear that she didn't share her father's preference for the stout, self-important lord.

Stella could almost admire the girl's ingenuity in trying to scupper her father's plans, even if her ill-conceived plot had landed her chaperone in Halston's disreputable company. "You and I are victims of my cousin's scheming, my lord."

One dark eyebrow tilted in enquiry. "Oh?"

"I believe I was meant to catch the two of you alone together and report the indiscretion to Lord Deerforth."

"With what purpose?" Halston frowned. "I'm too downy to let some presumptuous miss gull me. I've weathered plenty of scandals. I can weather another one. If she relied on me to propose to save her reputation, she relied in vain."

"I very much doubt that she expected you to propose. It's your dreadful reputation that made her settle on you."

Another grunt of laughter escaped him. "By all means, don't spare my feelings."

Stella didn't bother apologizing. Her manners or lack of them didn't matter at this stage. "She wants her father to send her back to Hamble Park in disgrace. She's been begging to leave London since she arrived."

Amusement creased his cheek. "She's an unusual debutante, then."

"She is. And clever, if at times impulsive." Stella might have plumbed the reasons behind Imogen's behavior. But the puzzle remained of what Lord Halston was doing out here alone in the cold. "Why on earth did you agree to meet her?"

This time, his chuckle held a rueful note that she couldn't help but like. "Perhaps because I hoped that if I drew the ewe lamb aside from the herd, the sheepdog might follow."

"The sheepdog?"

"You're not that slow, my dear Miss Faulkner. I've already told you that I want to seduce you."

He had, hadn't he? And she'd dismissed his statement as purely opportunistic. Imogen wasn't here. She was. But now his intentions toward her sounded more calculated. And to her alarm, they sounded like they predated this meeting in a freezing gazebo. "Me?"

"Yes, you."

Something vague that had worried her earlier suddenly clarified in her mind. "You know my name."

"Of course I know your name."

"I don't understand," she said, backing away and wrapping her arms around herself. Against the cold, and against the stirring awareness that if she'd noticed Lord Halston, Lord Halston had also noticed her. It was frightening. It was unacceptable. It was gratifying.

She couldn't let it be gratifying.

He shrugged. "It's quite simple. One lady in your family has escaped ruin in my company. I'm hoping you'll offer yourself up in your cousin's place."

Shock had her regarding him wide-eyed. "You...you've never given any sign that you noticed me."

He shrugged. "My attention would single you out, and that would only result in your banishment from London's ballrooms."

One shaking hand rose to her throat, where her pulse pounded like a drum. "I can see that you've devoted some thought to this." Her voice hardened. "But I'm still not sure why you'd be interested."

"In a middle-aged spinster of no distinction?"

Stella wasn't insulted. After all, she worked very hard to be unobtrusive. "As you say."

"Except a diamond remains a diamond, even when it's hidden at the bottom of a dark hole."

"A diamond?"

He smiled. "Chasing compliments, Miss Faulkner?"

"No, I'm doubting your sanity, my lord."

"How old are you?" Through the gloom, she felt his gaze focus on her. "Thirty?"

"Twenty-nine," she said shortly. It was lunatic to mind that his guess added a year to her age.

"Still a few years away from middle-aged."

"On the shelf, though."

"Only because that's where you place yourself."

"I have no fortune. I have to make my way as best I can."

"As a paid companion?"

"If I must." Although her uncle never paid her any actual money.

"Which means wearing drab clothes and torturing your lovely hair and biting your tongue."

She was surprised – appalled – at how much Lord Halston had noted without her registering his curiosity. Over the years, she'd learned to identify and discourage unwelcome male interest. Yet she'd have wagered every penny of her paltry savings that Lord Halston didn't know she was alive.

Now the question was whether the male interest was indeed unwelcome.

There was an illicit thrill in bandying words with this clever devil, just as there was an illicit thrill in eating him up with her eyes without fearing censure. "I haven't bitten my tongue with you."

"I'm sure that's been a relief."

It had, plague take him. She'd always been aware of his surpassing physical appeal, but this strange freedom that she felt in his presence was even more disastrous to good intentions. She had to keep reminding herself that they'd never met before. This felt too much as if she picked up an engrossing conversation that had gone on for years.

Stella straightened. Despite the danger – or perhaps even because of it – she'd enjoyed these last few minutes with Lord Halston more than she'd enjoyed anything in years. Which was a signal to bring the meeting to a close. All that could happen now was that she'd start to yearn for what she could never have.

She'd had quite enough of that, thank you.

He might talk about seducing her, but it was never going to happen. If she was wise – and to her regret, she had to be – this was the last time that she'd even speak to Lord Halston alone.

Her arms lowered to her sides, and she curled her toes to restore the circulation to her feet. While she wasn't wearing flimsy dancing slippers, her shoes weren't thick enough to keep out the cold. "My lord, all of this has been intriguing and rather flattering, but I must find my cousin."

Lord Halston was a diversion. Right now, she needed to find Imogen and give her a blistering lecture. Although the question remained that if the girl wasn't here risking her reputation in Lord Halston's company, where was she?

A wry smile curled his lips. His humor was too cursed appealing. The man she'd fantasized about in the privacy of her bedroom had been a cardboard cutout lover. The real Grayson Maddox, Earl of Halston, was considerably more interesting. Which only undermined her hard-won acceptance of her humble status and the dreary years to come.

"For shame, Miss Faulkner, you're running away. I thought you were made of stouter stuff."

Stella didn't smile. She knew enough to understand that sharing jokes was the first step on the road to ruin. And while her uncle's house mightn't be heaven, it was at least a roof over her head. "Then you mistake me, sir. I'm too dull to hold your interest."

She was still astounded that he'd noticed her at all. His taste ran to pretty opera dancers and racy society widows. Even when she was younger and wilder, she hadn't been in his style.

How it irked that she'd paid him enough attention to pinpoint what sort of woman he liked to bed.

Her interest in this notorious rake had been difficult enough to curb when he remained a stranger. Now she knew that against all the odds, he was curious about her, too.

Trying *not* to think about Lord Halston promised to take over her life.

He made another dismissive gesture. "We've already put paid to that ridiculous statement." Before she could argue, he went on. "When can I see you again? I realize that if you stay out here too long, people will remark on it, and there's always the chance that we may be discovered."

The unflattering truth was that he probably feared that anyone who found them together would question his taste. As a rule, he didn't waste his time on unimpressive creatures like her. "I assume we'll attend the same balls. Imogen seems to be invited to all the parties this season."

That brought on another grunt of amusement. "I don't mean when will I see you sitting against the wall with all the old tabbies."

Stella knew that he hadn't meant that, but it was time to bring this disturbing conversation to an end. Already every reckless cell in her body yearned toward him. Once before when she'd followed her wayward impulses, she'd barely escaped disaster. Never again.

"Then I fear this delightful encounter is to be our lot, my lord."

Although her tone was ironic, the sad fact was that the encounter had been delightful, even if unnerving. For the first time in years, she felt alive. She'd forgotten how her blood sang when she played flirtatious games with a good-looking man. Tolerating her role as Imogen's sedate companion would be harder than ever now.

Damn Lord Halston and his perfect profile and his powerful shoulders and his commanding height. And his smile and his humor, and the way he seemed to understand her in a way that nobody else had in years.

Her denial didn't chasten him. She didn't expect that it would. "That would be a pity," he said in a neutral tone.

"But inevitable." It took far too much effort to turn away. Whatever magic this dissolute man possessed, it was powerful. And bewildering. Leaving him seemed wrong, yet what was wrong was remaining in his presence. "I bid you good night."

He didn't move to stop her. "Good night, but not goodbye."

Her stupid heart leaped around like a drunken grasshopper, and she did her best to quell the excitement bubbling in her veins. Excitement was poison. Lord Halston was poison.

It was almost impossible to resist such a man. But resist she must. "You're doomed to disappointment, sir. There can be nothing more between us than a brief conversation in the moonlight."

He stepped past the brazier. While he verged within touching distance, he didn't touch her. "You sound very certain."

Stella turned back for a few forbidden seconds, imagining how it would feel if he swept her up against that hard-muscled body and kissed her. Did more than kiss her.

It had been so long since a man had touched her in passion.

She pushed the image away and when she spoke, her voice rang with sincerity. "I am certain. I beg you as a gentleman to abandon any thought of pursuing me."

His lips stretched in one of those devilish smiles that made her stomach clench in wanton longing. He might be wicked, but by heaven, he was beautiful, too.

All the urges that Stella had spent ten years ignoring and deriding and crushing howled in protest. Common sense demanded that she run, that she should have run the moment she realized that Imogen wasn't about to elope with this handsome libertine. Yet every feminine instinct insisted that she stay to find out whether Grayson Maddox could make her shake with pleasure.

With the moon shining full on his face, his speculative expression was visible. "Whoever told you that I was a gentleman was a damned liar."

"And don't you sound so proud of that?" Her tone was flat.

He shrugged. "I take what I want. I suspect that's one of the things you like about me. You don't strike me as a woman who wants a man to fuss and hesitate and play propriety, my dear Miss Faulkner."

Lord above, how could this man read her secret soul? Several times during this astonishing exchange, she'd been afraid. And intrigued and amused and attracted.

But hearing him speak to her hidden desires turned her blood to ice. If he'd paid that level of attention, no appeal to convenience or manners, let alone a spurious claim to indifference, would put him off.

Against every dictate of self-preservation, Stella was interested. However heartily she might wish she wasn't.

One unsteady hand lifted to clutch the shawl tight to her throat. Through stiff lips, she responded. "I'm not your dear Miss Faulkner, sir. I'm a woman of no fortune, with nothing to smooth my way in the world but my good reputation. If you deprive me of that, you destroy me. It's unworthy to pester a penniless lady who has so much to lose."

She tried to shame him into retreat. But when those clever eyes subjected her to a thorough inspection, she felt as if he ran his elegant hands over her naked body. This shiver was more desire than dread. Halston, so experienced with her sex, would know that, curse him.

"It's a damned pity that a magnificent creature like you has to play nursemaid to a spoiled child like Imogen Ridley and pretend respect to a puffed-up jackanapes like Deerforth."

Magnificent? How utterly ridiculous. She was nothing of the kind.

"Imogen isn't spoiled," Stella retorted, knowing that Halston would note that she didn't defend her uncle. "If anything, she's too good-hearted."

The earl's striking face was only part of his charm. He possessed a sharp mind, too. Too sharp for her liking. Like now when he observed her with a perceptiveness that made her shift from one icy foot to the other. "And you have a loyal heart."

She shrugged. "My cousin is easy to like."

Except at this moment when she wanted to strangle the little cat for getting her into this situation. The girl's scheme might yet cause a scandal that would ruin her in the world's eyes and see Stella tossed out onto the streets.

"Most women in your position would be jealous of her good fortune and resentful of her privileges. After all, you're as wellborn as she is, yet you have to take her orders and serve her fancies."

Stella's mouth opened in amazement. What a lot he'd found out about her. She struggled to respond. "Most women in my position are grateful to have a home and three meals a day. You have an unrealistic picture of the choices available to a poor gentlewoman. Blue blood doesn't fill an empty stomach."

"You speak as if your life is over."

"I have my entertainments." She shot him a pointed glance. "Although I'll wager they wouldn't impress a sophisticate like you."

He didn't react to the sting in her comment. Instead, he countered her direct glance with a direct glance of his own. "I find myself contemplating entertainments, too. Of a variety that would entertain us both."

The word "entertain" in that lazy drawl made her skin prickle with sensual curiosity. "I doubt you mean *entertainments*..." She added bitter emphasis to the word. "...that befit a virtuous spinster, my lord."

He arched expressive black brows. "You understand what I mean."

She did indeed. She was no naïve miss, convinced that a man's interest meant poetry and flowers and a chaste kiss in the rose garden.

Halston hitched one hip higher than the other in a casual stance that told her he wasn't serious about any of this. Why would he be? Stella was well beneath his notice. This was a connoisseur of fashionable beauty. The present taste favored pretty little blondes with sweet expressions. Stella had always been slender and tall, and possessed of features that people praised for their character, rather than their winsomeness.

Which meant that his lordship's interest in her couldn't be real. He was just playing cruel games. What a fool she was to read anything more into their conversation.

She sucked in a relieved breath. Lord Halston was just passing the time because Imogen had let him down. He might speak nonsense about wanting to engineer a meeting with Stella, but he'd no doubt be just as happy to flirt with Imogen as with Stella.

"You can't help yourself, can you?" she said in a considering tone.

She'd startled him. He stopped looking like Lucifer contemplating the potential of hell's latest recruits. "Can't help myself from wanting you?"

Stella shook her head, on firmer ground with every second. "No, from attempting to gain the interest of any woman you meet. My cousin isn't here, so at a pinch, her plain companion will do. Even though she's not up to your usual standard."

His laugh was low and knowing. "I have a dreadful suspicion that I'm the one who doesn't meet your standards, Miss Faulkner. In every way except the worldliest, you're a superior person to my sinful self."

If only he knew the truth. "You don't mean that."

This was a man at ease with himself. If he'd sinned – and he most definitely had – he wasn't eaten up with remorse about his misdeeds. "Don't I?"

"I must find my cousin, my lord." She stepped back, determined to go, if only because the lure of staying was so strong. "If she's not here, she could have come to grief on her way to this rendezvous."

His audible exhalation expressed contempt for that remark. "I doubt it. This is a very respectable corner of London. Lorimer Square isn't exactly Seven Dials."

"There are dangerous men everywhere. It doesn't matter whether they're wearing rags or evening dress."

As if she made a point against him, he bent his head. She did. She couldn't imagine him forcing himself on her cousin. He wouldn't have to. One glance from those heavy-lidded eyes would make any woman melt.

"It's been an enchanting interlude." He straightened. "I look forward to furthering our acquaintance."

"I'm sure," she said with a hint of sarcasm.

"You don't believe me?"

"No, I don't."

"Ah."

On the verge of leaving, she couldn't resist questioning his strange response. "What does that mean?"

"That means now I understand why you stopped looking like a frightened sheep."

She gave a short laugh, much as she resented the sheep comparison. "You've got better targets than a shabby governess from the provinces. I spoke of my reputation. But what of yours? Gossip says that only diamonds of the first water catch your eye. I'm beneath your touch."

"You will be beneath my touch, my appealing and far too certain of herself Miss Faulkner. You'll be beneath *me* before I'm done."

Her brief rush of confidence fizzled away to nothing. The cold that overwhelmed her had nothing to do with the wintry air.

She had no idea why, but London's greatest rake had set his sights on lanky, undistinguished Stella Faulkner. His tone told her that he didn't like the way she dismissed his blandishments. More than that, his answer vibrated with a conviction she couldn't mistake.

Although how she wished she could.

Her knees turned to water and those grasshoppers in her stomach grew into elephants, as she realized that she was in genuine danger out here alone with Lord Halston. If only because what he offered her was so infernally tempting.

This time when she spoke, nerves made her voice quaver. "I must go."

Without waiting for a response, Stella made her unsteady way down the steps. Then abandoning dignity, she picked up her skirts and sprinted along the dark path until the French doors leading to the ballroom appeared in front of her.

CHAPTER TWO

As Halston watched Miss Faulkner dash away, he returned to propping his shoulder against the wall. Her sure-footed speed belied any claim to being middle-aged. Although two weeks of observation told him that she did her best to appear dull and respectable.

Some deep-seated instinct had always insisted that beneath her modest demeanor, she was pure flame. His instincts never led him astray.

This meeting just now proved him right. Sexual awareness had crackled between them like lightning in a stormy sky. He hadn't touched her, not because he hadn't wanted to, but because he feared that if he laid his hands on her, he'd never let her go.

Every gossip in London attended the Lumsden ball. It wasn't the place to further this seduction. When he and Miss Faulkner came together – as come together they must, because whatever she said, those honey-colored eyes betrayed her hunger for him – he wanted time and privacy to enjoy her.

In a furious scene that had culminated in a bullet in his hide, he'd broken with his last mistress. He'd spent a week, licking his wounds and wondering if perhaps he should steer clear of actresses and dancers.

The barks of frailty he'd taken under his protection in recent times hadn't been a roaring success, however decorative they were. Hetty had shown a tendency to droop and weep and whine. In comparison to Sally, a brick would come across as another Isaac Newton. And Francene, a soprano rather than a dancer, had lived up to her reputation as a diva and proven temperamental to the point of mania.

When an exhausted Halston offered to pay her off, she'd thrown a tantrum that they must have heard in Dover. Then she'd produced a pistol and winged him. Without failing to pocket the diamond necklace that he'd bought her to soothe the sting of rejection.

For pity's sake, he used to enjoy the chase, but these days, no woman offered much of a challenge. Since he was sixteen, he'd played the libertine. Perhaps now that he was thirty-five, the game lost its flavor.

Everything he did to pursue a woman seemed a repeat of what he'd done before. The initial interest. The drive to possess. The possession itself, never as satisfying as he'd hoped. The downward spiral into bickering with, on his part, an increasing lack of engagement and, on the lady's part, endless nagging.

When Francene shot him, he admitted that he'd been neglecting her. Before the final break, he hadn't called on her in almost a month. He'd long ago tired of her constant demands for attention. By God, he might as well get married as suffer all the inconvenience of a wife's haranguing.

He'd always loved women. He loved looking at them. He loved the back and forth of the games that led to surrender. He loved fucking them.

But these days, if he set his sights on a female, her surrender was too quick. Whether she was an actress or an artist's model or an audacious society lady, the affair followed a predictable arc. It always ended when he retired from the fray, leaving some fabulous bauble behind to pacify ruffled vanity. This last affair left him bloodied, but that was the only thing that made it stand out from the rest.

He was spoiled with his own success, and he knew it. But knowing that didn't restore his interest in life.

Then a fortnight ago, Halston caught sight of a woman who wasn't his usual prey at all. At a ball that he'd attended because he was bored, he laid eyes on Stella Faulkner, and for the first time in months, perhaps even years, he wasn't bored at all.

In the general course of an evening's entertainment, his attention never wandered to the chaperones ranged against the wall. Why would it? He wasn't interested in old women or paid companions or poor relations.

But this particular night, something drew his attention. Or rather someone.

A woman younger than the others, although she tried to fade into the dreary crowd. A woman in a plain gray dress that somehow made every other female in the room look like an overdressed clown. A woman with a wealth of tawny hair, scraped back in a simple knot that only served to emphasize the purity of her bone structure.

She did her best to present an appearance of modesty, but the sheer effort that she made to disappear created its own whirlpool. This was a lioness trapped amidst a herd of sheep, and every cell of Halston's body had burned to make her his. The reaction was extraordinary, unprecedented, but inescapable.

Also inescapable, to his irritation, were the tight restrictions placed around a woman in Miss Faulkner's position. He soon discovered her name and role in the Ridley family, although despite his best efforts, he learned little more about her.

Apart from what his eyes told him. What he found out only made her more intriguing. She seemed determined to behave like the perfect companion. She regarded society with a sardonic amusement that she strove to hide. She seemed to like her cousins Imogen and Eliot. She had difficulty concealing her contempt for that posturing windbag, Lord Deerforth.

Halston would wager every penny of his vast fortune that she'd noticed him, too. The powerful connection between them made his skin tingle whenever her eyes were on him. Over these past two weeks, his skin had tingled frequently.

Perhaps Stella Faulkner just watched him because of the latest scandal. But he didn't think so. He was used to people talking about him. He was rich. He was a rake. For God's sake, his mistress had just shot him, a fact that must have enlivened many a conversation over Mayfair's breakfast tables. Yet he couldn't help believing that Stella Faulkner watched him for the same reason that he watched her.

Because she couldn't look away.

He'd spent the last fortnight, trying to work out the best way to approach her. Which immediately made this affair more interesting than his last dozen.

Halston wasn't chummy with her cousin Eliot, who was altogether a more upright citizen than his disreputable self. Even if he moved in Eliot's circles, he couldn't ask her cousin to forward the seduction.

Miss Faulkner hadn't made friends with any women who might make the introduction. When she sat with the old biddies, she kept very much to herself.

Her good name would be in shreds if he took the shocking step of crossing the room and asking her to dance. So a direct approach was out of the question.

Halston didn't wish the woman any harm. He wanted to seduce her for their mutual pleasure, then leave her with some happy memories. But as a poor relation, she was exposed to the world's judgement in a way most of his *inamoratas* weren't.

He'd reached the point of deciding to pay a servant in the Ridley household to spy on her so he could engineer a meeting. Then out of the blue, a note arrived from another woman who he'd never spoken to. A rather presumptuous little message, that suggested a rendezvous in the garden at the Lumsden ball. Halston was so notorious that women often propositioned him, but he'd never expected the popular debutante Imogen Ridley to be among their number.

In most cases, he ignored such blatant invitations. This time, his shout of triumph made his butler Philpott drop the breakfast tray with a great crash.

Because while Lady Imogen held no appeal for Halston, Lady Imogen was the path to the woman he wanted with increasing desperation.

Fate must be on the devil's side tonight, because he hadn't even had to deal with the pretty innocent. To his jubilation, he'd made contact with Miss Faulkner at last.

He wasn't a fool. His cynical side suggested that he convinced himself into this infatuation because it roused him from his lethargy. The most likely outcome was that a woman who appeared to be so dull might in fact *be* dull.

But Stella Faulkner had met his expectations, and more. She was clever and brave. And willing to put herself out for someone she loved, which he admired. She was also beautiful, but he'd recognized that from the first.

She wasn't sure about pursuing the acquaintance. While she might find him attractive, his interest left her far from dazzled. This was a woman who knew herself and the world.

Her self-possession intrigued him, impressed him. Their meeting in a chilly garden showed him that she was a prize worth winning. Even better, Halston had decided just how he meant to achieve that.

He'd spent two weeks picturing her in his bed. Slender. Naked. Long-limbed. Passionate. After tonight, she'd still feature in his extravagant fantasies, but now he'd dream with the certain hope of possessing her.

Breathless, Stella paused on the terrace, keeping to the shadows. Again, the cold night worked in her favor. In more clement weather, the Italianate balcony overlooking the lamplit garden would be crowded with guests taking the air or seeking a moment's privacy. Tonight it was empty, as the garden had been empty of everyone except Lord Satan peddling temptation.

Her heart was racing, not just because she'd fled Halston with humiliating haste. The fear that made her take to her heels still thundered through her. Fear and reluctant excitement. Satan might have peddled temptation, but this particular daughter of Eve had without doubt been listening.

Even worse, she still had to venture back into the garden to look for Imogen. And give the irresponsible miss a scolding on the dangers of being too clever for her own good.

Stella drew the shawl closer around her shoulders, but it didn't keep out the cold. If she ended up with the sniffles, thanks to Imogen's scheming, she'd have even more to say to the chit.

Her gaze ranged across the glittering crowd. A quadrille was in progress. Her uncle danced with Lady Lumsden, his hostess. The Lumsdens were active in politics, and Deerforth fancied himself as a man of influence in the nation.

Heaven help the nation if that came to pass.

If he hoped his skills as a dancer might forward his ambitions, Stella suspected he hoped in vain. He was already puffing and red in the face and while she watched, he fumbled one of the changes, earning him a glare from his partner.

In another set, her cousin Eliot danced with the notorious widow, Lady Verena Gerard. Deerforth wouldn't approve of his son and heir seeking such disreputable company. Eliot was meant to maintain an unsullied reputation to further his political ambitions.

Stella's gaze sharpened on her cousin. As he smiled at his ravishing partner, he looked quite besotted. With a muffled sigh, she predicted trouble to come. Her uncle had a dominant personality. If things didn't go his way, he wreaked his displeasure on everyone in the vicinity.

When her attention slid to the right, surprise and irritation rose in equal measure. It seemed that she'd wasted her time, combing the garden to find Imogen. It seemed, from what she could see, that she hadn't needed to brave the dark and cold to find her pestilential cousin at all.

Imogen, pretty and smiling in her azure gown, was dancing with Anthony Comerford, the Lumsdens' oldest son. She'd grown up with the Comerfords. Harriet Comerford was her best friend and made her debut this season, too.

Skipping across the floor to the lilting music, Imogen looked happy. Which was more than could be said for Imogen's governess, standing fuming on a freezing terrace. Stella really would strangle the little minx before she was done.

She smoothed her hands over her severe hairstyle and straightened her skirts. Then, praying no trace remained of her brush with a dissolute rake, she found a door that led into an anteroom instead of the ballroom, and slipped back inside.

"That was a rotten trick you played on me tonight," Stella said in a hard voice, as she and Imogen shared the carriage back to the house that Lord Deerforth had rented for the season. Because of the traffic in Lorimer Square after the ball, they'd be stuck together for a while. Which seemed nonsensical when she could walk across the square in less than ten minutes.

But traveling to a social event on foot wasn't the done thing. Stella had never been to London before, and many of its ways struck her as contrary to good country common sense.

However tonight she applauded ridiculous custom. This was her first chance all night to talk to her cousin alone. She meant to take advantage of it to ring a peal of bells over that pretty, empty little head.

A quieter than usual Imogen was staring out the window. Perhaps she tried to avoid a reprimand, now that her cousin had worked out her rattlebrained scheme.

"Trick?" she echoed, facing Stella with an exaggerated innocence that only confirmed her guilt.

Imogen was an entrancing creature with milk-white skin and big blue eyes and masses of glossy black hair. Blondes might be in style, but nobody remembered that when they caught sight of Lord Deerforth's exquisite daughter.

"Yes, trick. Leaving that letter out where you knew I'd see it and sending me off into the cold to save you from a disastrous mistake."

"Why...why would I do that?" She still tried to act the offended innocent. It worked on most males, including her father. Stella however was wise to her cousin's wiles.

"So I'd catch you with Halston and tell my uncle, and he'd send you home in disgrace. I know you want to go back to Hamble Park, but destroying your good name to achieve that end is using a cannon to kill a fly."

Imogen looked sulky, although at least she stopped trying to pretend that she had no idea what Stella was talking about. "Papa doesn't listen when I say I want to go home."

"This isn't the way to change his mind," Stella snapped, thoroughly annoyed with her cousin and also nervous about what she might try next. Tonight's tomfoolery had been dangerous enough. "What if I hadn't seen the letter? What if someone else had caught you together? What if Lord Halston took you up on what you were offering?"

"Was he there?"

"He was." And the rogue had proceeded to remind Stella that she was a woman with wants and needs that life as a governess didn't satisfy.

"Was he angry that I stood him up?"

"I have no idea. When I saw you weren't there, I left." *Liar. Liar.*

"I wasn't sure he'd come. We've never met."

"I know. I couldn't work out how you'd managed to reach the point of an elopement, when as far as I was aware, you've never spoken a word to him. But then he's a rake, and rakes have their methods."

"I picked him because he's so infamous. If you told Papa that I'd fallen into Halston's clutches, he couldn't fail to exile me back to Gloucestershire."

Stella's lips tightened. As she'd told Halston, Imogen had a good heart. But her desperation to escape London had become such an obsession that she wasn't thinking about consequences for herself or the people around her.

"He couldn't fail to try and force Halston to marry you. Is that what you want?"

Imogen's snort indicated her disdain for that idea. The inelegant reaction would have shocked her admirers, who all treated her as if she was made of spun glass. "Halston wouldn't marry me."

"No? Then perhaps you'd prefer to see Eliot or your father shot with a dueling pistol, when they defended your honor against the man who had ruined you."

Imogen's confidence faded. "It wouldn't have come to that."

"Wouldn't it?"

"Anyway, I didn't meet Lord Halston."

"No, you just left me to deal with him."

"You said you didn't stay to talk to him."

"I didn't. But it was a nasty trick you played on him, too."

At last, Imogen had the grace to display a trace of guilt. "Actually it wasn't a trick when I offered to meet him, although I wasn't sure he'd turn up. Most of the time, he doesn't bother with debutantes."

"What if he'd tried to seduce you?"

"Oh, I knew you'd be on my heels. He wouldn't get very far before you turned up to rescue me."

"You placed a lot of trust in my power to stop him."

Imogen gave a huff of laughter. "I'd back you against any rake in England, my dear cuz."

"You took an awful risk." The compliment didn't mollify her. She sucked in a breath and fought to get a grip on her anger. The girl seemed blithely unaware of the danger that she'd been in tonight. "At least you saw sense and abandoned the scheme before any harm was done."

When Imogen looked uncomfortable, Stella's voice sharpened. "You did abandon the scheme, didn't you?"

"Not altogether."

"Imogen..."

She sighed and made an apologetic gesture. "You know how I hate London."

"You've told me often enough."

Imogen started to pleat her filmy blue skirts. "I realize now that perhaps I was a little reckless to risk scandal."

"A little?"

"But I was frantic, and this seemed a solution." Imogen avoided her eyes. "When Harriet mentioned the gazebo, I decided it was the perfect place for a rendezvous."

It had been. Stella hid a shiver as she recalled the building's isolation.

Where on earth had Imogen disappeared to, if she hadn't been in the gazebo with Halston? A host of wild possibilities rushed through Stella's mind, including the horrible idea of Imogen hiding in the bushes and overhearing that charged conversation with Halston.

"So?"

"So I went out and I found the gazebo, but nobody turned up. After a while I was getting cold, and I came back to the ballroom."

"Two gazebos?" Stella hadn't thought of that.

Her cousin responded with a miserable little nod. "There must be. Because if Halston waited in one and I waited in the other, there is no other explanation, is there?"

Stella released a relieved breath. "Don't you dare try anything like this again. Lord Halston may have been occupied elsewhere when you were in the garden on your own." Expressing an interest in her unsuitable self. "But he's not the only rake in London. Who knows who else you could have run into in the dark? You've taken twenty years off my life."

Imogen ventured an uncertain smile. "I promise I'll behave."

"You must know your father won't send you home. He's gone to so much effort and expense to give you a season. Most girls would be in alt to attend all these parties and put gentlemen in a spin over their beauty and charm."

"You must think I'm very unappreciative."

"I think you've set your mind against enjoying London." And wedding Lord Chippenham. An opinion with which Stella harbored a certain amount of sympathy. Not that she meant to share that conclusion with Imogen. "Give yourself a chance.

Give London a chance. Because I fear you're stuck here for the duration."

"I know," Imogen said. "I've decided home will still be waiting in a couple of months. I may as well settle down and accept my fate."

To Stella's surprise, she sounded reconciled to her situation. Ever since they'd arrived, her cousin had bewailed her dreadful misfortune as one of the most popular girls of the season. Imogen's perpetual complaints about what was in fact her great good luck had prompted several lectures from Stella about her lack of gratitude. All had fallen on deaf ears.

If tonight's escapade had convinced Imogen to throw herself into London life with better spirit, Stella was almost grateful that it had taken place. With no great conviction, she told herself that there would be no major repercussions.

Imogen's reputation remained intact. Her father was ignorant of her foolhardy actions, which would save the household from a tantrum. And while Stella might have come to a rake's notice, Lord Halston would find it impossible to pursue her. That was if in the light of day, he decided he was still interested.

All good, really.

"You took an appalling chance. Not least your gamble that Lord Halston would act the gentleman. But as no real harm came of it..." She hoped to heaven that was true, and it wasn't Imogen's virtue that she was thinking about when she formed that unspoken prayer. "...I suppose I'll have to forgive you."

"I'm so glad, Stella. You're the best of cousins."

"I am. Just promise me you'll never do anything like this again."

Imogen bent her head. Stella wasn't sure whether it was in contrition, or whether the girl was avoiding her eyes. "I promise I'll never threaten to run off with a rake again. It was a silly idea, and I hate that I caused you all this worry. I've learned my lesson, and now I intend to enjoy my season."

"Very saintly of you," Stella said drily.

"I'm sorry for sending you out into the cold." The sincerity in Imogen's voice at last convinced Stella that she felt some genuine remorse. "You're right. I launched this scheme without thinking too hard about how it could go wrong. Or what impact it could have on my family."

The heartfelt apology soothed Stella's temper. "Thank you."

A silence fell, and at last the carriage lurched into movement. The crush of vehicles must be easing. Imogen went back to staring out the window, while Stella struggled to forget quite how handsome Halston had looked presiding over a burning brazier.

She already thought of him as the devil. That should be enough to convince her that she wanted nothing more to do with him. But she was wicked, more wicked than anyone knew. Even if he swept her away to hell, she had a powerful inkling that in his arms, hell would become heaven.

"Was he as naughty as everyone says?" Imogen asked. Stella realized her cousin was staring at her. The torches ranged along the street outside Comerford House lent enough light to reveal her cousin's curiosity.

"I told you, I didn't speak to him. I saw him, then I came back inside."

"It's just that you were missing for quite some time." What a deuced pity that Imogen had noticed that. "And you looked rather flustered when you came back into the ballroom."

"It took me a while to find the gazebo. And I was frantic about what had happened to you."

"He's very handsome, isn't he?"

Yes, curse him, he was. "Handsome is as handsome does."

Imogen shot her an unimpressed glance. "I don't know why you always try to act as if you're a hundred years old. You're not that much older than I am, but you carry on as if you're as old as Methuselah."

Did she? "That's not very kind."

Imogen looked unrepentant. "You're pretty and funny and much more interesting than the woman you present to the world. Even when I give you a nice dress, you do your best to turn it into something a nun would reject as too dowdy. And every time I look at your hair, I get a headache that I'm sure must match yours."

What an altogether uncomfortable evening this turned out to be. It had started with Stella in a panic about Imogen's safety. It then turned into another panic when she discovered that Halston had targeted her. Now she had to endure honest criticism from the cousin she loved. Honest and well deserved.

Which didn't stop the remarks from stinging. Because twenty-nine wasn't old, even though she'd told Halston she was middle-aged. Hot, passionate blood still pumped through her veins. Stella only had to recall her powerful attraction to his licentious lordship to admit that.

Yet with every hour she spent in her uncle's house, her youth seeped away. One day soon, she'd be old in truth, and it would be too late to make a life for herself.

Yet what choice did she have? She knew that Imogen meant well, but Stella couldn't contain the hint of resentment in her response. "I'm paying the price of my poverty. You know that."

"I know that you're paying the price of your parents' recklessness."

It was true. Her mother, Lord Deerforth's beautiful younger sister, had rejected a wealthy marriage in favor of eloping with her handsome drawing master. "My parents loved each other."

That was true, too. They had. And they'd loved Stella. But none of that had put food on the table or offered Stella an ounce of security after they perished in a cholera epidemic. Her parents had set up home in Naples, and her father had scratched a living, selling portraits and landscapes to Englishmen on the grand tour. Once the war started on the Continent, even that unreliable income had dried up.

After her parents died, Stella had been left alone, penniless, and battling a grief that left her bewildered. For a while, she'd tried to manage by selling her own watercolors, but it was hopeless. She wasn't as talented as her father, and a woman besides. Then, not long after that, she ended up with more terrifying things to deal with than earning a living.

The French invaded the Kingdom of Naples, and all of a sudden, as the child of English parents, she was in genuine danger. When the Royal Navy sent a ship to evacuate all British citizens, she was grateful to find a place on board.

It was also lucky that her mother had a network of friends among the rich foreign residents of the city. In worldly terms, Anne Ridley might have made an unfortunate marriage, but she remained the daughter and sister of an earl.

Lady Benstead had known Stella's mother as a girl and had kept up the acquaintance. She'd taken responsibility for Stella and made sure she was delivered safe to Lord Deerforth's estate.

Her uncle's charity had been so grudging that it made Stella's skin itch. But with the Marchioness of Benstead insisting that it was his duty to take in his niece, he'd had little choice but to offer Stella bed and board.

Still grieving her parents' deaths and the loss of the only home she'd ever known, not to mention shaken and sickened by the scenes she'd witnessed during the invasion, Stella found herself playing the part of a poor relation at Hamble Park.

Since then, Deerforth's charity had become even colder. There was never any question that he and his late wife might accept Stella as a valued member of the family and offer her the advantages they offered their own daughter. She was in the house on sufferance, and everyone knew it.

Everyone except Imogen, who could have treated her abominably, with nobody to say her nay. Yet Imogen had provided the one glimmer of brightness during these last dark years.

And they'd been hard years, especially for someone as overburdened with pride as Stella. She'd worked as Imogen's unpaid governess and now companion. After her aunt's death, she'd also taken over running the household.

Imogen's searching stare seemed to see more than Stella wanted to reveal. "Don't you want someone to love you?"

Imogen didn't know how the question stung. Once someone had loved Stella. Not just her parents. A man who had brought magic to her life. That sweet, forbidden memory had helped her to survive the endless humiliations of life with her uncle.

Her lips tightened, and her response was stiff. "I want to keep my place, where someone feeds me three meals a day and I've got a bed to sleep in. My uncle wouldn't appreciate it if I decided that your season is my season, too."

"I wouldn't mind if you shared my season."

"No, but your papa would."

"When I marry, you can come and live with me." Stubbornness firmed Imogen's jaw. "I'll make sure that you're treated in the manner you deserve."

Startled, Stella studied her cousin. Not because of the offer of a future home, although she appreciated the thought, even if she didn't count on it. There were two people in any marriage, and a new husband mightn't welcome his bride's indigent relatives moving in. It was the rest of the statement that had her agog.

"Married? You've always been set against the idea."

The prospect of entering the marriage mart had formed a large part of Imogen's objections to coming to London. If Halston's name hadn't distracted her when she found that letter, she'd have wondered why a girl who didn't want a husband was all of a sudden embarking on an elopement.

"I was," the girl said, once again avoiding Stella's eyes. "That was one of the reasons that it seemed a good idea to meet Lord Halston. If I was ruined, nobody would want to marry me, and Papa would leave me in peace when it comes to Lord Chippenham."

"You'd get tired of everybody slighting you as a scarlet woman."

The girl shrugged. The coach had stopped again, and this time Stella didn't mind. This conversation was proving too interesting to interrupt. "I have my garden, and anyone who is my true friend won't care about the gossip."

Imogen devoted her life to rebuilding Hamble Park's extravagant gardens. To date, her father had indulged her interests. Although Stella doubted he'd be so generous if Imogen's behavior sparked a scandal that blighted his ambitions.

She'd been at a crucial point in constructing a parterre when her father whisked her away to London. All she'd talked about since she'd arrived was how much she wanted to go back home and make sure the workmen were following her instructions. Imogen had always been much more interested in plants than she was in any young men who might want to court her.

"Yet now you speak of marriage." The girl had said that she was happy to continue with her season, too. Stella shot her pretty cousin a suspicious look. "Did you meet someone you like tonight?"

"How could I?" The faint flush along Imogen's cheekbones firmed Stella's suspicions. "It was all the same people that we've seen every night for the last two weeks. I danced with Lord Chippenham and Anthony Comerford and Eliot and a couple of Eliot's friends, who were obviously doing him a favor. Nothing out of the ordinary."

Stella didn't believe her. Although short of calling Imogen a liar, she couldn't say anything. She determined to look out for the young man who had taken her fancy.

Someone had. Lord Chippenham hadn't ignited that glow in Imogen's lovely eyes. He was almost fifty, and Imogen considered him a pompous boor.

Was it one of Eliot's friends? Eliot, while not a boor, was almost as respectable as Chippenham, and his cronies were all upstanding young gentlemen. If Imogen set her cap for one of them, perhaps her father might approve the match.

Imogen looked like a dainty little blossom, but she had a will like a mule. In the end, Deerforth would have to accept the failure of his plans for his daughter to cement his access to Chippenham. Chippenham with his connections to mining and shipping and political influence.

"I'm glad you've reconciled yourself to staying in Town," Stella said in a matter-of-fact tone. "The household will be happier at least."

Although a quick departure for Gloucestershire might be safer for Stella. She couldn't forget the determination ringing in Halston's voice when he threatened to pursue her.

CHAPTER THREE

"Lord Halston has called, my lady."

At the butler's announcement from the doorway to the crowded room, Stella's head jerked up from where she bent over her embroidery.

She'd spent all morning in a strange, jittery mood. Despite not getting home until after two, she'd had trouble sleeping. That encounter with a roué had been enough to set her wanton blood rushing in a way it hadn't since her last meeting with Niccolo ten years ago. She'd hoped that time might blunt her powerful response to a handsome man. Yet it seemed that when temptation was strong enough, she was as susceptible as ever.

This afternoon, Imogen was at home to callers, and the drawing room was heaving with giggly young girls, not to mention an assortment of older women. Mothers. Aunts. Godmothers. The occasional chaperone like Stella. A few older brothers were also present, escorting their sisters.

Stella only realized when she heard Halston's name that she'd been awaiting his next move. Whatever reassurances she'd given herself last night, she'd known that there would be one. Wondering how he meant to proceed had left her in horrid suspense.

A reverberant silence descended upon the largely feminine crowd. Everyone present was respectable, and any potential suitors were younger and less jaded than Lord Halston. The unexpected arrival of a man of his reputation would cause talk.

Given that Halston possessed both a great name and a substantial fortune, and that he was yet to choose his countess, gossip would focus on whether he'd found a wife at last in Imogen Ridley.

"Please show his lordship in," Imogen said, looking very bright-eyed. She'd know just what a compliment this was and how it would enhance her standing. Halston's call was the final accolade to confirm Imogen's social success.

His lordship strolled in, looking as spectacular as ever. He didn't glance at Stella on her chair near the fire. It was a warm, unobtrusive corner, and she'd spent far too long in it this afternoon, letting the conversation wash over her while her mind dwelled on notorious lords.

He bowed to Imogen and raised her hand to his lips. "I'm delighted that we were introduced at last, Lady Imogen. I've admired you from afar since your arrival in London. I'm just sorry that my injury makes dancing impossible at present."

Introduced? Stella had missed that. It must have happened when she accompanied Harriet to the retiring room to help repair a torn hem.

Interesting that Imogen hadn't told her. Her eyes sharpened on her cousin, who sat a couple of chairs away. The girl looked dazzled. And dazzling.

Last night, Stella had wondered if some gentleman had caught Imogen's interest. What a fool she was not to count Halston as a potential husband. He was well past the age where he was due to find a chatelaine for what was reported to be a magnificent estate in Buckinghamshire. And Imogen was without doubt eligible.

Imogen said that she'd chosen Halston for her scandalous rendezvous because of his bad reputation. Now, looking at them together, Stella couldn't help wondering if she'd also chosen him because she harbored a penchant for him.

He was too old for her, Stella's heart keened, as her hands clenched around her embroidery frame. Although he wasn't. He must be fifteen years younger than Lord Chippenham, and considerably more vigorous. Nor was he at all starchy.

Any girl would consider Halston an appealing suitor, despite his taste for wayward women. Lord Deerforth would find nothing to object to in such a match. He sought a son-in-law with money and influence. Halston had both. The Prince Regent was reported to adore him.

What a crown a marriage to Halston would place on Imogen's season. It would be accounted a triumph. While Halston gained a pretty wife with a loving heart and a sparkling personality. Why the devil wouldn't he court Imogen?

Except he's mine, Stella's lonely heart cried. *Except he spoke to me last night as if we met soul to soul. Except he said that he wanted me.*

Could he be so depraved as to scheme to wed the earl's daughter and seduce her humble companion at the same time? Growing up on the back streets of Naples, Stella had seen wickedness that would make the angels weep. Men without care or conscience in regard to money or power or women. As she'd said to Halston, evil men lurked in all stations, from the poorest laborer to the richest aristocrat.

Halston was reputed to be a devil with the ladies. But last night, he hadn't seemed so lost to goodness as that. When he'd expressed an interest in Stella, he'd seemed honest.

He'd seemed honest? What a nitwit she was. She'd fallen for the oldest trick in the world. Of course, he sounded honest. The best liars always did.

"Thank you for the gorgeous flowers," Imogen said, with a flutter of the eyelashes that she'd learned since she left Gloucestershire.

Flowers? That made his intentions toward Imogen clear. As happened after every ball, the house was inundated with floral tributes from Imogen's dancing partners. Stella had stopped paying much attention.

"You knew they were for you?"

"I don't think you'd send lilies to my father and address the card 'To a fair stranger.'"

His brief grunt of amusement was so familiar from last night, when he'd seemed to hang on Stella's every word. Just as he hung now on Imogen's.

The deceitful swine. How he must have snickered at Stella's gullibility. Although there was some consolation in remembering that she hadn't offered him much encouragement. With luck, he had no idea how powerfully he drew her.

Stella glanced around the room to see if anyone had noticed her startled reaction to Halston's arrival. But who would be interested in a mere companion when Imogen and Lord Halston offered such rich pickings for tattle? The guests who had been due to go because they'd used up their half hour made no attempt to move on. And there was little conversation, as dozens of ears pricked up to catch every word of Imogen's dealings with the earl.

"No, I doubt that Lord Deerforth would appreciate such a tribute."

The edge of excitement in Imogen's giggle made Stella wince. Had she sounded quite so beguiled in the gazebo? She had a sick feeling that she had. "No, I don't think he would."

"I saw his lordship at his club this morning and obtained his permission for you to attend a small house party at my estate in Buckinghamshire at the end of the week. Unfortunately, he's detained with political business and won't be able to come to Prestwick Place, but I'll do my best to entertain you in his absence. I hope these arrangements meet with your approval."

"Oh!"

This time attention focused on Stella, who to her mortification went as red as a beetroot. Her finger stung like blazes and had started to bleed. She'd dug the needle in hard. But this invitation to Halston's house was a particular mark of favor that could very well be the prelude to a marriage proposal.

"Miss Faulkner, are you unwell?" Halston asked, stepping toward her.

"I stuck myself with a needle, my lord." She surged to her feet and spoke in a rush that she regretted at once. If only she could sound cool and composed.

What she wanted most of all was a moment's privacy to tell him that he was a lying toad for saying he wasn't interested in Imogen. But she wasn't likely to get that any time soon.

She struggled to steady her voice. "No real harm done."

"Stella, you poor thing. You're bleeding all over your lovely embroidery, too," Imogen said, dashing over to take her injured hand. "I'll ring for a maid to attend you."

"No, no, I'm perfectly fine. Really it's nothing. Really." The curious stares made her skin crawl. "I'll go upstairs and wash it."

Halston withdrew a white linen handkerchief from his pocket and passed it to her. "Here."

She broke free of Imogen and accepted the handkerchief with a shaky curtsy and a reluctance that she was sure he noted. "Thank you, my lord."

"Give me that embroidery," Imogen said, leaving Stella free to wrap Halston's handkerchief around her bleeding finger.

"May I help you to the stairs?" he asked.

"It's not serious, my lord." She kept avoiding his eyes. Oh, how she'd like to tell him just what she thought of him, but she was too aware of the audience for their small drama. "Please don't let me interrupt your visit."

"It's no trouble."

At last, she sent him a quick look that she hoped conveyed her utter contempt for his machinations. Even if she wasn't suffering a painful dose of pique, she knew Imogen deserved better than this deceitful snake.

He raised his eyebrows in a silent question that he must know she couldn't answer here. Much as she'd dearly love to tell him just how much she detested his double dealing.

"Let me offer my arm."

Over his shoulder, she saw faces turned in their direction. Although she was sure that the interest still focused on Imogen and Halston, rather than a nonentity of a companion. Any further objections from her, though, might change that.

"Thank you, my lord," she said between her teeth.

"Do you want me to come with you?" Imogen said from beside Halston. Stella had to admit that they looked wonderful together.

"Please don't spoil your callers' time here." Her hand was stinging, but nowhere near as much as her pride was. "I'll come down the minute that I've put a bandage on it. It's almost stopped bleeding."

She wasn't a naïve ingenue like Imogen, with no experience of men and their tricks. Yet somehow she'd taken one look at Lord Halston and every scrap of good sense had flown away to far Cathay.

Halston curled his hand around her arm. "Come, Miss Faulkner."

Heat sizzled through her. She raised startled eyes to his, for a fleeting instant forgetting her resentment. And any curious observers.

Stella only took an instant to recover, but the sensation had been strong enough to make her fear his power over her. Even worse, something in those glittering eyes told her that he, too, felt the searing connection.

He'd never touched her before. Last night in the gazebo, despite the tension crackling between them, he hadn't laid a hand on her.

She wanted to snap at him to let her go, but a poor relation didn't order a peer of the realm around. When she lurched forward, her unsteadiness had nothing to do with her minor injury.

As she stumbled, his grip tightened. Her heart galloped so fast that she felt light-headed. For pity's sake, she needed to get away before she made a complete fool of herself.

Damn Halston. And she damned herself, too. Why did her good sense and her sensual inclinations have to be at war over the sweet-tongued swine?

Out of the corner of her eye, she saw Imogen place the ruined embroidery on the chair that Stella had vacated. She also noted the way that every woman in the room watched Halston as he escorted Stella toward the door. He was one of those men women couldn't help noticing.

Noticing? Gossip granted him conquests from John o'Groat's to Land's End. He was accounted irresistible, the scoundrel.

Well, Stella meant to resist. If he thought to fulfill his contemptible plan to have both cousins under his thrall, she intended to thwart him.

"You can let me go now," she muttered, as they reached the empty hall outside the drawing room.

He ignored her. She'd known he would. Deciding that she despised him didn't alter her affinity with him. Last night, she'd felt as if they communicated with more than words. She still felt like that. Another rake's trick.

"I need to see you," he said in a low voice.

"No, you don't," she replied in a snarl, and this time when she tried to get away, he let her go. "Go back inside to my cousin before you cause any more talk."

The gathering comprehension in his expression had her going red again. Because however much she wished it otherwise, if she heard the note of jealousy, so did he. "By God, you can't think…"

To her relief, Frederick, one of the footmen, appeared at that moment. He cast them a glance, but at least his presence saved her from further conversation with Halston.

"Thank you for your help, my lord," she said in a carrying voice. "I'm fine to go upstairs without assistance."

His narrow-eyed attention warned her that he wasn't finished with her, but he stepped back and bowed. "I hope your hand gives you no more trouble."

She hoped that *he* gave her no more trouble, but she wouldn't lay money on it. His jaw was set with a masculine resolve that told her this matter was far from closed. Which was rich, when he was flirting with Imogen and inviting her to his house and sending her flowers.

"I'm sure it won't."

Walking away was harder than it should have been, but Stella managed it and made her way up the stairs without a backward glance. She felt Lord Halston watching every step she made. Or at least she thought she did. When she looked back from the top landing, the hall below contained neither Frederick nor her bugbear.

Plague take Halston, he was turning her into a complete ninny. And she had days of his company ahead, unless she came up with some excuse not to accompany Imogen to Prestwick Place. The bleak truth was that as a lowly servant, whether related to the family or not, she didn't have the luxury of refusing to go.

Only when she gained the sanctuary of her narrow, spartan room next to Imogen's more opulent apartments did she realize that she still clutched Lord Halston's handkerchief, sadly bloodstained now, in her good hand.

CHAPTER FOUR

The next morning, the memory of Halston's call still disturbed Stella. She was in two minds over whether to warn her cousin about the conniving earl. The problem was that romantic young girls often found a Lothario irresistible.

Imogen was beside herself about the prospect of visiting Prestwick Place. They left in a few days and would be away almost a week. Stella had tried to warn her uncle against allowing his daughter to attend a house party hosted by an acknowledged rake. But Deerforth was so blinded by the chance of Imogen attracting a proposal from a society leader like Halston that he'd refused to listen.

At least there was one benefit to this mess. Deerforth had stopped haranguing Imogen about neglecting Lord Chippenham.

Stella told herself that she disliked the idea of Halston pursuing Imogen because they were unsuited. But she had an unwelcome feeling that she was just a dog in the manger. Despite everything that she knew of the reprobate earl, she wanted him for herself. Her few hours of sleep last night had confirmed that unfortunate fact. His satanic lordship had featured in feverish dreams that had her blushing when she woke.

Yesterday when she went upstairs after pricking her finger, she'd gone looking for Halston's bouquet. Straightaway, she knew which flowers were his.

Most of the floral tributes massed around Imogen's sitting room and bedroom were pretty posies of spring flowers. So many, that Stella wondered why the overpowering perfume didn't give Imogen a headache.

A few extravagant gentlemen had even gone to the expense of ordering hothouse roses. One gentleman alone had sent a sheaf of exotic red lilies. That seemed an odd tribute to a debutante.

Knowing that she overstepped her rights, Stella couldn't help sneaking a look at the card. Crisp white board scored with a vigorous, slanting hand. Many men asked their secretary to order flowers for the beauties of the moment. Something about this convinced Stella that Halston had written the message himself.

"To my fair stranger, I hope when next we meet, we will be strangers no more. Yours, Halston."

An odd message to send a debutante. An odd message to match the odd choice of flowers.

Odd or not, the lilies had found favor with her cousin. She'd set them in the place of honor on her dressing table.

With a heavy sigh, Stella pushed open the garden's back gate. Everything was getting very complicated, and she had a headache that had nothing to do with flowers. Other than red lilies.

She was on her way to return some books to the circulating library. The membership might be in Imogen's name, but Stella was the one who did most of the reading, unless the book was about garden design. Imogen was still asleep, no doubt dreaming of Halston. At last night's ball, she'd danced twice with the earl. His wounded arm hadn't seemed to cause him any difficulty.

Dolly, the young maid who accompanied her on errands, dawdled a dozen yards behind her. "Miss Faulkner, I forgot my handkerchief. You go on ahead, and I'll catch up."

"Make sure you do," Stella said.

The morning was cold, and the girl had left her alone before, when she'd decided she'd rather loiter in the warm kitchen than come outside. Stella thought it was absurd that a woman of close to thirty and with no value in the marriage market needed a chaperone to go two streets from home. But those were the rules of London society.

Once past the busy stables, she turned into the narrow alley lined with high brick walls that brought her out onto Lorimer Square. One of these walls enclosed the overgrown garden of Fleetwood House, where the reclusive Duke of Alwyn lived.

She was in such a stew over the forthcoming house party that it took far too long to realize that an unmarked carriage had rolled forward to block her exit. Only when the door opened from inside the vehicle did she recognize her danger.

"Come along, Miss Faulkner. Don't hang about. Get into the carriage. If I've got out of bed at this ungodly hour, the least you can do is fall for my wicked stratagems."

The speaker's identity was no surprise. Of course it was Halston.

Stella stopped as uncontrollable physical awareness flooded her. She was unsure whether she wanted to scuttle back to safety or stay and give the reprobate a good scolding – and also a warning to take care of Imogen and her reputation, if his intentions were honorable.

Honorable? How on earth could they be honorable if he'd taken to lying in wait for Imogen's companion?

"It's not my responsibility if you decide to keep Christian hours," she said, despite herself venturing closer so that her voice wouldn't carry.

The plainly dressed coachman maintained his stolid stare over the horses' ears. The carriage was older and shabbier than she'd expect for someone as high in the instep as Halston.

"See? Already you're proving good for my character. With only a morsel more of your attention, redemption is a distinct possibility."

"I'm not sure you're worth the effort," she said flatly.

"Oh, cruel angel," he said, and she couldn't stifle the warmth that stole into her heart at his absurdity. Before she could question the wisdom of what she did, she stepped right up to the carriage.

Lord Halston sat in the shadows. She supposed that he was doing his best to be discreet, but she couldn't suppress a shiver. The thought was inescapable – if she joined him, she moved from bright morning light to darkness.

"I'm no angel." That was truer than he could imagine.

His smile conveyed acres of sin. Goodness, it was only nine o'clock in the morning. Too early for seduction, surely. "That's what I'm relying on."

Stella couldn't control a blush at that. "If you bribed Dolly to leave me alone with you, the news will be all over the household before luncheon."

She kept her tone matter-of-fact, even as a disagreeable mixture of anger and apprehension and reluctant fascination churned inside her.

He shook his head with a weary patience that made her want to hit him. "O ye of little faith."

"You're taking a very biblical bent this morning."

"More of your beneficial influence on my character."

"I doubt it."

Eyes glinting with laughter met hers, and despite all the curses that she'd laid on his head over the last few days, something hard and constricted inside her loosened. "I think you're dashed ungrateful, after I struggled all last night not to spare you a single longing look or whisk you out into the garden for a kiss or two. My neck aches with the effort. There I was, dancing with all those little poppets who bore me stiff, while the woman who really makes me stiff refused to give me as much as a smile."

She pretended not to hear that brazen comment. "You danced with my cousin. Twice."

While she'd sat with the chaperones, afraid that Halston might make some move toward her. Then she came home depressed, because he hadn't glanced at her. She'd tried to tell herself that was what she wanted. To her regret, she didn't believe it, although if the earl tangled her up in a scandal, her uncle wouldn't think twice before he threw her out. Then inevitable destitution awaited.

Smugness should never be attractive. On Lord Halston, it was enthralling. "You noticed."

Stella didn't smile back. "And you sent Imogen flowers and a suggestive message. And you called on her yesterday, when you invited her to your home. Are these attentions the prelude to a proposal, my lord?"

Her boldness didn't unsettle him. "I could do worse than to marry the chit." His tone turned thoughtful. "She's pretty, and livelier than most of the other girls on the marriage market this year."

No, no, no. Her stomach contracted at the thought.

He paused, while Stella struggled to come up with an adequate protest. Or a protest that avoided admitting that her main reason for loathing the idea of him marrying Imogen was that she was attracted to him herself.

He continued on in the same musing note. "If I marry Imogen, you and I will become cousins. How cozy will that be?"

She regarded him in horror. It seemed her suspicions had been correct. "You—"

"Unless you want to try and talk me out of my villainous plan. There's an idea. Why don't you get into the carriage and tell me why I should change my mind?"

"She's too good for you," she said through lips that felt like wood.

"Undoubtedly."

Her eyes narrowed on him as she climbed into the carriage and dropped onto the seat facing him. With a shaking hand, she set the heavy bag of books beside her.

She was taking a dreadful risk, but at least inside the coach, she was safe from prying eyes. What she intended to say needed privacy. Out in the alley, one of Deerforth's grooms could wander up at any time. "I won't let you marry Imogen if it's the last thing I do."

She had time to register Halston's satisfaction as he slammed the door shut, enclosing them in a twilit space that felt uncomfortably intimate. The blinds were down for discretion's sake, she supposed, although sitting in this confined cabin didn't seem discreet at all.

"'Step into my parlor,' said the spider to the fly," he purred from the seat facing forward. A gentleman would take the seat facing backward, but he'd already told her he was no gentleman, hadn't he, the blackguard?

When the coach lurched into motion, Stella linked her hands in her lap to hide their unsteadiness and grimaced in displeasure.

"Your parlor smells like it needs a good clean, Sir Spider. You'll need to do better than this decrepit conveyance, if you hope to impress Imogen," she jeered, then cringed. Curse her, could she make her jealousy any clearer?

His soft laugh made her skin tighten with desire. How could she want him and despise him at the same time? She'd known the urgency of sexual craving before, but all those years ago, her brain hadn't been in such opposition to her appetites.

As Stella's vision adjusted to the gloom, she studied Halston. Dressed in a dark coat and breeches and boots, he leaned back against his seat. She wasn't used to seeing him in such casual attire. For the ballroom, he was always turned out *comme il faut*, and yesterday for his call on Imogen, he'd worn an elegant blue coat.

The black silk sling still supported his injured arm. To her irritation, the effect was as dashing as ever. His long legs stretched across the well between the seats, so she had to crowd against the side to save her skirts from tangling with those gleaming boots.

"I don't want to impress Imogen. I have no interest in your cousin at all, as you would know if you applied an ounce of your enormous intelligence to the matter, my sweet little nincompoop."

Her lips straightened. "I'm not sweet. I'm not little. And I'm certainly not yours, my lord."

"And you're not a nincompoop." His chuckle rippled over her like warm water on a cold day. "You're just a tad bamboozled."

She was indeed, but that didn't stop her from injecting a sour note into her response. "You must be desperate to dig up a compliment, if you're stuck with commenting on a woman's cleverness."

"You underestimate me. Good conversation is one of life's great pleasures."

"And you're a great connoisseur of life's pleasures, aren't you? Clearly the world has misunderstood your interest in opera dancers, my lord. You pursue them because you want to discuss the latest poetry, not because you want to bed them."

She broke every rule in the young lady's book of etiquette by mentioning his affairs. But there was a heady freedom in not guarding her tongue.

"I didn't expect you to be a snob, Miss Faulkner." She caught the gleam of his eyes as he surveyed her. "Surely you more than anyone know that poverty doesn't necessarily stem from stupidity."

"You're right to chastise me." This time, she flushed with shame. "I don't know those women. I shouldn't make assumptions."

"No, you shouldn't. Although you've made a number of assumptions about me, which I'm pleased to say have brought you here now."

Something in her refused to cower. "You've kidnapped me," she said coldly. "Bravo. They'll give you a medal."

Another of those low laughs. "That's a rather theatrical interpretation of a short trip around some of the better areas of the capital. Especially when you climbed in of your own volition."

"You're the one who mentioned spiders and flies and stepping into parlors."

Straight white teeth flashed in a smile. "You're much too pretty to be called a fly, Miss Faulkner. Even in that inexecrable dress that's the wrong shade for you."

Nearly all her clothes were the wrong shade for her. Her warm tawny coloring was so different from Imogen's striking white skin and rich black hair.

"If I'm shabby, I match this carriage," she retorted. "Are you sure you're not in Queer Street and looking for a rich heiress to marry?"

"And after I took so much care to hire a vehicle that wouldn't attract notice. I'm hurt that you don't give my efforts to protect your good name the credit they deserve." He paused. "Actually if I'm being strict with the truth, my coachman Terry found the vehicle. He took my instruction to locate a carriage that nobody would associate with the Earl of Halston a little too much to heart."

"Is your coachman to be trusted?" She was too angry with him to be nervous. "I assume that's Terry up there and not the hackney's usual driver."

"Yes, he's my man. All my staff are to be trusted. They're paid damn good wages to keep their mouths shut."

"Yet still your doings are discussed on every corner."

He shrugged. "My mistresses aren't always as circumspect as my servants."

Her lips firmed in disapproval. "If you're hoping for a Devonshire arrangement when you wed Imogen, my lord, I won't play the third side of the triangle."

Last century, the Duke of Devonshire had maintained a famous *ménage à trois* with his wife and his mistress, his wife's best friend.

Halston tutted like a schoolmaster disappointed in a lazy pupil. "I would have thought a clever girl like you would be awake to my scheming."

"I am." Her tone remained sharp. "You want a pretty, respectable wife. And a mistress within call as well."

"I want a mistress, at least. I told you before that I don't want your cousin."

"Then why the attention to Imogen?"

"Must I explain myself? It's a devil of a bore."

The carriage slowed. Although the blinds prevented Stella from seeing outside, she guessed that they'd reached the main road and heavier traffic. "If my company no longer amuses you, my lord, I'm sure I'll survive the disappointment when you take me home." She paused. "Or to the circulating library which is where I planned to go."

A short laugh escaped him. "I'm not your deuced coachman, damn your impudence."

"No," she said in a hard voice. "Right now you're an abductor and a tormentor. And I hope that's all. I'd hate to place more serious crimes on your doorstep."

"Come now." Halston made a derisive gesture toward his injured arm. "A four-year-old child could best me. I'm not about to leap on you and have my wicked way."

Stella didn't really think he would, bullet wound or not. If she did, she'd never have got into the carriage, no matter how she itched to box his ears. "I imagine you prefer a more luxurious setting for sin."

His chuckle filled her with alarm. Her hands gripped each other until they hurt. "My dear, I'm so desperate that I'll take you wherever and whenever you give me the word. Which should tell you what you ought to know already. It's you that I'm interested in."

The alarm deepened, but unfortunately so did the hunger. She'd wondered if the moonlight had sparked the storm of attraction she felt in the gazebo. But every time she saw him, she wanted him more. His admission that he wanted her, too, did nothing to dampen her lustful impulses. "Then I'm afraid you'll have to tell me what you're up to."

Only when his smile deepened did she realize what she'd revealed in that answer. The wise choice would be to inform him in no uncertain terms that he wasn't going to have her at all. Now it seemed too coy to backtrack and claim a modesty that she didn't in truth possess.

He sighed and settled back against the cracked leather of the seat. "Will you come and sit next to me?"

"No."

"Pity. How's your hand?"

She was in such a flurry that she didn't understand the question. "My hand?"

"You hurt it yesterday."

"Oh. Yes. Yes. I did." When he'd invited Imogen to Prestwick Place, and she realized that she'd have to go, too, to supervise the burgeoning courtship.

"So how is it?"

"I'll live. I'll launder your handkerchief and return it to you."

"Don't bother. I have others."

To her mortification, she'd slept with that stained square of linen under her pillow. How he'd snigger if she told him that. For heaven's sake, it was as if she was begging him to ruin her.

The coach came to a complete stop. The street was a chaos of people and carts and horses, but inside the carriage, Stella and Halston shared a private haven that belonged in another universe.

That thought was as dangerous as anything that he'd done. Perhaps even more dangerous. Because if Stella really did live in a world where following her impulses had no unfortunate consequences, it might be her leaping on Lord Halston. She'd like to discover just what all that rakehellery had taught him about pleasing a mistress.

"In the first place, one of my footmen made an assignation with Dolly. Your name wasn't mentioned."

She sucked in a breath to calm her jumping nerves. "That's how you knew where I'd be this morning."

"See what straits you put me to? A peer of the realm turning spy."

She should be annoyed, but nobody had taken this sort of trouble over her in years. Her anger, already shaky, shifted out of reach. She missed it. Its departure left her too defenseless against other more insidious feelings. "I imagine riding in this coach feels like more of a sacrifice than perpetrating a little subterfuge."

"Anything for you, my darling."

The sugary endearment provoked an unimpressed huff. "Only if it fits with your plans. I won't have Dolly used and abandoned. If your man goes beyond a few kisses, he'll have to wed the wench."

An exaggerated sigh. "Dolly shall be safe. You have my word on it." He paused. "Although you mightn't be."

The mortifying fact was that with every minute in Halston's company, safety lost more of its appeal. "And Imogen?"

Again she'd missed an opportunity to put him in his place with a decisive "no, thank you." She feared that she moved beyond the chance to speak those words. At least in a way he'd believe.

"Can you see me with the chit?"

"Yes, I can. She's not silly, and she's very pretty, and while her father's no prize, she's wellborn enough to be your countess."

He frowned as if her response was a disagreeable surprise. "Are you trying to talk me into proposing to the girl?"

She shook her head. "No. She deserves better than you."

"Ouch."

She didn't smile. "She's pure, and she's good, and I'd hate her to be disillusioned by the man she marries."

"Whereas you have no illusions at all."

"No, I don't."

"You knew what I meant when I said you made me stiff."

Startled, she sat up straighter as the carriage jerked forward, bumping across the cobblestones. There was shouting from the street, but she paid it no heed. The squabble outside couldn't compare to the war that she fought in this private space. A war that she seemed to be losing.

The problem was that she faced attack on two fronts. Lord Halston wanted her to succumb to him. So, to her disgust, did everything untamed and free that had lurked in her heart for the last ten years.

"Did you think you pursued an unworldly spinster?"

He gave a derisive huff of laughter. "Wide-eyed innocence isn't my style."

"So why did you send flowers to Imogen?"

"Haven't you worked it out yet?" His hand sliced the air. "The lilies were for you. I assumed you'd guess. They're not suitable for a young girl. The message should have told you, if nothing else."

Could that be true? Had she been so blinded with jealousy that she'd missed the most obvious answer? From the first, something had seemed off about those flowers and that message when she tried to match them up with Imogen.

"Imogen was a stranger to you, too."

"Imogen is a means to an end. I told you in the gazebo that I've been trying to work out how to gain your attention."

"And the house party invitation?"

With a speaking expression, Halston glanced around the coach's dilapidated interior. "In the country, I'll find it easier to arrange time alone with you."

Time alone with her? A naughty thrill that she didn't want to acknowledge ripped through her. "You're taking a lot of trouble to create an opportunity for fornication."

He shrugged. "I'm sure my labors will receive adequate reward."

Her laugh was wry. "Are you? I'm not."

Halston arched his eyebrows. "Miss Faulkner, I'm counted a fine judge of women. If I deem you worthy of notice, odds indicate that you are."

Stella studied him, profoundly perturbed. She'd started out convinced that the dangers of an affair with this decorative libertine outweighed all other considerations. Now she seemed to be contemplating how they might manage a liaison.

"If my uncle ever learns that you and I were involved, I'd be out on the streets. You risk nothing in this game. I risk everything."

"I know." For once, his tone held no challenge. The unexpected gentleness undermined her caution as nothing else could have. "Which is why I'm trying so hard to keep our affair a secret."

"We're not having an affair," she retorted, although if she heard fading resistance in her voice, so could he.

God save her, could she do this shocking thing? The perils were enormous. Unthinkable. Yet something told Stella that if she went to Halston's bed, the rewards would be even greater.

She'd struggled to reconcile herself to surviving without excitement, physical pleasure, even any genuine purpose. Halston reminded her that she was a woman with feelings and desires. Life since she'd left Naples had done its best to suffocate her ardent nature. The grim reality was that the years to come would achieve that goal.

This might be her last chance to revel in a man's passion. It might be her last chance to reciprocate that passion. Whatever else Lord Halston was, she knew he'd prove to be a breathtaking lover. The future promised to be bleak and lonely. Memories of a rake's touch might offer a little warmth to hold against the endless cold.

Halston watched her with an unwavering stare. His voice was soft. "We're not having an affair *yet*."

"Yet," she echoed, peering at him through the dimness and wondering if she could trust him. Wondering if she'd gone past the point where she'd hesitate even if she couldn't trust him.

Stella waited for some sign of triumph, because they both knew that she teetered on the brink of consent. But the eyes that met hers were serious and conveyed a sincere concern that she feared relying on. "Will you come to me when we get to Prestwick Place, Miss Faulkner? I'm ravenous for you, and I have a suspicion that you might feel a slight yen toward me, too?"

"A slight yen?" she repeated with a hint of mockery.

That mobile mouth quirked. "Do I dare to suggest that I underestimate your interest?"

"Devil take you, Halston." She sighed as she gave up the fight. His victory had been ordained since she'd first seen him across a crowded ballroom and her starved heart had kicked into a frantic gallop of greedy desire. "You'll dare more than that before you're finished."

"By God, I hope so," he said in a fervent voice as he seized her gloved hand.

Stella didn't try to pull free. After yesterday, the shock of contact shouldn't catch her unawares. But her ungovernable heart slammed to a dizzying stop, and the breath crammed in her lungs.

"What do you say, Miss Faulkner?" He paused. "Damn it, I can't keep calling you Miss Faulkner."

Amusement turned down her lips. "No, I suppose not. Not if this really is going to happen. My name is Stella."

Silly, given she agreed to allow him all kinds of liberties, that inviting him to use her Christian name felt like she broke some taboo.

Halston firmed his grip. "Stella." Her name sounded beautiful on his lips. "So you agree to be mine?"

Heaven help her, heaven help both of them, it seemed she did. "Yes," she said on a shaky exhalation as delicious heat flowed up her arm. "We...we have to make a few things clear."

"Anything," he said urgently.

Her laugh cracked. "Careful. You don't know what you're promising."

"I don't care. I'll do anything to have you."

Astonished, she tried to make sense of this. He'd had so many women. Why should she be anything special? "You sound like you mean that."

"Don't you know that I'm mad for you?"

That should terrify her. Not least because she feared that when they came together, she'd prove a sad disappointment. But every word Halston spoke sent need pulsing through her blood.

"You...you have to protect my good name. You know what all this can cost me."

"You have my word."

Perhaps she shouldn't believe him, except that he'd already gone to extraordinary lengths to conceal his interest in her. In London, the world's gaze followed his every move. In the country, they might find a chance to be alone and unobserved.

"The affair ends when I say. It won't extend past our time at Prestwick Place, in any case. Once I'm back in London, you and I go back to being strangers."

He frowned. "Will that be enough for you?"

Stella already knew that it wouldn't be, but what choice did she have? "If we come together in London, people will find out." She paused. "I thought you'd like that condition. Your dalliances aren't noted for their longevity."

His wince was theatrical. "I don't know why I like you so much. I've never met a girl so candid about my failings."

She didn't smile back. All this was so fraught for her. She might have consented to come to Halston's bed, but she was wide awake to the dangers of her decision. Even if she was discreet, discovery was possible. Even likely.

"I suspect that I'm only of interest because I'm a novelty. You, too, may stop the affair any time you like. I promise I won't make a scene. That should make a nice change for you."

"I won't call an end to things before I have to."

The certainty in his voice set her heartbeat leaping. "We'll see." Before he could argue, she went on. "I can't risk a child. You must finish outside me."

She expected her frankness to disconcert him, but he merely nodded. "As you wish."

"Thank you." She sucked in another breath. The realization seeped in that she'd committed to become Halston's lover. Even worse, she couldn't muster a moment's regret about the decision. "Now I think you should take me home."

His devilish smile set her secret places clenching. By heaven, he was a beautiful man. How could she, how could any woman resist falling?

"Not quite yet. We need to seal our deal."

A sudden attack of nerves made her disentangle their fingers. Her hand rose to the base of her throat where her pulse raced fast enough to win the Derby. "You said you'd wait until..."

"Until we get to Prestwick Place." His smile intensified. "I did. But I'm sure that a woman who makes such a businesslike contract to come to my bed can spare me a kiss on account."

CHAPTER FIVE

*H*alston watched her eyes darken. Stella Faulkner had such an expressive face, especially now that she stopped guarding every reaction. How difficult it must be for this passionate creature to restrain all her natural impulses when she was in her uncle's house. Life had been ghastly unfair to this exceptional woman.

The carriage began to move faster. An opening must have appeared in the traffic. With every second, the charged atmosphere inside the vehicle intensified. When they came together at last, the explosion would rock the world.

"Kiss?" The slide of her tongue moistening her lips shuddered through him like gunfire.

"Yes." He made another wry gesture toward the sling. "If I were in full fighting order, I'd take you into my arms right now. As it is, I'll have to ask you to come and sit beside me. Will you do that?"

Her lips twisted. Self-deprecating humor was such an essential part of her. "It seems absurd to hesitate when you have my promise that I'll come to your bed."

"But right now, it would be easier if I could sweep you into my embrace and make the world go away?"

"Yes."

He held out his good hand. "Come kiss me, my darling. I hunger for you."

Her smile faded, and he caught a glimpse of the depth of her craving for him. She'd stopped pretending that she had any more choice in what happened between them than he had.

He liked that. He liked that very much indeed.

Halston couldn't remember the last time that he was in thrall to a woman, the way he was in thrall to this one. His craving made a mockery of propriety and caution and prudence. The idea that he might experience this volcanic yearning alone was unbearable.

It turned out that he wasn't alone.

Stella trembled when she took his hand and shifted next to him. As she'd pointed out, the old carriage held traces of twenty years of former passengers. Unwashed humanity. Stale tobacco. Dust and dog hair. But she was so close now that something fresh and citrusy tinged his deep breath of relief. He caught a hint of something else, too. An alluring female warmth that must be the scent of her skin.

She turned toward him, and her gaze found his as she took off her plain bonnet. For a long moment, they studied each other. The hubbub of London, the seedy surroundings, the threat of discovery, all dissolved to nothing. The world shrank to this woman and his compulsion to claim her.

This close, he could see the pupils dilate in her golden-brown eyes. Her lips parted as her breath rushed out, and her breasts swelled against the unbecoming gown. By God, if she was his mistress in truth, he'd dress her to match her leonine beauty.

But he already knew that this affair would be brief and intense, and a matter of secret assignations. He'd never get the chance to set Stella Faulkner up with a house and a carriage and a bed that he had a right to share while he paid her bills. She wasn't one of his pretty light-skirts, contracted to stay as long as he was interested in pumping them.

Perhaps Halston should be grateful for that. He wouldn't have to watch this initial enchantment fizzle away into boredom and bitterness. It must be the force of his current desire that had him convinced that this time his interest wouldn't fade, that this time the fascination would only grow.

To his surprise, his hand was unsteady, too, as he cupped the delicate line of her jaw. The shock of his skin on hers slammed through him, the way it had when he'd taken her arm yesterday afternoon.

Stella gasped when he made contact, and her eyes widened. She felt it, too.

The day was cold, but her skin was warm and smooth. He rubbed his thumb against her cheek and leaned in closer. He was near enough to taste her breath. It carried a hint of mint tooth powder, because it was still so early in the morning. Most people he knew would still be sleeping off last night's excesses.

With a gentleness in opposition to the storm raging through him, he tilted her face up to position her for his kiss.

"Halston…" she whispered, and the longing in the sound had him quaking. He couldn't remember the last time a woman had made him shake. Stella made him shake without even trying.

"Yes, sweetheart?"

She curled her gloved hand behind his neck to bring him closer. "Stop teasing me, curse you."

"I'm savoring the anticipation."

Her eyes sparked. "You devil."

His hold firmed, and he closed the distance between them. When his lips met hers, the world flared into blinding heat. There was no hesitation, no seeking for the best way to proceed. Her mouth opened, and she welcomed the thrust of his tongue.

On a choked sound of surrender, she curved closer. Pleasure flooded him and a sense of rightness that he'd never known before. His tongue flicked against hers, encouraging her to join in the play of lips and teeth. She needed no second invitation.

He groaned and released her face to curve his good arm around her. His head was swimming, as his body readied itself to go beyond mere kissing. Although mere kissing didn't begin to describe this experience.

She speared her fingers through his hair and tugged. The faint discomfort built his need. He leaned forward, pressing her against the side of the coach. She followed his lead as sweetly as honey drizzled on fresh bread. Her murmurs against his lips indicated approval.

By all that was holy, he had to have her now. They had privacy. A woman who devoured him with her kisses wouldn't deny him. He twisted on the worn seat and reached out with his other arm to shift her so she could take him.

Red-hot pain sliced through Halston, and his groan this time wasn't a reaction to pleasure. He wrenched away from Stella and pressed a shaking hand to his shoulder. "Damn it, I forgot my injury."

She slumped against the faded pattern on the wall. The unabashed desire in her expression did nothing to quell his pounding urge to possess her.

Her thick honey-brown eyelashes drooped over heavy eyes, and her mouth was full and damp after his kisses.

"Are you all right?" she asked, her voice husky.

The pain started to recede. "You make me forget everything else."

"It's the same for me." Her hand moved in a helpless gesture. "Practice has made you a wonderful kisser. It leaves me wondering what else you can do to me."

Arousal thundered through him with a force that vied with the ache in his arm. "You're not coy."

"Do you mind?"

"No, I like it. I always imagined that beneath the prim exterior, there was a woman who matched me in desire. I'm delighted to discover I was right."

Stella didn't pretend affront at his statement. With every second, he fell further under her spell. She'd kissed him with a voraciousness that made him mad for her.

Taking care with his arm, he kissed her again. She met him with a lack of shyness that had him hard and throbbing. How in tarnation could he contain himself until they reached Prestwick Place?

When she pushed at his chest and tugged her lips free, it was almost as painful as jarring his arm.

"I have to get back." Her voice shook. So did she. "We can't come together here."

"I know that." Halston heard his furious regret. "Although for a moment there, I forgot. You took me to a new world."

Her smile made his heart lurch. She looked as captivated as he felt, damn it. It seemed a sin against nature that he couldn't steal her away this instant.

"I want you now." He couldn't remember the last time a woman had obsessed him like this. "I've hardly had a thought that doesn't involve you since the day I first saw you. Now I've kissed you, I won't be fit for anything else until I can hold you in my arms again."

Her features softened, and she stroked his face with a tenderness that made his heart squeeze tight as a walnut. Even through the thin leather glove, her touch sent heat roaring through him. "You shouldn't say such things."

He lifted his good hand to press her palm against his cheek. "Why not? They're true. Can I see you again before we go to the country?"

She was drifting back from the realms of sensual pleasure. As the dreamy light faded from her eyes, she became alert to the risks they ran. To confirm those risks, someone swore just beyond the window, the curse so loud that the man could be inside the carriage with them. Halston and Stella might pretend the city outside didn't exist, but if he pulled up the blinds, they'd be in full view of the busy street.

"You'll see me tonight at the Wetherby musicale, if you intend to come."

"You know what I mean."

Her smile basked in his desperation. He liked to see her accepting his need for her as her due. When they'd met in the garden, she hadn't trusted his interest. "I do."

"Well?"

She withdrew her hand. The cessation of contact felt like the fall of an ax.

By George, she had him in a spin. The power of this desire threw a stark light on how his recent affairs had seen him just going through the motions.

"I think it's too dangerous."

With a moody sigh, he sat back and scowled at her. "You have no pity for me."

"You know there will be more inconveniences than you're used to."

"I know you're going to drive me to lunacy with wanting you."

"You promised to preserve my good name."

"Yes, I did. But that was before I kissed you. How in Hades do you expect me to act as if we're strangers now?"

Her expression turned stern. "Lord Halston, if you won't abide by my conditions, we can't continue."

Aghast, he stared at her. "You'd turn your back on an attraction as powerful as ours?"

Stella returned to the other seat, and she spoke with an implacable tone that he had to believe. "If I'm exposed as your lover, I'll lose any security I have. At worst, you'll suffer a bit of gossip. The world will shrug its shoulders and say the notorious earl has made another conquest. I didn't lay down my conditions lightly, my lord. Tell me now if they don't suit you, and we'll shake hands and part, with no rancor on either side."

Astonished, annoyed, offended, he surveyed her. She spoke as if it wouldn't hurt her to forsake him, whereas the thought of letting her go devastated him. Already. When he hadn't yet taken her.

What state would he be in by the time he bedded her?

He didn't like the shift in power. When he'd decided to seduce this improbable chaperone, he'd imagined that he held all the cards. It turned out that Stella Faulkner had a power of her own. More, it was a power she intended to exercise.

"You know the lengths I'm taking to protect you."

"I know that you'll need to double your care for me. Are you sure I'm worth the inconvenience?"

"By God, yes," he groaned, picking up her hand. Damn it, he couldn't even take off her glove because of his gunshot wound. Francene's theatrical gesture was turning out to be a blasted nuisance.

Stella lifted his hand to her lips and kissed it. She was more demonstrative than he'd expected. He liked that. In particular, he liked the idea of her devoting that boldness to him when he got her to himself in Buckinghamshire. The problem was that he needed to last until then without shattering in frustration.

"Then we have an agreement, my lord." She inspected him. He saw that his fears of her coolness were unfounded. Those caramel eyes were smoky with hunger. "Let me help you with your sling. It's coming off."

"Thank you." He rapped his knuckles on the roof of the carriage to tell Terry to retrace his route to Lorimer Square. Or a discreet alley around the corner from it.

Halston sat vibrating with desire as she moved next to him to fix his sling and straighten his clothes. Every touch thundered through him and reminded him that in this affair, he was vulnerable in a way he'd never been before.

When she'd finished tidying him up, she raised unsteady hands to her hair. "Do I look like I've been kissing a disreputable gentleman?"

He smiled, almost reconciled to letting her go. After all, he'd never intended to seduce Stella in this ramshackle vehicle. She was so perfect in his arms that he'd got ahead of himself. Which was a surprise in itself. Lord Halston never approached a liaison without making all the calculations. "A little."

It was more the languorous glow in those brilliant eyes than anything obvious like disordered clothing. He'd got bloody excited, considering that he hadn't undone a single button on that severe frock.

She looked dismayed and started to smooth her hair. Halston watched her with intense pleasure. He couldn't remember being this interested in a conquest since...

Well, since never.

"Come and kiss me," he murmured. "So I have something to keep me going until we reach Prestwick Place."

The gaze she leveled on him was hot enough to get him all het up again. "Is that a good idea?"

"Do you care?"

She looked troubled. "I fear you're a rash devil, and you're going to cause me a lot of bother."

"I hope so. Even if just in a private capacity."

A reluctant laugh escaped as she slid closer. "I wish it was Saturday and I was at Prestwick Place."

"So do I." He curled his good arm around her and drew her unresisting body against his.

Stella placed her hands on either side of his head. "Kiss me, Halston."

Their lips met, and once again everything beyond their embrace disappeared. He took his time, tantalizing her until she sighed with pleasure. Then he lost himself in a passionate exploration that threatened to turn his blood to steam.

When he raised his head, she'd collapsed against the seat. She looked as overcome as he felt. Her hands curled over his shoulders. "I wish I didn't have to leave you."

He'd wanted confirmation that what they did affected her as deeply as it affected him. He'd wanted to regain his power over her. Now he did. Yet there was no triumph, just pleasure in knowing that whatever this glorious insanity was, they suffered together.

"Then don't. Come home with me now and let's feed on each other until we're sated. If ever a woman was born to rule a sensual kingdom, it's you. It's an offence to nature for you to be a dried-up stick of a governess."

For one resonant moment, he wondered whether she'd throw away everything that trapped her in her uncle's house. He found himself praying that she'd agree. Together, they could handle any disaster that followed.

Then, as part of him knew she must, she pushed herself up to sit apart. "Tempting as that offer is, Halston, we live in the real world."

"I haven't felt like I lived in the real world since I first kissed you."

Stella dismissed his ardent comment with a laugh. "Then it's a good thing that one of us is trying to be practical." She paused. "The carriage has stopped."

"Has it?" Halston couldn't look away from her face, soft and rosy after those tempestuous kisses.

"Does that mean we're back in Lorimer Square? I'm not game to show myself."

He didn't move straightaway. "If it does, you'll leave me."

Her lips turned down. "I must." With a shaky laugh, she once again smoothed her fiercely restrained hair. "What you do to me."

With great reluctance, he lifted the blind far enough to confirm that they were on a side street off Lorimer Square. Blast it all, he felt like he'd only been with her for five minutes.

Halston sent Stella a hopeful look, even as he knew that it wasn't fair to ask her to stay. "I hate sending you back to servitude."

She shrugged. "It's not so bad. At least Imogen isn't a little tyrant. Don't imagine I've suffered this last ten years."

Except that he already knew she had. He'd caught a glimpse of the vivid creature who lurked under the controlled exterior. He hated to think of Stella spending years concealing her true self beneath that prim manner. And while she seemed to accept her life, it couldn't have been easy to humble that proud spirit.

"One more kiss?"

She shook her head, but the longing in her eyes told him that she didn't want to go. Hell, sometimes – often – he loathed society with its curiosity and its judgement and its endless rules. But never did he hate it so much as now. What harm would it do to the world if he took Stella Faulkner away with him now?

"One more kiss will turn into two, then three."

And after that, more than kisses. Passion like this wouldn't long be content with kisses. Sucking in a shuddering breath, Halston tried to console himself with a reminder that they'd have their chance in a few days.

It wasn't enough.

He began to doubt if anything he did with this woman would be enough. Although that thought must stem from the unusual restrictions placed around this particular affair. He never pursued respectable women. In particular, respectable women with as much to lose as Stella. In general, he despised those unprincipled swine who took advantage of servants who weren't in a position to say no.

That wasn't Stella, thank God. But they were both aware of her precarious situation. Not even a whisper must escape that buttoned-up Miss Faulkner had fallen prey to a rake's advances.

Right now, letting her go felt like someone sliced at him with a razor, but he was in the throes of wanting without possessing. Once she'd surrendered, surely he'd grow bored, surely whatever power she wielded would fade. He'd solve her mysteries and when he did, as always happened, she'd lose her allure.

But as Halston stared into those golden-brown eyes, it didn't feel like that would ever happen. When he stared into those golden-brown eyes, he couldn't help but wonder if this was the one woman whose appeal would last.

Romantic nonsense. After all his experience, he should know better.

The scoffing voice lacked conviction. Because if this was the woman whose appeal never palled, where did that leave him?

CHAPTER SIX

" *My* goodness, Stella, it's magnificent!"

Stella raised her head. She'd been pretending to read a book for most of the trip from London. She hadn't taken much of it in because her thoughts dwelled on Lord Halston's kisses.

Beside her, Imogen's maid snorted awake, but when she saw they were still traveling, she closed her eyes again. Nancy was a good-hearted girl, but inclined to laziness when she could get away with it.

Imogen leaned out the carriage window, one hand holding her stylish chip straw bonnet in place as she drank in the scenery.

"Sit down, Imogen, unless you want to look like a wild hoyden when we arrive at the house. You'll have plenty of time to see the estate over the next few days."

"But look, Stella."

Feeling as if she gave into sinful temptation, she put aside her novel. "You'll have to shift away from the window before I can see, you ridiculous girl. One would think you've never seen a country house before."

As she settled back in her seat, Imogen gave a self-conscious laugh. "I know I'm being frightfully gauche, but Prestwick Place is more impressive than our house. I'm looking forward to touring the grounds. They're supposed to be among Capability Brown's best work."

Stella rolled her eyes. When she was alone with Imogen, she didn't need to conceal the saltier parts of her personality. "So you've told me about five hundred times. If I hear one more word about follies or terraces or the placement of oak groves, I swear I'll throw myself out of this carriage."

Imogen smiled without a trace of remorse. "I fear I'm a dreadful trial to you."

Stella smiled back. "Perhaps not a *dreadful* trial."

"You're too good to me. But I've wanted to see Prestwick Place for years. I've been trying to achieve some of the same effects at Hamble Park, but Papa is proving uncooperative."

"He didn't let you dig three new lakes. I remember that. I can't imagine your suffering, you poor deprived creature."

Imogen laughed again. She was in a notably good mood. She'd been in a notably good mood since she'd been introduced to Lord Halston a week ago.

As Stella studied her cousin, with her bright eyes and rosy cheeks and air of barely suppressed excitement, disquiet pricked her. Was Imogen hoping that this house party might produce a proposal from Halston? He'd stated that he had no interest in Imogen, and Stella believed him. But she didn't want her cousin's feelings hurt either.

Imogen had never shown much interest in the male sex, beyond their ability to shift mounds of dirt or chop down trees. It would be a pity if her first romantic stirrings ended in tears.

"It was only two lakes, and one wasn't much more than a pond." Imogen gestured toward the window. "You haven't looked yet. I would think a woman who loves the countryside as much as you do would be beside herself to get out of London for a few days. But you've had your nose in a book the whole way."

"How do you know? You've been asleep for the last three hours."

"Have you looked outside?"

With a long-suffering sigh, Stella glanced out the window, then couldn't contain a gasp of admiration. Imogen was right. The approach to Prestwick Place was magnificent indeed.

They'd come through the estate gates twenty minutes ago and driven through a forest. Now the vista opened up to reveal an idyllic landscape of marble temples and silvery lakes and lush parkland, scattered with the groves that so took Imogen's fancy.

It was perfect. More perfect than Hamble Park, which despite Imogen's best efforts, included too many disparate elements to make a satisfying whole.

Stella was already too close to being smitten with Prestwick Place's owner. She refused to fall in love with his house as well. Especially as she had no chance at all of ever becoming its chatelaine.

In fairy tales, the handsome prince might rescue Cinderella from her servitude and whisk her away to a happy ending as his princess. In real life, rakes took poor girls to their beds then tossed them out to survive as best they could, once they'd served their purpose.

Stella couldn't even resent Lord Halston for what he offered her. He'd been honest about his expectations. He made no promises beyond short-term pleasure. She wasn't a candidate to become his countess, and they both knew it.

But as her wondering gaze took in the approach to the gracious old Jacobean house in its lush valley, she couldn't help wishing that she was an eligible lady who might one day take charge of this impressive property.

"Didn't I tell you?" Imogen asked.

Stella leaned back and battled to stifle her powerful and unacceptable reaction to Halston's beautiful home. She was a temporary denizen in this particular Eden, just as she was a temporary denizen in his life. If she ever let herself forget that, she was in trouble. "You did."

"I wonder if Lord Halston will introduce me to his head gardener."

For a moment, a nonplussed Stella regarded her cousin. This last week, Imogen had acted like every other society miss, interested in what she wore and keen to attend the next in the endless round of social engagements. "Imogen, I doubt you'll have time for that. You're one of the guests, and manners require you to stay with the other visitors."

"Don't be so starchy, Stella. Lord Halston told me that things are free and easy here at Prestwick Place and he just wants me to enjoy myself."

"Which doesn't mean you can spend all day talking compost and drainage with the outdoor staff."

Imogen shrugged and turned her attention back to the superb view. "Not all day."

With that, Stella had to be satisfied.

When they arrived, Stella braced for her first sight of Halston. Since that astonishing carriage ride through London when he kissed her into a daze, she'd seen him at a distance at two balls and the Wetherby musicale. In a crowded room, hiding her interest was difficult enough. In his house, among this select gathering, she'd have to be even more careful than usual.

But the butler who greeted them said that his lordship was occupied with urgent business and he'd see his visitors at dinner. The other guests had already arrived and retired to their rooms to recover from the journey.

According to Imogen, Halston had invited about twenty people to stay. Stella couldn't help but find the pains that he'd taken to bring her here without arousing any curiosity flattering. Even her first love hadn't gone to such lengths to get her alone. But then, the rules of courtship in Naples were looser than they were in London. At least when it came to a young man pursuing a poverty-stricken foreigner.

To Stella's surprise, when the maid showed her to her room, she wasn't sleeping in the dressing room or next to the nurseries. She was yet to sleep in the servants' quarters when Imogen stayed with friends or extended family, but her lowly status was always clear.

"Are you sure this room is for me?" She stepped aside as two footmen brought in her shabby luggage, which looked very out of place amidst this Renaissance splendor. The high ceiling was gilded with suns and moons and the Maddox crest, a rather disgruntled-looking unicorn in gold chains. A four-poster bed hung with brocade curtains dominated the room, which was paneled in oak and decorated with paintings of mythological subjects and two huge, ornate mirrors.

"Yes, miss. His lordship arranged for you to be next to Lady Imogen." Behind the maid, the footmen carried her bags through a door that seemed to lead to a dressing room for her exclusive use. "Her ladyship's dressing room is next to yours, although the connecting door is jammed at present. Her bedroom is the one along from that. Shall I unpack for you?"

"No." Troubled, Stella collapsed onto a tapestry-upholstered window seat. The lavish room offered a fine view of the three lakes that so aroused Imogen's envy. "No, thank you."

The girl curtsied. "Very good, Miss Faulkner. George will bring you some refreshments. There's hot water in the dressing room if you'd like to wash. Or we could arrange a bath."

A bath? What a luxury. "No, thank you, but some tea would be welcome."

"Very good, miss."

Feeling overwhelmed, Stella watched the servants leave, then wide-eyed she surveyed her surroundings. Never had she experienced such opulence. It felt wrong on so many levels, although her automatic panic that people would guess that Halston intended to visit her here had subsided. She was well below the notice of the other guests. Nobody other than Imogen was likely to set foot in this richly decorated apartment that was so inappropriate for a humble companion.

As if summoned by the thought, her cousin appeared in the doorway. "This is lovely, Stella."

She raised her head. Imogen still wore her travel dress, although she'd taken off her pelisse and bonnet. Her excitement was even more apparent than it had been in the carriage.

"I think there's been a mistake."

Imogen shook her head. "I gather it's the only room where you can be near me. Nancy is sleeping in my dressing room."

"It doesn't feel right."

"Oh, you drive me mad sometimes," she sighed, coming in uninvited and plopping herself down on a gilded sofa. Why should she wait for an invitation? Stella was her minion, after all. "You're almost wallowing in being poor. Your life doesn't have to be sackcloth and ashes. You should let yourself have fun now and again."

A memory of forbidden kisses flashed through Stella's mind. If only Imogen knew. "But a room like this just makes everything else more painful." She shook her head and struggled to muster a smile. "I'm being ungracious. If the house is so crowded that a mere companion gets to sleep in these glorious surroundings, how can I complain?"

Imogen's nod was approving. "That's the spirit."

"Is your room nice?"

"Palatial. And about a mile square. You'll have to come and see it later."

"Later?"

"Yes, Harriet wants me to have tea with her. She sent a message when she saw us arrive."

Imogen's best friend, the Lumsdens' second-oldest daughter, also attended the house party, along with her parents. That was one of the reasons that Lord Deerforth had been willing to send Imogen away under Stella's sole supervision. "Shall I come?"

"Why don't you enjoy a little time to yourself? You've been running after me every minute of the day since we got to London. I've noticed this last week that you've been tired and distracted. You can have a nap. I'm hoping this will be a little holiday for you."

"That's very nice of you." Moments like these explained how Stella had managed to endure ten years with the Ridleys. Imogen was often kind, when she didn't have to be. "I'm sorry if I've let the side down."

A careless hand waved away the apology. "As if you'd do that. But you've been a little less...present these last few days. A stay in the country should do you good."

Stella hoped that she wasn't blushing. To her relief, her tea tray arrived at that moment, saving her from having to come up with some explanation for her distraction. And not the real one. She knew exactly what caused her to neglect her duties. Or rather who.

"I hope so. A ball isn't half as much fun when one is the observer as it is when one is beguiling London with one's charm."

Imogen giggled. "You have your own charm, you know."

If she did, it would forever remain a secret from society. She rose and wandered across to the table. Not only was there a pot of tea, but sandwiches and cakes. It had been a long time since they'd stopped for lunch at one of the big coaching inns. Stella's stomach gave a rumble that proved she was a peasant and no princess.

She stripped off her gloves and picked up a chicken sandwich without stopping to remove her pelisse. "In that case, seeing you have other fish to fry, I'll have my tea and see you before dinner."

The footman finished setting up the tea and bowed before he left. As Stella ate her sandwich and then another one, Imogen almost skipped out of the room. She really was in alt about this visit.

Stella stared after her cousin with growing consternation. Was Imogen persuading herself into a penchant for Halston? She hoped to heaven not.

Once the door closed, she gave a heavy sigh. She subsided onto one of the delicate mahogany chairs to nibble one of the exquisite little cakes and drink her tea. Why did everything have to be so infernally complicated?

The hot fragrant liquid was like heaven. She closed her eyes and felt some of the tension leach out of her. Solitude was so rare, these moments felt like a gift. Perhaps Imogen was right, and she shouldn't talk herself out of enjoying her stay at Prestwick Place. After all, this was as close to being a kept woman as she was ever likely to come.

"Do you like your room?"

Shock made her hand tremble until her tea splashed into her saucer. She surged to her feet and whirled to face the intruder. "Halston!"

CHAPTER SEVEN

Halston smiled to have the woman he wanted above all others here in his home. For once, front and center in a setting that befitted her.

Now if only he could get Stella out of that hideous green traveling ensemble that was far too young for her and designed for a curvy little poppet like her cousin. And when he said get her out of it, he wasn't just thinking about the sensual possibilities.

"Welcome to Prestwick Place, Stella."

He'd hoped to surprise her. If her wide-eyed astonishment was any indication, he'd succeeded. "How on earth did you get in here? Have you been hiding the whole time?"

With a low laugh, he leaned a shoulder against one of the barley sugar columns that rose from the base of the bed to hold up the elaborate canopy. "Grant me a little dignity, please."

"You didn't come through the door." She set the cup and saucer on the table. "Did you come in through the dressing room?"

She was regaining her composure. He'd make sure that didn't last, by George.

He was surprised himself at quite what enormous pleasure he got from seeing her at Prestwick Place. "Don't be a silly widgeon. That wouldn't be very discreet."

"No, it wouldn't." Her exasperated look pleased him, too.

Halston loved that neither his title nor his rakish reputation overawed her. From the first, Stella had seen him as the man he was, without the deceiving glamour that gossip lent him. Only with her did he realize what a burden it was always to play a role.

He indicated the paneling in a shadowy corner beside the bed. "I chose this room because a hidden passage leads to the earl's apartments."

"I didn't hear anything."

He smiled. "Yesterday I spent a donkey's age oiling the door so it doesn't creak. See what lengths you've driven me to?"

She frowned. "So you can pop into my room whenever you feel the urge?"

"Only at your invitation."

Her eyes narrowed on him. "I didn't invite you this time."

He shrugged. "I must have misheard you."

She burst into laughter. "To the devil with you, Halston, you're an impudent beast."

He straightened. "I am at that."

"I suppose the passage was a priest's hole. The house is old enough."

Sardonic humor curled his lips. "I suspect that a previous earl built it so he could visit his mistress without his wife knowing."

"Now you're using it to visit your mistress."

"Do you mind?" She didn't sound as if she did.

"That I'm here to share your bed? No. Although perhaps you should knock on the wall or something before you come through."

"As you wish. Shall I lock the door to the corridor outside?"

"No, if Imogen finds it locked, she'll ask too many questions. She's off having tea with Harriet Comerford. That should keep her occupied for at least an hour. Probably two." Stella studied him with a critical eye. "You're not wearing your sling."

He glanced at his wounded arm. "It was a damned nuisance."

"Does it still hurt?"

"Getting into this coat had its moments." He paused. "But when I'm naked, I should have no difficulty."

A faint flush marked her cheekbones. "I think my difficulties might start when you're naked."

"I hope so."

She made a helpless gesture. "They said that you were busy with important business."

His smile widened. "I am."

She understood straightaway. How Halston loved that quicksilver intelligence. "Oh."

"Perhaps it's time to start negotiations."

She looked wary. "Now?"

"A small taste, at least." His smile faded, and he let her see the hunger that had gripped him since their last meeting. "These past few days have been torture, seeing you and not being able to touch you."

She took a step forward. "I tried so hard not to stare at you as if you're the center of my world."

He covered the distance between them and swept her into his arms, ignoring the pull on his healing scar. His mouth crashed down on hers. Their conversation, as so often, had been prickly and full of wry humor. This kiss was as serious as life and death and burned with the desire that had eaten him up since he'd last held her.

Immediate heat flared. With a soft growl of enjoyment, she kissed him back, using her tongue. Her hands raked through his hair as she held him close.

She gave another of those beguiling little murmurs and sucked his tongue into her mouth. It was the most carnal thing that he could remember in a lifetime of carnal encounters.

He swung her toward the bed, setting off another twinge in his shoulder, and pushed her down onto the mattress. Kneeling over her, he met her gaze in the shadows. Her eyes were large and dark, the color of old brandy, and her bosom swelled against the jacket of her traveling ensemble.

"Let's see what's under this horror of a coat," he said roughly, unfastening the row of plain buttons down the front.

She gave a splutter of laughter. "You never like what I wear."

"Do you?"

"Not much."

Halston pushed aside the edges of the pelisse and started work on the second set of buttons doing up her frock. As he uncovered her down to the edge of her plain white shift, his heart slammed against his ribs in a way that it hadn't in years, even when he'd undressed the most celebrated courtesans.

He kissed each inch of olive skin that he revealed, relishing her rich female fragrance with its tinge of salt. He hadn't even given her time to wash after her journey. He was such a barbarian. But he'd been watching for her arrival, the way he'd once watched in vain for his mother to visit him at Eton.

Nor was Stella a passive partner in this gathering tempest of desire. She shifted under his kisses, releasing intriguing little sighs that rose to a hoarse cry when he kissed her neck. Her hands danced across his shoulders and arms. Somewhere in all that frenzy of caresses, she got out of her pelisse and untied his neckcloth. When she stroked his bare chest under his loose white shirt, he shuddered in response.

Halston lifted his head from her bosom and kissed her again with all the fierce need rising inside him. Still kissing her, he seized her skirts and pulled them higher. She was more delectable than honey, hotter than flame.

"Halston, we're not safe." Shaking hands pushed him away. "Imogen could come back."

She was right. They weren't safe. "Damn Imogen," he almost snarled, rising on his elbows. "I want you."

He knew that he couldn't take Stella now. He'd never planned to. But once he touched her, every good intention fled. Over these last days, he'd starved for her. Seeing her across a crowded ballroom had only deepened his relentless craving.

She summoned a wry smile. "I want you, too. But you know that. I can't hide it."

He frowned, as he gazed down into her striking features. Passion lent her face a softness that turned her into the loveliest woman he'd ever seen. "Don't hide who you are. Never hide who you are. Not from me."

"It's frightening to put aside my mask." Her gaze focused on his face. "I've lived behind it for ten years."

Halston kissed her again, taking his time to savor her. When the kiss started to catch fire, he drew away. He felt more than just physical hunger for Stella, but at this moment, unsatisfied desire threatened to sweep everything else away. "I'm delighted that I can offer you a few hours of freedom."

"I was free growing up. Perhaps too free." Her eyes were troubled. "I'm not a virgin, Halston."

"That doesn't make me think less of you."

She looked rueful. "It matters to most men. At least when it comes to things like marriage, or my ability to guide a young girl into adulthood."

"Nobody could question your devotion to Imogen." He rolled off her and sat up to lean against the bedpost again. Lying on top of Stella was too tempting.

"She's a darling. It's not hard to love her. Even if I wanted to wring her neck when she played that trick at the Lumsden ball."

A smile lengthened his lips, as he raised a knee and rested one arm on it. "I'm forever grateful to her for that. If she hadn't, I might still be pining for you from afar."

Stella pushed herself up until she rested against the headboard with her legs stretched out in front of her. "I still don't know why you noticed me."

He tilted his eyebrows at her. "Even after those kisses?"

A wave of her hand dismissed his question. "That's after the fact."

"You'd noticed me."

She rolled her eyes. "You're very noticeable, as you well know."

He frowned, trying to put the inexpressible into words, even as he curled his hand around her leg just below the knee. He couldn't have her, but by God, he'd touch her while he could.

"So are you. Or at least you are to me. The first time I saw you, I thought of a trapped flame. And having seen you, I couldn't *not* see you, if that makes sense."

"I suppose it does. I felt the same, although you seemed far beyond my reach."

"You were the one out of reach." He stroked her leg, pushing up her skirts to reveal shapely calves in serviceable brown stockings. "I've never pursued a woman so hedged about with thorny fences. All those stern old biddies quite daunted me."

She didn't smile. "You could choose any lover."

He shrugged. "I don't want any lover. I want you. You ask why I noticed you? Was it fate? Who knows? But I looked across that room and saw a woman whose manners screamed propriety and whose eyes glittered with fire. I knew she was the one for me. That feeling has only deepened since."

"Oh, Halston..." she sighed.

He couldn't resist the melting surrender in her golden eyes. Surging up the bed, he lashed his arms around her, kissing her until his blood turned into a hot torrent.

By the time he lifted his head, they were both breathless. He had to stop now, or he wouldn't stop until he thrust inside her. The prospect made him as hard as granite. Telling himself that his chance would come in a few hours didn't soothe the ache in his balls.

Stella looked delightfully ruffled. The severe knot that confined her hair showed signs of collapsing, and her lips were full and red after his kisses. He itched to sweep away these trappings of the prim governess, trappings that had so little to do with the real Stella.

Tonight.

"You should call me Gray."

"Should I indeed?"

He gave her a quick kiss. "It's what I want to hear you scream when you're shaking in my arms."

Her laugh held a hint of irony. "And of course you'll make me scream."

"That's the plan."

She brought his head down for another kiss. He loved that she took the initiative. When she shifted to meet his eyes, she looked pensive. "You weren't surprised."

"When I kissed you?"

She shook her head. "When I told you I'm not a...virgin."

"Ah."

"Why?"

"I'd guessed." Halston settled against the pillows and drew her into his side. Cuddling Stella was damnably pleasant. "Nothing we did shocked you."

"I was shocked at how I felt."

"That's capital." He glanced down at her, fearing that he must look completely besotted. "Why should I mind? I'm no virgin either."

She smothered a snort. "I'm hoping you'll give me the advantage of your experience."

"Perhaps I'm hoping you'll give me the advantage of yours."

A flush heated her cheeks and made her look younger. She might claim to be a woman with a romantic past, but she possessed an essential innocence that called to him. Which was strange because he wasn't a man who dealt in innocence. "I'm not...I'm not that experienced."

"But you knew enough to tell me to finish outside you. I like that I needn't coax you through each step to intimacy. We can get to the good stuff faster, if I don't have to talk you over the first hurdles."

She laughed again. "You're such a man."

He smiled, even as he thought about what she'd said. "I'm guessing there's been nobody since you came to live with Deerforth."

She shook her head. "I haven't known a lover's touch in over ten years. I haven't wanted a lover's touch."

"Until you met me."

"Until I met you." Her glowing eyes settled on him. "It was lucky I didn't want to pursue a flirtation. My uncle wouldn't have approved, and life was hard enough as it was."

Halston drew her closer. "I hate that things have been so difficult."

"I've been safe." She paused. "And now I'm not safe, but I'm happy."

That made him kiss her again and again, until his control threatened to crack. This was torture. This was bliss. This was too risky to continue, blast it.

Halston pulled away and settled her head upon his shoulder. "Talk to me," he said gruffly, despite his words, brushing his lips across the top of her hair. "If we keep kissing, I won't be responsible for what happens."

"I haven't felt like this since I was a young girl in the throes of first love. I'd always imagined that the fires burned lower as one got older."

He groaned and closed his eyes. Her scent was the air that he breathed. Sensible lemon soap. Something warm and female that had nothing sensible about it at all. "If you keep saying things like that, you'll find yourself compromised in the blink of an eye, my girl."

She lifted her head to land a clumsy kiss on his jaw. "What shall we talk about?"

He fought against reacting to that kiss with more kisses. She'd escaped a good swiving by a hair's breadth, but he knew his limits. "I believe you were telling me about your colorful past."

She frowned in puzzlement. "Do you care?"

The stark truth was that he did, and not just about her first lover. He wanted to know everything about her. "Indulge me."

"Very well, but please stop me if I'm boring you."

He gave a grunt of amusement. "I'll try to stay awake."

"I'm sure you've heard that Mamma rejected a rich marriage and ran off with Papa to Italy. It created a massive brouhaha. After that, Papa made a meager living as an artist, but we were happy together and we had one another. And I loved Naples."

"That's where you and your lover met?"

"Yes. We planned to marry, but Niccolo was killed fighting the French. Mamma and Papa had died in an epidemic the previous year. I'd spent months trying to manage on my own, but it was impossible. Even more impossible when Napoleon ordered his armies into the city. I was lucky to get back to England where my uncle took me in."

"I'm sorry about Niccolo." More, Halston couldn't bear learning that she'd been alone and afraid. "You loved him?"

The golden eyes were full of such grief that Halston hardly needed to ask. No question that she'd loved him.

"When he died, I felt like my life was over. But I was just nineteen, and a broken heart only kills people in stories."

Halston struggled against a painful and unworthy stab of jealousy. He could imagine how tough life had been for Stella, left destitute and grieving in Naples, then arriving in England to bear the weight of the scandal of her parents' elopement. "Does your uncle know about Niccolo?"

She rolled her eyes. "Good heavens, no. It's bad enough that I share my mother's wild blood. If he knew I'd gone to a man's bed, he'd never give me the time of day. He believes that whipping is too good for a fallen woman." Her expression darkened in a way that disturbed Halston. "As it was, he gave me a pompous lecture on controlling my reckless impulses. The threat was clear that if I didn't toe the line, I was out on my ear."

Another reminder, should Halston need one, of what risks she took, now that she succumbed to this attraction. "The swine."

"He's not a swine." She pursed her lips. "He's just a self-important prig with a narrow range of understanding. I'm even grateful to him. He's been good to me, according to his lights. It would have been easy to ignore my appeal for help." She stopped. "Although if Mamma's aristocratic friends from the English community in Naples hadn't written to him and extolled my good character, he'd never have taken me in. Don't forget he placed his daughter in my care. My virtue or the lack of it does matter."

"Do you still love him?"

"My uncle? I doubt I've ever loved him."

"No, you absurd creature. Niccolo."

The delay before she answered felt like torture. Which was mad. Love was never part of Halston's dalliances.

While he couldn't remember wanting a woman the way he wanted Stella, and he liked her more than anyone else he'd met lately, this was only another short-lived affair. Hell, she'd told him that it was over, once they returned to London. Even for Halston, less than a week was brief for a liaison.

"Does it matter?"

It shouldn't, by God. After all, they were both aware of their arrangement's parameters. A few days of sensual pleasure before they retreated to their respective corners. "I'm interested in you."

Her glance was unimpressed. "I know."

He laughed. "Not just as a bed partner."

"So you want us to be confidants as well as lovers?"

"A little conversation will fill the gaps between lovemaking. We'll need to get our breath back now and then. You pointed out that we're both advancing in years." His voice became serious. "And you can talk about these things with me, knowing there's no danger. There's not even any judgement. It would be the height of hypocrisy to condemn you for one adventure, when the angels have stopped keeping track of mine."

Halston expected her to smile, but instead she studied him. Her attention stirred a vague discomfort. He had an unwelcome inkling that she saw all the way down to the vacuum where most people had a soul. In general, that lack didn't worry him. But something about this unusual woman made him wish to be a better man, wish to be worthy of her.

"Part of being free?"

"If you like."

"Then, yes, I still love him."

Halston stopped himself from grabbing Stella by the shoulders and ordering her to think of no man but him. Only just. The red mist obscuring his vision meant a few seconds passed before he realized that she was still speaking.

"Although it's truer to say I remember loving him. He was a sweet boy, and I was a sweet girl when I met him. If I hadn't sketched him so often and kept the drawings, I wouldn't even remember what he looked like. It's been ten years. I doubt he'd like the woman I've become." While she sounded sad, it was an old sorrow.

The thought of Stella weeping over drawings of her lost love made him want to punch his fist through the wall. When he had no right to be jealous of what she'd done ten years ago. And with a dead man.

"So you're not pining for handsome Niccolo?"

Her smile was wistful. "I still think about him and how unfair life was to him. He was killed trying to save his brother from a French patrol. He deserved better."

"You did, too."

"Perhaps." He admired her lack of self-pity. "How did you know that he was handsome?"

"I guessed." The image of a liquid-eyed Italian Adonis only stoked his shameful jealousy.

"Niccolo was dark like you, but in a very different style. He was a black-eyed angel, whereas you've got all of Satan's wicked allure. He was also ridiculously chivalrous. I had to drag him into bed. He was determined to wait until we spoke our vows. But I was mad for him. This might make me sound like a brazen hussy, but I'm not sorry I gave him my maidenhead. Or that we came together half a dozen times after that. Knowing that I made him happy, even for a few short hours, has been some consolation. Deerforth is right. I share my mother's wild blood."

Halston frowned. "Your mother fell in love, and you did as well. Wanting to take that love to its rightful conclusion doesn't turn either of you into the Whore of Babylon."

Stella was a passionate creature. He'd sensed that from the first. Her kisses in the hired carriage, and even more during the tumultuous minutes he'd spent in her arms this afternoon, only confirmed that.

He suspected that she'd been the dominant partner in her tragic amour. Her description, terse as it was, gave him a fair idea of what Niccolo had been like. Charming. Beautiful. Romantic. Perhaps a little weak. Something told Halston that however powerful her first love, the years might have revealed that she needed a man capable of standing up to her.

Curiosity sparked in her lovely eyes. "You're kinder than I imagined you'd be."

Halston shifted in embarrassment. He was used to women admiring his looks or his virility – or most often of all, his large fortune. A compliment on something like kindness felt unwarranted. "I'm trying to lull you into trusting me."

"I'm about to go to your bed. My reputation is in your keeping. I'd better trust you, or I'm an empty-headed little fool."

He dropped another kiss onto her disheveled hair. "You're certainly not that."

When she turned her face up, he pressed his lips to hers. Even that brief kiss was too disturbing. "You must have known frustration as well as sorrow."

Her smile wasn't far off a grimace. "What do you think?"

Arousal ripped through him, as he pictured what she might do in the privacy of her bed. "I think you must have spent many nights touching yourself and imagining that the hands were Niccolo's."

Her lashes fluttered down. "It's a sin."

Halston made a contemptuous sound deep in his throat. "Most things that give us pleasure are called sins." He swallowed to moisten a dry mouth. "We should stop talking about this."

Her eyes opened wide. "Are you disgusted to know that I sought my own satisfaction?"

This time, the sound he made was closer to a groan. "For God's sake, Stella, quite the opposite. It's far too stirring, when I have to keep my hands off you until tonight."

The color in her cheeks deepened when she glanced down to where his cock tented his trousers. In so many ways, he'd been right to call her innocent. "Oh."

"Oh, indeed." He caught her hand and brought it down over the front of his trousers. This time, his groan was long and fervent and expressed frustration as well as pleasure.

A gloating smile curved her lips. "I'm glad I don't suffer alone."

"Your frustration ends tonight. Mine does, too."

Her smile intensified. "I do hope so."

Halston kissed her with rising ardor, even as he recognized that there was no point to all this excitement. When he raised his head, he met eyes glittering with a sensual interest to match his own.

"There's something else that you should know." Her voice was low and husky and combined with her touch to heighten his agitation.

At this rate, he'd need a swim in the icy lake after he left her. Or he'd be in no state to play host to all these damned annoying people that he'd invited to his house to disguise purely private intentions. "Oh, yes?"

"Yes." Her eyes looked even more like gold. "Since I first saw you, I don't picture Niccolo when I touch myself. The man I think of when I'm alone in my bed is you, Gray."

As he struggled to come to terms with her confession, her hand moved under his and she shaped his erection. "Stella..."

Halston dragged her into his arms, ignoring another complaint from his injury, and kissed her with open-mouthed urgency. He pushed her down onto her back. A few rough tugs followed, and the sound of ripping fabric.

Her breasts spilled free into his trembling hands. His heart slammed against his ribs with such force that he feared they must crack. Her breasts were so damned pretty. Not large, but sweetly formed and with delicious light brown nipples pointed with arousal.

He shifted onto his side and cupped one delicate curve. A perfect fit in his palm, just as he was sure their bodies would fit together when he slid inside her.

His thumb brushed the sensitive tip. On a broken cry, Stella arched up to encourage him. When his tongue teased her nipple, she tasted delicious. Scraping his teeth across the beaded tip, he began to fondle her other breast. She cried out again and dug her fingers into his scalp.

It took far too long to notice that she wasn't caressing him. She was pulling on his hair and saying something. Dazed, he raised his head to meet eyes heavy with need.

"Gray, if you keep going, I won't be able to say no."

Regret that involved a fair measure of guilt pierced Halston. Hell, this was torture. He wanted to feast on her without worrying about anything else. Stella looked forsaken, too, spread across the bed in an abandoned pose that did nothing to fortify his control.

They must stop. Even recognizing that, it took an almighty effort to remove his hand from her bosom. She was no longer touching his dick, which was a good thing.

Or at least so he told himself.

He couldn't remember a woman who swept him away from the real world the way Stella did and into a realm where all that counted was desire. The sad irony was that with this woman, the real world and its judgements counted more than with any other lover.

He rolled onto his back, taking her with him so that she straddled him. When her torn bodice sagged, he couldn't resist fondling her breasts.

"We really have to stop," she murmured, bending down to crush her lips to his in a desperate kiss that made him ache.

Their wriggling had put paid to her coiffure. A tawny tangle tumbled down to form a veil around his face, as her lips drove him insane. He tunneled his hands through the silky mass, while their mouths waged a battle of ferocious pleasure.

When at last she pushed up against his chest, she was rosy with arousal. He smiled at her. In pain, but just so damned delighted with her, he almost didn't mind. "You don't look like anyone's governess right now, Miss Faulkner."

She gave another of those huffs of laughter that he found so charming, perhaps because they were nothing like the tinkling giggle that most of the women of his acquaintance cultivated. Her eyes completed a survey of him that threatened to set him ablaze. "That may be the case, but you certainly look like a libertine, my dear Lord Halston."

Laughing and catching her by the waist, he turned until she was beneath him. When he rose on his elbows, she stroked the chest revealed under his gaping shirt.

Halston quaked beneath her touch. Wherever her hands strayed, they trailed magic.

"We must be sensible," he forced out and heard a complete lack of conviction in the words.

Stella drew him toward her. "I think that's what I should say."

More kisses. More heat. More luscious frustration, but in the end, they came to rest against the pillows, entwined in each other's arms, and he was almost glad that she'd escaped a swiving. At least before he had time and privacy to do her justice.

She murmured with disappointment when he drew away. He liked that Stella owned her desire. Hell, so far he liked everything about her, except the fact that he couldn't take her to bed right now and keep her there for a month.

"I'm sorry," he said, his throbbing prick reminding him how much he wanted her.

"Don't be sorry. I love it when you touch me."

He gestured toward her bare breasts. "If you don't want me to touch you again, you might want to pull up your dress. Next time, I can't promise to stop. Nobody has ever driven me as wild as you do."

When she didn't move to obey, he ground his teeth and reached across to hitch up the bodice of that ugly green dress. Eventually he covered her. That seemed like the sin, not what Stella did to herself in the lonely nights.

"Stop looking at me like that." The hunger in her expression made him want to kiss her again. "It's just inviting trouble."

"I can't help it. Do you know why I said yes to you?"

"Because you want me?"

"Well, that, obviously."

"And?"

"And because while I've missed a man's touch, one man alone has tempted me to his bed."

After that, what could Halston do but lunge forward and kiss her again? Even though he knew that it would worsen his torment. By all that was holy, he'd tumble her all night, once he got her to himself. He cursed the hours that stretched ahead before he could possess her.

She flattened her hands on his chest and held him away. "You should go."

"I should," he said, and this time he meant it. "I'll come to you, once the house is quiet."

"I can't wait."

He groaned. "I'll think of you every second."

"You're such a flatterer." Amusement lit her eyes. "No wonder you make the ladies swoon. You have such a way with a seductive phrase."

"Are you seduced?"

"I hope to be."

He chuckled and kissed her again, lingering long enough to torment himself with wanting more. The taste of her lips flung him high into heaven. When she gave herself to him, the world would burst into flame. Having to wait until midnight seemed like punishment.

"Until later," he whispered.

"Until later," she repeated, her eyes making sensual promises that he'd make sure she kept.

He shifted off the bed. "It's agony to leave you."

Her smile's cynical edge told him that she didn't believe him. He was trapped in the liar's dilemma. When he made extravagant declarations to Stella, he spoke the truth. Yet his reputation for smooth-tongued seduction meant that she took all his remarks with a pinch of salt.

"I'll see you at dinner."

His sigh held a sulky tinge. "When I have to pretend that we're strangers. When I have to pretend that I have an ounce of bloody interest in the tribe of blockheads infesting my house."

She was still laughing at him. After Francene's dramatics, Stella's coolness should be welcome, but Halston wanted her to suffer the way he did. Damn it, he just wanted her. When he held her in his arms, he glimpsed a need to match his own, but she regained her sangfroid far too fast for his liking.

By heaven, he'd shake her up tonight. That ironic distance would disappear forever, once he took her to paradise and back.

"I'll make it up to you."

He directed a theatrical scowl at her. "By George, you'd better."

Her low laughter followed him, as he disappeared behind the hidden door.

CHAPTER EIGHT

Stella sat on the bed, watching in wonder as the secret door opened on a dark passageway, then closed behind Halston without a sound. She had a strange feeling that she turned into a heroine in one of the gothic romances that she devoured with such gusto.

She scrambled to her feet and crossed to examine the wall. Unless one knew about the door, one would never guess that the clandestine entrance existed. Excitement roared through her, as she realized that the next time the panel opened, it would admit a man who meant to use her body.

She could hardly wait.

Stella still quivered after those passionate kisses. How foolish she was to think that she understood desire. She'd wanted Niccolo with all the urgency of first love. What she experienced in Lord Halston's arms wasn't at all the same. It was powerful and dark and irresistible. It seemed to draw her deep into a turbulent ocean.

Despite the tragic end to her affair with Niccolo, their love had been full of joy. When she kissed Halston, she succumbed to danger and desperation.

Yet she craved Halston's touch in a way that eclipsed even her passion for her handsome Italian suitor. Niccolo had called to her innocence. Halston called to the shadows lurking in her soul and left her craving more of his touch.

When she caught a glimpse of herself in one of the baroque mirrors, a shocked cry wedged in her throat. A shaking hand rose to clutch at her torn bodice.

Halston was right. She didn't look like anyone's governess. Her clothes were disheveled. Her hair coiled around her face, and her lips were full and red.

Disturbed on so many levels, she stepped closer to the mirror. She and Halston had stopped short of sexual congress, but nobody who saw her now would believe that. She looked thoroughly tumbled. Worse, the brown eyes in the mirror brimmed with sensual languor.

Stella had spent ten years suppressing the vibrant, voluptuous woman who gazed back at her. She'd managed it at nineteen. Would she manage it again, after she and Halston parted?

She'd agreed to his sinful proposition because she wanted him to give her pleasure such as she'd never known and would never know again. But what on earth would she become, once the pleasure was done?

The ormolu clock on the mantel chimed five. The eyes in the mirror rounded in horror as she realized how late it was. If Imogen saw her like this, there would be the devil to pay.

The first thing she had to do was get out of this dress and hide it away. She dashed through to the dressing room. The fabric ripped again before she managed to bundle the rag into the armoire. Memories of Halston touching her bare breasts didn't help to steady her hands.

She managed a quick wash in water that was now ice cold. Even when she'd finished, she could still smell lust and Lord Halston on her skin.

In the nick of time, she hauled her shabby peignoir out of her bag. A soft knock sounded on the door, and Imogen came in without waiting for an invitation.

While Stella loved her cousin, she'd always hated that her servile role meant she had no right to insist on the most basic privacy. Uncontrollable heat rose to her cheeks as she imagined the fuss if the girl had marched in fifteen minutes ago.

"Harriet's room isn't half as nice as mine," Imogen said, settling herself on the edge of the rumpled bed. Stella had hoped to restore it to order before Imogen turned up. As it was, she was just grateful that her cousin hadn't discovered her close to naked in Halston's arms. "In fact, it's not half as nice as this one. She doesn't have a view of the lakes."

"Poor Harriet." Stella's smile was teasing, as she tightened the belt on her robe and came forward into the room from the dressing room doorway. "How will she survive?"

Imogen gave a short laugh. "You always think I'm trying to get one up on Harriet."

"How very odd that you say that."

Lady Harriet Comerford was golden fair. When she and Imogen were together – which they usually were – the effect was dazzling.

Imogen surveyed the room with a curiosity that made Stella jumpy. "Did you manage to have a sleep?"

"Yes," Stella said.

"You must have had nightmares." Imogen frowned, as she studied the wreckage around her. "This bed is a battlefield, and your hair is a complete bird's nest."

Stella raised a nervous hand to her tangled hair, while she injected as much conviction as she could manage into her answer. "I dreamed of Italy."

When compassion softened Imogen's gaze, Stella felt guilty for playing on her feelings. "I'm sorry. I remember you had bad dreams for years after you came to us."

To Stella's horror, she realized that Halston's neckcloth lay at her feet. Such carelessness was unforgivable. She'd been so overtaken by passion that she'd been lost to the danger of discovery.

Placing one foot on the length of white linen, she tried to sound like her normal self. She didn't dare try and kick it under the bed, in case the movement attracted Imogen's attention.

"I haven't had bad dreams for ages." She summoned a purposeful tone. Outside, the sky over the lovely landscape darkened toward nightfall. "You should go and change for dinner. You want to look your best."

Imogen's nonchalant shrug rather surprised Stella. The girl had been so excited to come to Prestwick Place, presumably because it meant the chance to flirt with Lord Halston. "Nancy always performs miracles." Imogen's eyes sharpened. "I've asked her to come to you once she's finished with me."

"But..."

Imogen stood, and Stella edged around to hide the neckcloth. "I know you'll say it's not the done thing, but Papa isn't here to disapprove. I hate to see your pretty hair bundled away as if it's a shameful secret. Look at it now, it's magnificent. Like a lion's mane. And I'm the only person who knows about it."

After today, that wasn't the entire truth. More heat flooded Stella, as she recalled Halston's hands buried deep in her hair as he drew her down for yet another intoxicating kiss.

"I'll lend you my pearls, and perhaps Nancy can do something with one of your dresses."

"I'm only your companion," Stella said, as the impossible vision of appearing before Halston as a woman of consequence floated before her.

She was poor, she was a child of scandal, and she had a checkered past. She'd long ago given up any futile hopes of entering society as an equal to the highborn ladies who graced the ton.

Imogen's sniff was dismissive. "You're an earl's granddaughter and an earl's niece. You're my cousin. You have a perfect right to take your place in my world."

"Your father doesn't agree."

"Papa will never find out that you loosened up a little at a country house party. Be brave, Stella. I know you try to hide yourself away, but you don't have to. Not for the next few days anyway."

"You're...you're very generous."

"Pfft." Imogen treated that statement with eloquent contempt, as the clock chimed the half hour. "I'll come and fetch you, once we're both dressed. We'll go downstairs together."

The moment Imogen left, Stella scooped up Halston's neckcloth and shoved it into a drawer with fumbling hands. Nancy had sharp eyes and was a gossip besides, however much of a genius she was with hair and clothing. Stella was torn between a longing to look pretty for Halston and fear at how close she already verged to scandal.

When everyone gathered downstairs for dinner, the size of the house party surprised Stella. Halston hadn't exaggerated when he said he'd done his best to hide his private intentions toward her. From what she knew of him, too, this was a more respectable crowd than he ran with most of the time. No notorious widows. No men of doubtful reputation. Definitely no pretty opera dancers or courtesans.

This sudden change in behavior caused comment. Halston had been clever there, too. Stella had feared his invitation might rouse speculation about a proposal to Imogen. If word spread that such a connoisseur had considered then rejected her cousin, it would harm the girl's prospects on the marriage market.

Young ladies from good families weren't his usual company of choice. But he'd invited four of the most popular debutantes, any of whom would make him a suitable countess.

Nobody observing him with his guests would notice particular signs of favor to Imogen or Harriet, or Lily Bilson or Elizabeth Tierney. None of them sat next to him at dinner, which to Stella's surprise had proven enjoyable.

Whether it was her less forbidding coiffure or the fact that manners were more relaxed in the country, the gentlemen on either side of her didn't seem to resent having to speak to a woman without fortune or connections. Even better, they turned out to be interesting conversationalists. The worst part of the meal was trying to avoid staring at Halston, who was at his satanic best in formal black. He'd placed Mrs. Bilson on his right and Lady Tierney on his left. Both of those ladies were beyond the age of pursuing their host.

"You're looking very pretty tonight, Miss Faulkner," Lady Lumsden said, sitting beside Stella when the ladies retired to the drawing room after dinner.

Stella smiled without her usual reserve. She liked the whole Comerford family, and Lord and Lady Lumsden were among the few people in society who treated her like Imogen's cousin and not her servant.

"Thank you. Imogen decided that I needed to come out of my shell."

Lady Lumsden took a sip of her tea, as her perceptive blue eyes assessed Stella's altered appearance. "Good for her."

Self-consciously Stella touched the soft arrangement of curls that Nancy had created from her unruly hair. She wore a dress that she'd made herself in a subdued shade of blue. It suited her coloring better than any of her cousin's castoffs. The borrowed pearls around her neck made her feel for once like a lady and not the hired help.

"It isn't appropriate," she said.

"Nonsense." Annoyance thinned Lady Lumsden's lips. "Just because your uncle treats you like a lackey doesn't mean that's what you are."

"My uncle took me in when I had nowhere else to go," Stella said, trying to sound suitably grateful.

"And has played on your sense of obligation ever since." With a decided clink, Lady Lumsden set her teacup and saucer on a side table. "I'm sorry. I'm being too frank. But your mother would hate to think of you as Lord Deerforth's drudge."

Lady Lumsden had been friends with Stella's mother and was one of the few people Stella had met in England who spoke of the late Anne Ridley with any fondness. Her uncle almost never mentioned his sister. If he did, it was in tones that suggested she'd committed some irredeemable sin.

In this sophisticated, acquisitive milieu, Stella supposed that marrying a poor man for love did count as a sin.

She struggled to come up with a response, but Lady Lumsden went on, thankfully on a different topic. "I wonder what Halston is up to with this house party."

Stella choked on her tea. As she struggled to catch her breath, Lady Lumsden took her cup away before she spilled its contents.

"I'm sorry. I breathed in at the wrong moment," she gasped, once she managed to speak.

Dear Lord, she'd better polish her skills at being surreptitious or her reputation was doomed. She feared that she must be as red as a radish.

Glad to have an excuse for avoiding Lady Lumsden's gaze, she found her handkerchief and wiped her eyes. The problem was that Stella felt like she had a big black and white sign pinned to her back, announcing her naughty intentions toward the Earl of Halston.

During her coughing fit, heads turned in her direction, but interest faded as her coughing subsided. She must stop jumping like a startled cat whenever she heard Lord Halston mentioned. For a start, it was bad for her health. So far, she'd drawn blood with a needle and almost choked.

"Are you all right?" Lady Lumsden asked. "Shall I call a footman to help you upstairs?"

Stella shook her head. "Thank you, but there's no need. I'm sorry."

"Don't apologize. I wondered if you had any idea what prompted the spectacular if disreputable earl to invite a crowd of strangers to his country seat in the middle of the season. It isn't his normal style."

"To have a house party?"

"Oh, he's had a few of those, but the guests are never marriageable maidens and their parents and chaperones. One might almost imagine he was ready to settle down at last. But so far, he's paid no special attention to Harriet. Nor as far as I can see, to Lily or Elizabeth or Imogen."

Stella felt uncomfortable discussing Halston. "I have no insight into his lordship's intentions. How would I? I doubt he even knows who I am." In her ears, she sounded stiff and unconvincing.

To her relief, Lady Lumsden took her words at face value. "I'm not suggesting that he confided in you, but I wondered if he'd shown any particular preference for Imogen before you left London."

"He sent flowers and called after they met at your ball," Stella said, guessing that neither of those things would be news. Imogen told Harriet everything, and Stella suspected that Harriet kept few secrets from her mother.

Lady Lumsden made an unimpressed mutter. "I know that. And he's danced with her at every ball this week. But then he's also danced with Harriet and the other two girls. If he does offer for one of them, it will be the coup of the season. Many a matchmaking mamma's heart has broken over dashed hopes of snaring the elusive earl for her daughter. These last few years, he hasn't frequented many ton parties. They must seem like dull potatoes, compared to the exotic fare of his cyprians and actresses."

At last, Stella felt composed enough to look at Lady Lumsden. She spoke with more candor than usual. Her improved appearance must be lending her confidence. "Would you like him to offer for Harriet? She'd make a beautiful countess."

After this afternoon's passionate demonstration, Stella knew that she was his current object of desire, but at heart she was a realist. Halston had an old title and a massive fortune. He owed it to his name to marry and have children.

It might not happen this season, but sometime in the future, Stella would have to hide her devastation when he announced his betrothal to a suitable miss. She already knew enough of her feelings for Lord Halston to understand that she'd suffer when he married someone else.

She even recognized, through the clamor of furious denial in her heart, that if he picked Harriet or Imogen, he'd gain a sweet-natured consort. She didn't want him to be unhappy.

Lady Lumsden frowned, as she contemplated the prospect of Harriet as Lady Halston. "It would be a great feather in her cap. But he's so much older and more jaded than these young girls."

"It's the way of the world that men of experience marry well-bred maidens."

Lady Lumsden shook her head as if banishing a troublesome thought. "I suppose if Harriet loves him, I won't stand in her way. I made a love match. I'd like the same for my daughter."

"Do you think she loves him?" Stella stopped in horror. "I'm sorry. My new hairstyle has stolen all my manners. That's none of my business."

"You have a right to an opinion." Lady Lumsden smiled. "After all, you've spent such a lot of time with the girls. Harriet is so fond of you. As are Lord Lumsden and I."

Shock crashed through Stella, and for once it was a shock unrelated to the man who she intended to bed tonight. "Really?"

Lady Lumsden gave a short laugh. "Don't sound so surprised. Both my husband and I have remarked on your intelligence and your devotion to your cousin. Anyway, I wanted to talk to a sensible woman about this situation." She glanced around the room and lowered her voice. "I'm not sure anyone else here qualifies."

Stella gave a startled giggle, even as part of her wanted to refute any claim to being sensible. She was on the verge of being very imprudent indeed. Even worse, she could hardly wait to go to the bad.

Lady Lumsden went on. "And as far as your question goes, no, I'm rather relieved that Harriet isn't in love with Lord Halston, although I suspect if he made a genuine effort to attach her interest, she couldn't resist. Heavens, I'm a middle-aged wife and mother, and I've been in love with Pelham from the day I met him, yet even I get a thrill when Halston levels that naughty green gaze on me."

"He's very handsome." Stella hoped her tone didn't betray that she was in thrall to their host.

"He is. But it's more than that. He's clever, and you sense that somewhere under all that decadent charm, there's a man of character. I'm just unconvinced that a chit of twenty will unearth any unplumbed depths in his soul. Does Imogen like him?"

"Lord Deerforth does," Stella said, before she remembered that she was a mere companion and a damned indiscreet one at that.

"Of course Deerforth does. He wants to cut a dash in the world, and Halston moves in the highest circles." Lady Lumsden paused. "If I were a young girl, I'd find Halston preferable to that windy bore Chippenham."

So would Stella, but she'd already said too much. She summoned a polite smile. "I'm sure my uncle is doing his best to find a suitable husband for Imogen."

"Very diplomatic, my dear." Amusement sparked in Lady Lumsden's eyes. "But I imagine you want Imogen to be happy."

"Very much. But if she's set her heart on someone this season, she hasn't confided in me." Her eyes found Imogen, chatting with Harriet and Lily and Elizabeth on the other side of the room. The four girls made a picturesque group. Any one of them would make a fitting match for Halston.

She'd known and liked Harriet for years. The other two were new to her since she'd arrived in London, but Stella liked what she'd seen of them. So did Imogen, and while she might be young, she was no fool when it came to judging people.

Perhaps only wishful thinking convinced Stella that Imogen hadn't set her cap for Lord Halston. She certainly appreciated the attention that his notoriety gained her. A girl who aroused Halston's interest was always worth a second glance, or so the world believed.

While it mightn't be Halston, someone had caught Imogen's eye. Stella was sure of it. She hoped to goodness that whoever it was didn't turn out to be a heartbreaker.

"You wouldn't tell me if she had."

Stella smiled. "Probably not."

"Which is just as it should be, I suppose. I'm just a nosy old woman."

Stella always appreciated Lady Lumsden's self-deprecating humor. "Is it possible that Lord Halston has no ulterior motives and he's just decided to vary his guest list for once? Miss Bilson's father is active in business, and Lord Tierney is a power in parliament. Lord Lumsden is good company. Perhaps we're wrong to concentrate on the feminine guests and should instead think about the men he's invited."

"You could be right," Lady Lumsden said without sounding persuaded. "I imagine everything will become clear over the next few days."

The gentlemen chose that moment to join the ladies, which hinted that their host's interest didn't focus on the influential men he'd invited. They hadn't lingered over their port to talk business or sport or politics.

Halston prowled in last, and Stella couldn't help watching as he gravitated toward some of the older ladies beside the blazing fire. Her shiver of awareness had nothing to do with the cold night.

"See what I mean?" Lady Lumsden murmured, proving to Stella's dismay how closely she observed her. "He just has to walk into a room and every woman goes daft."

Stella made herself smile, although she was mortified that Lady Lumsden had noticed her reaction. "Even humble companions."

Lady Lumsden cast her a sharp-eyed glance that made her cringe and fear that she might have shown too much interest in the handsome earl. "You know, I never think of you as humble, Miss Faulkner."

"I..."

Lady Lumsden waved away her protest. "You might do your best to fade into the background so your uncle doesn't cut up rough, but at heart there's much more to you than you let on."

"Thank you." Halston had said something similar. "I think."

Lady Lumsden's amusement was kind. "It's a compliment, in case you're wondering. Although I'm sure that life these last ten years would have been easier if you were the dull creature you pretend to be."

"I think you overestimate me, my lady."

"Do you? I don't. Anne Ridley's daughter was bound to be interesting."

"My mother made some disastrous choices," she said through stiff lips, as old grief pierced her.

"She and your father were happy, weren't they?"

"Oh, yes."

"And they loved you?"

"Very much."

Lady Lumsden shrugged. "Then their choices weren't disastrous. Society's view of life isn't always the full story, you know."

Startled anew, Stella looked at Lady Lumsden. "You're being very nice to me."

"I hate to see a woman of your quality wasted. If life with your uncle ever becomes unbearable, don't assume that you're friendless."

Her amazement grew. "You've never spoken to me like this before."

"A house party provides more opportunity for conversation than London."

"But you could have drawn me aside in Gloucestershire."

"I could, but it's only since we came to London that I realized quite what a tyrant Deerforth is. You're his sister's child. He shouldn't treat you like a skivvy."

Stella couldn't summon the hypocrisy to defend her uncle again. "I could never leave Imogen, but thank you. I loved Mamma dearly, but here in England, nobody has a kind word to say about her. Except you. That in itself makes me grateful."

Sadness dimmed Lady Lumsden's bright gaze. "She was a good friend, and I see so much of her in you. Not least the passionate heart."

Stella's lips firmed. "A beggar can't afford a passionate heart."

Lady Lumsden took her hand and pressed it. "Remember I'm your friend, too." She mustered a smile, although Stella could see it was an effort. "Now I've monopolized you long enough. I promised to make up a fourth at cards. Would you care to join us?"

"No, thank you." If Stella tried to concentrate on cards, she was afraid that her distraction would cause comment. "Good luck."

"Thank you." Lady Lumsden rose and crossed to speak to Mrs. Bilson.

What a surprising, uncomfortable conversation, although Stella appreciated Lady Lumsden's generosity. In this last week, two people had offered help if she needed to make a new life. Imogen said that she'd give her a home after she married, and now the Lumsdens extended their support.

At present, she had no plans to leave her uncle, although if Imogen wed, that would change. But it was a relief to know that she didn't face the future alone.

She doubted that either offer would survive a scandal, though, which made it even more imperative to hide her affair with Halston. Lady Lumsden had called her sensible. That sparked cynical amusement. A sensible woman would never fall into a rake's clutches.

The awful truth was that she had no wish to disentangle herself. She only wanted to entangle herself further. Those kisses this afternoon had stoked her hunger. It had been years since a man had touched her in desire. The hiatus had strengthened her responses. She hadn't yet gone to Halston's bed, and already he'd taken her into a new universe.

Stella just prayed that disaster didn't ensue, once she surrendered. Even as she realized that when she was so set on sin, praying was probably a waste of time.

Since he'd come into the room, she'd struggled not to look at Halston. He'd avoided looking at her, too. Now she couldn't help sneaking a glance.

Even though his back was to her, he must sense her gaze. She saw his shoulders stiffen. It was dangerous to watch him for too long. She feared that her face might betray her longing. But nonetheless her gaze lingered.

When he shifted, his eyes met hers across the room with an impact like lightning. Then with a deliberate motion, he turned away, before anyone noticed where he was looking.

The rake was more careful with Stella's reputation than she was.

CHAPTER NINE

$\mathcal{S}$ tella stretched out in her extravagant bed, jittery with nerves and excitement. The room was dark, apart from the glow of the fire. She appreciated the extra touch of comfort. Her uncle didn't waste such luxuries on his despised niece, and there had been occasional winter nights when she'd curled up next to Imogen to keep warm.

The clock on the mantel chimed the quarter past midnight. She had no idea when Halston would come to her. He'd said it would be after everyone was asleep. She could have a long wait.

It would be sensible to try to snatch a little sleep, but her heart raced and the blood fizzed in her veins like champagne. She'd never felt so wide-awake in all her life.

She'd just decided to get up and fetch her book – although she knew that she wasn't likely to concentrate on a story either – when a panel moved in the wall.

Her heart had been galloping for an hour. The sight of that secret door opening made it stop with a mighty thud. Shaky with apprehension, she pushed up against the pillows and watched as Halston emerged from the dark gap.

In the flickering light of his candle, he appeared breathtakingly tall and his features took on a fiendish cast. He was still dressed. Or mostly. He'd removed his fashionable coat and the crimson silk waistcoat, leaving him in shirtsleeves and dark trousers.

The familiar sardonic smile twisted his lips. "You look like you've seen a ghost."

"Do I?" Stella stammered, raising one hand to where her pulse hammered in her throat.

It was absurd that only now did the full reality of what she was about to do hit her. For ten years, she'd stuck to one path. What happened now took her a million miles away from that.

He stepped closer. "Boo."

The silliness brought her back to earth with a jolt. Self-disgust edged her huff of laughter. "I need to stop reading gothic novels. They're playing on my imagination."

"Ghoulies and ghosties and things that howl about the battlements?"

"Something like that." She shifted to sit on the edge of the bed and ran a hand through her fall of hair. She'd unbound it before she lay down.

He raised the candle to reveal her. "My purposes are definitely of this world."

"I know they are. So are mine."

His smile intensified. "I'm delighted to hear that. Shall we go?"

"Go?" She frowned. "Aren't we staying here? I thought that was why you gave me this lovely room."

"As a bower of sin?" He set the candle on the chest of drawers. "No, I gave you this lovely room because I wanted to do you honor."

More of that dangerous warmth filled her. Dangerous because it had nothing to do with desire and everything to do with blossoming emotional intimacy. Desire was powerful, but simple in comparison to her increasing liking for Halston as a man.

Stella hoped to finish this affair with both reputation and heart intact. Every moment that she spent with the licentious earl put her heart in jeopardy. Nobody had made her feel special since Niccolo's death. It was a feeling that she couldn't allow herself to get used to. Life would be barren enough as it was, once she went back to London.

He went on, unaware of how his kindness unsettled her. "And because it's at the end of a secret passage."

Without thinking, she held out her hand. "So where are we going?"

When Halston took her hand, heat swamped her uncertainty. It was years since she'd had a man in her bed, and she wasn't sure how she'd compare to his previous, far more worldly lovers. But anticipation made a mockery of her collywobbles. She wanted him. The chance to have him was too precious to sacrifice, however fidgety she was.

"My room. It's more private. You're going to scream with pleasure, remember?"

"You never know. I might make you scream."

"You might indeed." Appreciation glittered in his eyes. "Are you ready?"

She raised her chin and told the giant rabbits bouncing around inside her stomach to settle down. "Yes."

"That's my girl."

Before she could protest that she wasn't his girl – although she had a sinking feeling that she really was – he drew her close for a gentle kiss. His lips seemed to ask a silent question. When she melted against him and twined her arms around his neck, she gave the only answer she could.

Yes. Yes. Always yes.

By the time he lifted his head, her knees had dissolved into water and her head was spinning. Heaven help her when he took the seduction beyond kisses. She'd turn into a blithering lunatic.

She rose on her toes to press her lips to his. Lord Halston was so tall. Niccolo had been her height. Perhaps that was why all this felt so different.

Not to mention that she and Niccolo had been in love. There was no suggestion that love formed any part of her arrangement with Halston.

"Shall we go?" he whispered, taking her hand again and pausing to pick up the candle.

"Yes." *Yes* seemed to be her word of choice tonight.

She tightened the belt of her peignoir and squared her shoulders. The moment had come. Stella waited to feel some reluctance, but when she searched her heart, all she found was eagerness.

What she was about to do would make her a pariah, if society ever found out. Yet she was happy as she couldn't remember feeling since her parents died, all those years ago in Naples.

"Try not to talk in the passage," he murmured, approaching the gap in the paneling. "It runs behind the bedrooms and voices are audible, as you'll discover."

They stepped into the opening. In the narrow space, she fell behind him. Beneath her slippered feet, the wooden boards were bare.

"Shut the panel behind you," he said in a voice so low, it was closer to a vibration than an actual sound.

She clicked the panel closed, shivering in the cold air, now she was away from the fire. Then shivering again when thick darkness enclosed her. Halston's candle seemed a frail defense against the blackness. She bit back another half-joking comment about ghosts.

As if he sensed her sudden failure of courage, he pressed her hand. He was a perceptive man. At least when it came to her. She suspected that perception would translate into unforgettable pleasure when he used her body.

A subtle tug, and they began to make their way down the corridor. Stella was bristlingly conscious of the people on the other side of the wall. Imogen's room was quiet. The girl must be asleep. Stella took a moment to wonder who filled her dreams. She was almost certain that it wasn't the soft-footed man who drew her toward ruin with every step.

The Lumsdens were talking about Harriet's beaux, and Halston scored a mention. The Bilsons were arguing over Mrs. Bilson flirting with Lord Tierney over dinner. Guttural snoring roared from the Tierneys' room.

When Halston stopped, she collided with him. She pressed her hand to her lips, too late to muffle a gasp.

"There are steps ahead," he murmured into her ear.

This time, her shiver was pure pleasure. His breath was warm on her skin, and in the confined space, she felt drunk on his tangy scent. Sandalwood soap and something potently male.

He turned a corner and kept hold of her hand as they climbed a set of steps. Finally he stopped at a wall. With a couple of soft clicks, the panel opened on a large sitting room that put her opulent bedroom completely in the shade.

As Halston led her forward, Stella realized that they were in one of the gable ends of the house. He released her and reached back to shut the panel, closing them in.

Wide-eyed, Stella surveyed her surroundings. Candles lit the room to gold, and a fire blazed in the hearth. The room was decorated in cream and dark green, and vases of massed flowers perfumed the air. Lilies predominated.

She recalled her jealousy when she thought Halston had sent that bouquet to Imogen. As she drew in a breath tinged with exotic fragrance, her anticipation rose.

"Very convenient for a mistress," she said huskily, moving across to take a closer look at an enormous arrangement of spring flowers.

Smiling with unabashed satisfaction, Halston leaned against the wall and crossed his arms across his powerful chest. His loose-limbed slouch reminded her of a big cat. A leopard or a tiger. However relaxed he might appear, he was ready to pounce.

"Are you trying to find out how many women I've installed in your room for nefarious purposes?"

She shook her head. "I'm guessing you've lost count."

With a huff of amusement, he crossed to open the bottle of champagne on the sideboard. There was a pop as he released the cork. "Not exactly."

"It's none of my business."

"It's not. I don't kiss and tell."

Fascinated, she watched him fill two glasses and set the bottle back in the ice bucket. He was such a pleasure to observe. He turned the most prosaic action into art.

"For which I'm very grateful," she said, accepting the glass he held out.

Green eyes unwavering, he took a sip of his wine. That intense jade stare felt like a caress. She gave another of those delicious little shivers that were becoming a habit.

"But in this case, I'll break that rule."

"Oh?" Stella wasn't sure that she wanted to know about the army of beauties who had trodden that corridor to arrive at his bed. She wished she hadn't raised the subject.

"None."

"A nun?" she repeated, shocked even though she thought she was beyond the point where his sins might appal her.

Despite her dismay at his confession, his gentle laugh made her heart turn over. "No, you absurd creature. None. No women. No mistresses. I try and keep my nose clean here, where I live and where I'll one day bring my countess."

"I...see," Stella said, finding his circumspection almost more disturbing than some tale of profligacy.

"London is for fun. Prestwick Place is much too serious to play host to my wild women." He drank some more champagne. "Apart from you."

"I don't know what to say. I think I'm flattered."

Damn it, there he went again. Making her feel special, when she knew she wasn't. Not really. Except that she was more of a nuisance to get into bed than his usual paramours.

"So you should be, madam." His smile broadened. "There are some delicacies over there. Are you hungry?"

"Just for you," she admitted, shocked anew, this time at her boldness. It had become a habit to guard every word and action, but something about Lord Halston made subterfuge impossible.

His eyes flared as he stepped closer. "Stella..."

She took a gulp of champagne and swallowed it with a speed that did the fine vintage no justice. Dutch courage was more important than the taste. Her craving for Halston's hands on her skin became a mania.

Stella set her crystal glass on the nearest table. Her grip was so unsteady that liquid sloshed against the rim. When she turned to face Halston, he hadn't moved. The urgency sharpening his features made him look more like a fallen angel than ever. Lucifer tumbled to earth to seduce a mere mortal.

Lucky mortal.

She shook back the weight of her hair and reached down to untie her peignoir. Under Halston's burning regard, her fingers were clumsy. It took an eon to release the knot.

His unhidden interest stirred wanton pleasure. When she lifted her hands to slide the robe from her shoulders, she felt confident. More, she felt beautiful and desired, and equal to anything that happened tonight.

As the peignoir slipped to the floor, Halston gave a low growl of pleasure. "You wore it."

"Yes."

When she'd come upstairs, she found the exquisite golden silk nightgown draped over her bed. Now she displayed herself for the gaze that devoured her from top to toe.

She was naked beneath the silk, which was sheer enough to reveal every detail of her body. Her breasts swelled, and her nipples tightened until they hurt. Longing settled in her belly, and a deep throbbing set up in her secret hollows.

Halston's hand was unsteady, too, as he placed his glass beside hers. "You're glorious."

Stella spread her hands in welcome. "Let's do glorious things together."

CHAPTER TEN

Halston surged across the distance between them and caught Stella up in his arms for a passionate kiss. She met him with white-hot desire. No uncertainty, no coyness, no games. Her hands tugged and ripped at his shirt, as if she needed to touch his skin more than she needed to breathe.

It took an almighty act of will to lift his head. She looked wild and desperate, her eyes brilliant with hunger. She was gasping after that overwhelming kiss, and under the nightgown, her breasts rose and fell. He caught a glimpse of peaked nipples and a shadowy hint of the curls at the delta of her thighs.

The silk did little to conceal her body, but even so, he cursed any barrier between him and her nakedness. That nightgown had cost him a king's ransom, and right now he wanted to rip it to shreds until all he could see was Stella.

He dragged his shirt over his head and tossed it to the floor. "It's exciting that you want me."

While her gaze skittered across the raised red scar that the bullet had left, he was grateful that she didn't mention it. "I want you more than I can say," she admitted.

How he loved the frankness of her lust. His shaking hands plowed into that sumptuous fall of hair and when he brought her close, her breasts crushed into his chest. He kissed her again, feeling the slide of silk against his skin.

With arousing murmurs of enjoyment, she clawed at his back. He was already hard, but her unfettered pleasure in what they did made him swell against his trousers. Her hands explored his arms and shoulders, avoiding his injury, before tracing an incendiary line down his spine.

A grunt of shock escaped when she gripped his buttocks, hauling him into her body until he rubbed against her stomach. Their bodies fitted as if designed to meld together. She moaned against his lips, kneading his arse with a rhythm that only made him more frantic to be inside her.

She ripped her lips free of his and bit his neck. The sting thundered through him and stoked his raging desire. Her busy hands slipped between them, ripping at the fastenings on his trousers until he sprang free, throbbing and eager.

When her fingers curled around him, bright light blinded his eyes. The blast of heat threatened to blow his head off.

Halston caught her hips and hoisted her high. The movement pulled on his wound, but he didn't give a damn. She made a guttural sound redolent with approval and curled her legs around him, bunching up the nightgown.

When Stella opened to him, he caught a drift of rich female arousal. He staggered forward until her back slammed into the wall. Her hands hooked around his shoulders, as she rained greedy kisses over every part of him that she could reach. His face, his neck, his shoulders, the top of his chest. Each touch of her lips sparked a fire, until raging flame consumed him.

He jiggled her until she was poised, ready for him. Unable to hold back, he plunged deep. She cried out, and her hands turned into talons, scratching him.

Halston sucked in a great gulp of air. She was deliciously tight, and hot and sleek with need. Closing his eyes, he rested his head on her shoulder and let intense pleasure flow through him.

She shifted, and her grip eased to a caress. The silent invitation was irresistible. He began to move with hard, determined thrusts that knocked her against the wall. She pressed her cheek against his. Each gasp when he penetrated her played a magnificent symphony in his ears.

Those gasps rose until she clenched around him in spasms of ecstasy. Fumbling, shaking, aware of her quaking climax going on and on, he swung around and stumbled to the floor. As he descended, he banged his knees hard. He registered the pain at a distance.

Supporting her back, more careful with her than with himself, he lowered her to the carpet and thrust again. He wanted to stay inside Stella forever. Her body offered the closest glimpse of paradise he was ever likely to get.

It went against every masculine instinct to wrench free. With unsteady hands, he shoved up the crumpled nightdress to reveal her bare stomach.

Halston lost himself on her skin, groaning with unrivaled pleasure. He collapsed at her side, struggling for breath, feeling like he'd just run through a forest fire. He was utterly exhausted, utterly enthralled. Stella had taken all of him and wrung every drop from him. He wondered if he'd ever find the strength to get up off the floor.

Surprising him again, she took his hand. The link confirmed the bond forged out of that astonishing conflagration of pleasure.

After that astoundingly good fuck, this connection should seem trivial. Holding hands was something sweethearts did. Innocent children.

Whereas Halston was no innocent child. Nor was Stella.

But the warmth that stole over him with the chaste contact was as powerful in its way as that first, earth-shattering entry into her body. He curled his fingers around hers, unable to find words to express his pleasure in what they'd just done.

His heart slowed. He was no longer deaf to everything except the stormy force of his blood. He heard an owl hoot outside, then another owl answered. He heard the fire crackling in the grate.

And he heard something else, something that he needed a few moments to identify. His senses might reawaken to his surroundings, but his mind still wandered the outer limits of the stars, where this lovely woman had transported him in that delirious swiving.

Horror flooded him. And self-recrimination. He'd been staring unseeing up at the ornate plasterwork on the ceiling. Now he turned his head toward Stella. Even that small movement strained him. She really had used him up in a way that he couldn't remember before.

"You're crying," he grated out. "Devil take it, did I hurt you?"

To his regret, she released his hand and sat up, folding her legs beneath her. He'd suspected from the first that she had spectacular legs. He'd been right.

"No, of course you didn't." Her voice was clogged with tears.

"You were very tight, and I wasn't gentle."

Trembling hands wiped her face, as she answered in that same thick voice. "It was a bit of a shock at first." She directed a glance down to where his trousers gaped open and his dick lay flaccid against his thighs. "You're much larger than Niccolo."

Halston told himself that only a petty human being would appreciate hearing that. "You haven't had a man in ten years. I should have been more careful."

"It was wonderful." Her laugh was rueful. "The most exciting thing in my whole life."

He sat up, too. "Then why are you crying?"

"It's silly, but I've never felt anything like that before." Stella made an apologetic gesture. "I promise I won't howl my eyes out every time you take me."

He caught her hand and lifted it to his lips. "I don't mind."

To his surprise, Halston didn't, although feminine tears had long ago lost any power over him. Too many mistresses had used tears as weapons of war, to squeeze more jewelry out of him or a more generous settlement when an affair was over.

But Stella wasn't trying to manipulate him. In fact, it was clear that her overwrought reaction left her mortified.

She was starting to look happier, thank goodness, although a tinge of embarrassment lingered in the quick glance she shot him. "I'd forgotten what it's like when a man is inside me. I'd forgotten quite how...intimate it feels. Not just physically, but emotionally. For a little while, I wasn't alone anymore."

His heart was rusty when it came to poignant emotion. When it squeezed tight now, the effect was painful. "Oh, sweetheart," he sighed and placed his arms around her shoulders.

That turbulent, searing encounter hadn't contained a single trace of tenderness, but as he drew her against his side and kissed the top of her head, tenderness felt like it was eating him alive.

He'd always known that this affair would be unlike any of his others. It turned out that he'd had no idea how far it would take him from his usual pragmatic arrangements.

At least Stella wasn't crying because he'd hurt her or because she regretted what they'd done. He couldn't bear it if either of those were the case.

"I had different plans, you know," Halston said in a musing tone.

"I'm sure that's not true." She shifted to meet his eyes, but made no attempt to break away, he was pleased to notice. "You meant to take me to bed. I never expected anything else."

He gave a brief laugh and kissed her. "Bed being the point. I was going to ply you with wine and delicious morsels and share a little conversation, then take my time to arouse you, once I led you through into my bedchamber. It was all going to be frightfully civilized."

She stroked his hair. "I liked that it was savage and uncontrolled and unplanned. It felt wonderful to know how much you wanted me."

"There's no doubt about that." If she glanced down now, she'd see he wanted her again. How was it that he'd gone from fearing he'd never move again to sharpening interest in having her once more? "I promised to make you scream."

She started to look cheerier. "You did." She paused. "And you did. No wonder you're looking so pleased with yourself."

"I am, although I'm less pleased at my lack of restraint. One touch and I was lost."

"I think it's my turn to look smug."

As her amusement faded, he read longing in her golden eyes. That was another thing that was different about this affair. The thought of his previous mistresses yearning for him would have made him run a hundred miles in the opposite direction.

"I wanted you, too," she admitted. "It's been an eon since you kissed me in London, and then I thought this evening would never end. I can't think of anything but being in your arms. Now that I know what you can do to me, it will be even worse. You've lured me into the realms of sin, Gray. I fear they might become my permanent home."

He kissed her again. He loved the taste of her mouth. He loved the way that she surrendered her whole self to every kiss. "I'd like that."

Sudden shock had him going still. What the hell was he doing? What he said smacked of promises for the future. He never made promises to a lover.

When he'd pounded into Stella's body, the experience had eclipsed all earlier fucks. Now his emotional barriers cracked one by one.

Stella Faulkner was dangerous.

Halston should have recognized that before, but he'd been in such a frenzy to have her, misgivings went unheard.

Those misgivings had risen to a clamor, and he didn't know how to silence them. He couldn't countenance the idea of ending this affair. Not yet.

He told himself that was just because she was so wondrous in his arms and he still had things he wanted to do to her. But he had a bothersome inkling that having her would only make him want to have her again.

She watched him, a faint line between her tawny brows. Although her eyelashes were wet, she was no longer crying. "What is it, Gray?"

Shaking his head, he reminded himself that he was a notorious rake who sought sensual pleasure and nothing more from his amours. He refused to acknowledge how hollow that statement sounded, even in the privacy of his own head.

"Nothing." He shifted away and fastened his trousers. With his tackle waving in the air, he felt a little too vulnerable. "Let me clean you up."

"I can do it." She paused, then spoke in a tone that he hadn't heard since their first meeting. Back when she was convinced that he wanted to court her cousin. "In fact, I think I'd rather."

Blast it all, she'd sensed his withdrawal. It was frightening quite how attuned they were. Not just on a physical level.

That was what scared the life out of him, not the unparalleled delight of uniting his body with hers. Problems only arose when he wasn't fucking her.

Halston stood and reached out to help her up. He saw her consider refusing his hand, and he kicked himself for making such a bloody mess of this. Since they'd met in the gazebo, he'd plotted this chance to spend the night with Stella. Now because he lost control of his feelings, she was busy building barriers against him.

Feelings were always a catastrophe. Feelings could go to blazes.

The extent of his relief when she accepted his hand was out of all proportion to the action. "There's hot water in the dressing room."

"Thank you."

Halston fought the impulse to follow, to watch her strip off the extravagant nightdress and sponge his seed from her skin. He still hadn't seen her naked.

If he didn't mend this rift between them quick smart, he might never see her naked.

That thought summoned a desolation that provided a warning in itself. He couldn't remember the last time he'd feared a woman's rejection. Mostly – always – if a woman said no, there was always another woman to take her place. Although the sad fact was that they never said no.

Halston had a sick feeling that if Stella walked out of this room now, he'd rue the lack of her as long as he lived.

CHAPTER ELEVEN

When Stella came back into the room, Halston was sitting by the fire with two glasses of champagne set out on the low table in front of him. He'd cleaned himself off, although he hadn't put his shirt on.

Barely casting him a glance, she tied the belt of her peignoir with what he felt was unwarranted purpose. She didn't have to tell him that she used the garment as armor.

Damn these unwelcome, disturbing insights. He should be planning the next step in his seduction. "Come and join me," he murmured.

She didn't venture closer, and her eyes were wary in a way that they hadn't been since she'd agreed to become his lover. "I should go."

Dismayed, he surged to his feet. "You can't mean that."

One hand made a bewildered gesture, while the other clasped the neck of her robe high against her throat. There was little trace left of the wanton goddess who had let him take her up against the wall in that monumental explosion of bliss.

He'd broken trust with her, and his inchoate fears of where this liaison might take him dissolved in a flood of excruciating regret. "Stella, forgive me."

Her eyes remained cool. "There's nothing to forgive. I was silly to mention things like intimacy and hearts. That wasn't part of our arrangement. I don't blame you for feeling hounded. I hadn't prepared myself for how I'd react when I shared my body with a man again. I'm sorry you've taken all this trouble, only for me to spoil everything."

Dear God, she was blaming herself for the fact that he was a deuced coward. "You haven't spoiled everything."

"Yes, I have." She didn't go, but nor did she join him. "I saw your face."

He ground his teeth, cursing himself with every profanity he knew. "Sit down."

She still didn't move.

"Please."

She studied him for a long moment before she stalked across to sink into the chair opposite his. Despite his turmoil, he couldn't help noting that however often she might call herself a humble companion, humility was a quality foreign to her nature.

"You must have had love affairs that didn't work out," she said, still sounding like she talked about buying cabbages, instead of a torrid swiving. "It's not the end of the world."

Perhaps it would be the end of the world. At that instant, Halston realized that any opportunity to break away from her and return to the careless sod he'd once been had passed. It had passed back in London.

Now that he'd been inside her, he hadn't a hope in hell of conducting this love affair as if Stella

Faulkner was just another forgettable lover in a long line of forgettable lovers.

He spoke words that he never said to anyone. Words that sent a cold shiver down his spine. "Let me try and explain."

He hadn't set out to be changed. Yet already she changed him. God knew where he'd be when she finished with him. Useless to man or beast, he feared.

Stella's gaze remained watchful. He thought with nostalgia of the glow in her eyes when he'd held her in his arms. But at least she was still here and prepared, if not eager, to listen to him. "There's no need."

"There's every need," he said with a hint of heat. "I'm making a deuced dog's breakfast of this. I'm usually a more adept lover."

Faint color warmed her cheeks. "It's not your prowess as a lover that's the problem. You must know that when you made love..." She stopped and searched for another word. "...when you took me, you pleased me."

He did know. "No, it's my prowess as a human being that's in doubt."

She shrugged and twined her hands together in her lap. He noticed that she didn't rush to reassure him. "I can't blame you for worrying about horrible scenes and emotional demands, after the way I blathered on like a green girl. We agreed to part on cordial terms in a few days, and that will end all dealings between us."

He slashed the air with one hand, rejecting her attempt to play down the importance of what they did. "You mistake me."

A cynical smile turned down her lips. "I don't think so."

With a sigh, Halston raked one hand through his hair. "I'm not running scared because you're making unreasonable demands. I'm running scared because I have a horrible suspicion that the person who ends up asking for more will be me."

She frowned. "I don't understand."

"Neither do I." His smile was grim. "But right now, if you walk away, I'll miss you like the very devil."

Shock widened her eyes, and she pressed back against the chair as if trying to escape. But as well as shock, her eyes shone with gratification. She liked hearing that he was at her mercy. "That...that wasn't the plan."

"I know."

One hand crept up to her throat. With her, the gesture always expressed uncertainty. "I can't offer more than these five days. You know I can't."

He spoke before he weighed all the ramifications, but what he said struck him as the perfect solution to their dilemma.

Except the dilemma was his. Stella so far, plague take her, seemed perfectly satisfied with a short-term affair followed by a permanent parting.

"I don't know anything of the sort. In Deerforth's house, you're an unappreciated dogsbody. If you stay there, all your passion and fire will turn to bitterness and regret. You were born to illuminate the world, Stella."

This time, his compliment brought no softening to her expression. The hand clutching that damned ugly robe to her throat clenched. By God, that rag she was wearing was proof enough that she'd accepted a role in life that was well beneath her. "And I'd do that as your mistress, would I?"

His look was direct. "Yes."

"At least I might illuminate the demimonde. While I'm grateful for the offer, what happens next week or next month when you tire of me?"

She didn't sound grateful, curse her. "Perhaps I'll never tire of you."

The scorn in her laugh stung. From the first, he'd liked the way that she harbored no illusions about his lack of character. Right now, he'd sign over half this estate if she just gave him the benefit of the doubt. "And pigs might fly."

"I'm not in the habit of promises."

"I'm not asking for promises."

No, she wasn't. After a lifetime of discouraging females from expecting more from him than a few good fucks followed by a definitive goodbye, it seemed stupid to resent Stella's lack of demands.

Although by all that was holy, he did. How the mighty had fallen.

"What if I set you up with a house and a carriage and everything to ensure your comfort?"

Her lips tightened. "*Carte blanche*, in other words."

"Yes. I'll cover all your expenses while you're my mistress. I'm known as a generous lover."

"If not a steadfast one."

He winced again at the dry tone.

She went on. "And I suppose when you're finished with me, I must seek another protector."

No. By God, no.

That howl of denial must be a product of Halston's temporary madness. His affair with Stella had only just started. It was unrealistic to think that he'd remain as desperate to have her as he was now.

But even the voice of common sense couldn't convince him that he'd stand idly by while she turned to a new paramour. Still, his voice emerged flat when he replied. "If you like."

"I doubt that what I like will have very much to do with it. I'll be unfit for other employment, and I'll need to keep body and soul together. Especially if I become accustomed to a life of luxury as your *petite amie*." Her chin angled up with the pride that made Stella such an improbable servant. Her hand lowered to grip the arm of the chair, and she spoke with a firmness that he couldn't question. "Thank you, my lord, but I don't think I'm willing to throw away my good name and take up a life of vice."

Her refusal should bring him back to reality. After all, his affair with Stella was meant to be a short-lived diversion before his next short-lived diversion.

Halston struggled against acknowledging the boredom that weighed on him as he thought of the long line of women ahead. When had his life of endless hedonism palled?

He could answer that in one sentence. Since the day he'd first seen Stella Faulkner. "What if it's not a life of vice? You admit to wanting me. God knows I'm crazy for you. What if you stay until this fire burns out? Then you may choose your own path."

She looked troubled. "Once I become your mistress, I'll be notorious because you're notorious. My uncle would never take me back. No respectable person would associate with me."

He leaned forward. "What if I contracted to pay you an allowance after you leave? Or a lump sum, if you'd rather have nothing more to do with me. We can sort out the details."

Despite all his experience with liaisons, right now the idea of never seeing Stella again twisted his gut into knots. Even so, he liked the idea of her being independent better than he liked the idea of her leaping into some other bastard's bed.

Halston went on before she could object. He could already see that she wanted to object, dash it. "You can make your own decision about where you go and what you do. You could travel. You could go back to Italy. Or you could establish yourself as a wealthy widow somewhere obscure where nobody will ever know that you were once my mistress. As a rich *incognita*, you'll have choices that you'll never have in your uncle's house."

Her eyebrows arched. "You're talking about a major financial commitment."

"I'll make sure you have enough to live in comfort." He studied her face. "You may not need to worry about this for a long time. My craving for you is so strong that I won't be in any rush to end our association."

Her smile was unamused. "I suppose I should be flattered."

"Damn it, Stella, I don't want you to be flattered. I want you to tell me that you're no happier at the thought of leaving me at the end of this week than I'm happy to leave you."

She paled. "You sound like you mean that."

He spread his hands. "I do."

"But you hardly know me."

A scornful laugh escaped, and he leaned back in his chair. "Of course I know you. Didn't you, too, feel that instant recognition the moment we met? Think about it, my darling. For ten years, you've lived without a man's touch. Yet the second time we were alone, you agreed to come to my bed."

She looked even more troubled, which wasn't the reaction he'd hoped for. "You may be right..."

When she didn't disagree, he gave a soft purr of satisfaction. That earned him a narrow-eyed glare before she went on. "You may be right, but I don't like the idea of you paying for my company. I'd be as much at your mercy as I am at my uncle's. More. He doesn't have the power to trample my feelings. You do."

Halston smiled, wondering if she knew that she confessed to a vulnerability to match his. "I'm a rich man, Stella. If I can use those riches to provide comfort and security to the woman I want, all the better."

"But you must marry."

Startled, he sat up straight. "Not any time soon."

"If I stay with you, how will I feel to see you fall in love with some well-bred miss and then set her up as your countess?"

Old cynicism had him answering before he thought about how his answer might make him appear. "There's no danger of falling in love with my future wife. Love doesn't exist."

"Of course love exists." Stella regarded him with such pity that he shifted on his chair. "My parents loved each other. They loved me. I loved Niccolo. I love Imogen."

He shifted again. By now, he should be used to her talent for catching him off guard. "Then let's say love doesn't exist for me."

To his chagrin, the pity in her eyes deepened. "Have you never loved anyone, Gray? Has nobody ever loved you?"

"No to both questions," he said shortly.

"Some of the women you've taken to your bed must have loved you."

"Must they? I know they loved the jewels I gave them and the cachet my interest lent them. Not to mention the fact that I'm a good fuck."

Stella blanched. "Not all of them. I can't believe that. You're a charming man." Her voice lowered. "You'd be tremendously easy to fall in love with."

Did she know how much she admitted? He waited for the discussion of love to evoke the usual suffocating sensation. Instead, as he should now expect, he felt only a vast yearning.

For physical union. Desire was always present.

But for more than that. For understanding. For tenderness.

For...her.

"Kind of you to say so," he said.

Her expression told him that was an inadequate response. He'd received that particular look from women before. With Stella, as with so much else, the disappointment cut deeper than usual.

"What about your parents? They must have loved you. It comes with the territory."

He sighed. How had his attempt to secure her presence in his bed turned into an inquisition on his barren emotional life? "My father died when I was a baby. I never knew him."

"What about your mother? You're a beautiful man. You must have been a gorgeous child. I doubt anyone could resist you. Then or now. You must know that I can't."

Another admission from her. "My mother was a bluestocking, more interested in books than she ever was in her son."

He thought that he concealed how his mother's neglect had rankled. Again he recalled that lonely schoolboy at Eton, pining for his mother to visit.

But something in Stella's eyes told him that she guessed at the wound he still bore. He braced for smothering compassion, but her jaw firmed and she continued in a matter-of-fact tone. "Then she was selfish and unfair. But you must have had a nursemaid who loved you."

He shrugged. "I suspect a few of the servants were fond of me. But I pay them, don't I?"

"Oh, Gray…" Her sadness made his flesh creep. Good God, were those tears in her eyes?

He'd taken just about as much of this as he could. It felt like she turned his skin inside out. "Don't you dare feel sorry for me."

"Never." She mustered a smile. Not one of her most convincing efforts, he wanted to tell her. "You're the magnificent Earl of Halston, the envy of all he meets."

He hid a flinch, because if this difficult conversation had revealed anything, it was that the magnificent Earl of Halston was a failure at the most basic human relations. With a shock, he realized that when he was with Stella, he didn't feel alone.

Look what a disaster that created. Here he was, on a night meant to be all sensual fulfillment, and he was wittering on about his childhood. It made him feel pathetic.

Halston refused to feel pathetic. Especially in front of this woman who, above all others, he wanted to admire him.

With manufactured nonchalance, he raised his champagne and took a mouthful. It was warm and flat. "So will you consider my offer?"

Stella took a minute to answer. Blast it, how he wished he could claw back the last hour and redo everything from when he'd swived her. He wished he'd carted her off to bed then and there and never started this discussion.

Her regretful glance warned him of her answer. "No."

Frustration flooded Halston. And something that felt very like fear. He already worried about cutting a poor figure in her eyes. He'd always thought that it was a brave decision not to believe in the sentimental nonsense that people called love.

Exposing his lonely childhood didn't seem half so laudable. "You don't trust me to look after you?"

"I do. Although I worry that you'd think I only stayed because you paid me."

He'd said too much. His skin prickled with humiliation. She'd picked up on his comment about the staff here at Prestwick Place.

A hint of impatience edged his response. "I want my mistress to eat, if only so she stays alive to amuse me. You're too proud."

He thought that she might resent that remark, but she bent her head in acknowledgement. The regal gesture confirmed his statement.

"I'm sorry, Gray. I won't say I'm not tempted. I am. But I can't do it. I'd feel like I was selling myself." She went on before he could argue with that. "And if I ran off with you, the scandal would harm Imogen. It would reawaken all the old talk about Mamma. People would wonder whether the women in my family really are too wild to wed. She deserves better than that."

Halston sent her a piercing glance, even as he couldn't help accepting that Stella loved her cousin. For what else was that selfless devotion but love?

"Are you saying that you're happy to finish with me at the end of this visit?"

He caught a flash of overpowering emotion in her eyes, before those thick gold-tipped lashes veiled them. "Not happy, no." Her voice was grave and, to his regret, adamant. "But I'm used to putting aside what I want in favor of what I must bear."

Halston hated that this insight into her life underlined how spoiled he was. He'd never had to sacrifice anything. His life was devoted to endless self-indulgence that he had to make no real effort to enjoy. Which perhaps explained why his enjoyment faded more with every year. Not to mention that it explained his interest in Stella Faulkner. She was the first challenge that he'd faced in an age.

But he'd played enough politics, in the bedroom and in parliament, to know when to step away from a negotiation and let circumstances unfold to his advantage.

He couldn't let Stella go back to being a stranger, and while she might say no now, who knew what she might agree to, once he showed her how much pleasure he could give her? His campaign began to win himself not just a temporary lover, but a cherished mistress.

When she raised her glass, he reached out to stop her. It was the first time he'd touched her since she'd threatened to end the affair. Even such casual contact as the brush of his fingers across her wrist sent heat sizzling through him. He knew she felt it, too, because her gold gaze flew up to meet his.

How the devil could she be satisfied with mere days of passion, when the desire between them was as inescapable as an earthquake?

"Let me pour you a fresh glass. It's flat."

She regarded the glass as if surprised that she held it and put it back on the table. "I don't really want it."

"Shall we proceed to the bedroom?" Halston stood and extended his hand. It was time to start convincing Stella that life without him wasn't worth living. "If I've only got these few precious days, I don't want to waste them."

"And talking to me counts as wasting them?" she asked with an ironic tilt of her eyebrows.

He gave a soft laugh. "No. But conversation has served its purpose. Come to bed, Stella. The night is passing too fast, and I want to hold you in my arms."

Her eyes softened, and she took his hand as she rose.

CHAPTER TWELVE

Stella didn't find it so easy to shake off her reaction to those surprising, heartbreaking revelations about the emotional desert that Gray lived in. During her time in England, she wouldn't have been human without an occasional lapse into self-pity. But looking back, she knew she'd been loved. More, she'd loved in return. Even now, while her uncle didn't even pretend to love her, Imogen did.

Yet Gray seemed to have grown up without as much as a hint of unconditional affection. Something in his tone when he mentioned his mother told her that while he mightn't love her now, he'd loved her as a child. Her neglect had hurt him badly.

As the conversation continued, Gray looked more and more hunted. He hadn't enjoyed giving her that glimpse into his inner life. In fact, he'd found the whole process excruciating.

What was also clear was that he had plans for the rest of the night. Plans that focused on physical sensation alone. He meant to ignore anything that might taint the glamorous, careless picture he presented to the world.

Goodness, the picture had convinced her, hadn't it? Just as it was designed to.

Gray had hated revealing his vulnerability. He'd feared that she'd think less of him because he wasn't quite the dashing, uncomplicated libertine he pretended to be.

The problem was that while Stella found the handsome, heartless rake irresistible, it was the man deriding love who tugged at her heart.

When he'd told her that dismal story of loneliness and alienation, she longed to take him in her arms and comfort him, to tell him he wasn't alone, that she was here with him.

Good heavens, what a catastrophe that would have been. He'd abhorred even the small portion of pity that she couldn't hide. Worse, the depth of her compassion warned her that when she said he'd be easy to love, she wasn't speaking in the abstract. Plague take him, she was already half in love with the scoundrel.

That wasn't the plan at all.

Stella had agreed to this affair to steal some sensual delight from a life that offered nothing but grim duty. A few days in a rake's arms allowing her to gather some nice memories to warm the cold nights to come.

Yet already her foolish heart begged for more. When Gray offered to make her his mistress, she'd almost said yes. Although she knew in her soul that she wasn't made to be a kept woman. Even aside from issues like Imogen's reputation.

The Earl of Halston was a complex man and not altogether an easy one. She just had to recall his unconcealed horror after making that inadvertent remark about staying with her forever. Lord Halston was a renowned seducer and a wild man about town – and as skittish as a half-broken colt at the prospect of anything hinting at emotional involvement.

His expression now, as he drew Stella into his arms in the opulent bedroom, told her without words that the moment for confidences had passed.

She went willingly. The memory of that shattering climax still made her tremble. She and Niccolo had both been inexperienced when they came together, although they soon discovered the path to delight. But even those sweet recollections couldn't compare to the volcanic reactions that Gray had drawn from her body tonight.

If Gray meant to devote his next hours to more of the same, she'd accept that. Even while some silly, yearning part of her mourned his retreat from genuine closeness.

Under lowered eyelids, her hazy vision took in her surroundings. Another fire burned in the grate, and a candelabra in the corner provided light. But this room wasn't as bright as the sitting room, and the atmosphere was more intimate.

Behind Gray loomed the huge bed. The covers were turned down, revealing crisp white sheets and mounds of plump pillows.

Soon she'd lie under him in that bed. Anticipation tasted more delicious than champagne. After their explosive encounter against the wall, she shouldn't be so desperate to have him inside her again. But that first union only made her avid for the next. And the one after that.

Stella couldn't stifle a futile wish for the night to last forever.

Gray's kiss was hot as fire and told her that he still thirsted after her. He conquered her mouth with a ruthlessness that made her quake with wicked excitement. He used his lips and tongue and teeth on her until she sagged, panting with surrender.

He brushed aside her peignoir. For the first time, his headlong seduction paused. "You're not wearing your nightdress."

"It was…it was stained," she stammered.

"Damn fool idea to buy you a nightdress at all." At the sight of her bare breasts, his smile turned pantherish. "Let's burn the rag."

A gasp of horrified laughter escaped. "You will not burn it. It's beautiful."

And the most extravagant piece of clothing that she'd ever owned. From the moment that she put it on, she'd felt like a princess. If perhaps a princess offered as tribute to an enemy invader.

He took his time arousing her, until her nipples ached and desire churned in her stomach. When at last he took one crest in his mouth, she gave a broken cry and buried her hands in his hair to bring him nearer.

He cupped her breasts. They fit his elegant hands, but old insecurity gnawed at her, especially when she thought about the other women he'd tupped. "I'm not blessed with abundant curves."

Another of those big cat smiles lengthened his lips and sent a thrill skittering along her spine. "You're just the right shape."

As if to prove it, he placed a kiss on the not particularly mountainous swell of flesh. Stella started with pleasure and arched forward. When he drew on her nipple, a hot wire of sensation snaked down into her clenching womb. She moaned and hooked her hands over his sinewy shoulders as her legs threatened to crumple.

Through his trousers, his rod pressed into her stomach. Frantic to give him the same pleasure he gave her, she fumbled at the fastenings on his trousers. He made a soft growl of approval and teased her nipple with his teeth. She was so het up that she whimpered, and her attempts to uncover him became even more inept.

All this bumping and rubbing made her blood pump. She knew that it agitated Gray, too. He groaned with audible agony against her skin and lifted his head. His eyes were brilliant, and the skin clung to the chiseled bones of his face. "Are you trying to drive me insane?"

Stella gave a muffled laugh. "No, I'm trying to undo your trousers, but my hands won't cooperate."

"Let me help."

His hands weren't as deft as usual either. But in the end, he managed to push down his trousers and step out of them. On shaky legs, she stepped back to survey his nakedness. Their hunger for each other had been so overwhelming the first time, that neither had stopped to shed their clothes.

The breath jammed in her throat, and her racing pulse made her head swim. She'd called him beautiful. She'd had no idea.

Avid eyes drank him in. Tall, perfectly proportioned, muscled where he should be muscled, lean where he should be lean, he dazzled her. She hid a pained wince at the sight of the scar on his shoulder. He didn't want her pity for that either.

Stella surveyed the broad shoulders, the powerful chest, and the way curling dark hair accentuated his pectorals. That hair drew into a dark line leading down to his erect penis.

When he moved inside her, she'd known that he was large. The sensation of being stretched to her limits had been both uncomfortable and rapturous. Now her gaze focused on the impressive column of flesh that emerged from a nest of black hair between his strong, horseman's thighs. Deep feminine wonder stole her ability to speak.

She licked her lips and imagined tasting him down there, where he was most a man. She and Niccolo had experimented along those lines, and he'd loved what she'd done to him.

"Stella?" he asked, although he must realize how his nakedness affected her.

Why wait? She had mere days to accomplish a lifetime's worth of sin.

She stepped forward and dropped to her knees. Trembling hands cradled the heavy sacs, then she shaped her fingers to his virile power. By heaven, he was so hot. Male potency filled her hand and her senses. His musky scent was more intoxicating than wine, as addictive as opium.

His breath emerged in ragged spurts. When she fisted her hand around him and began to move it up and down, he groaned again and tilted his hips forward. "Don't...stop."

Gray gazed down at her with a hunger that was as clear as if it was written in a book in front of her. But she guessed that he wouldn't ask her to go further.

Lucky for him, he didn't need to ask. She firmed her grip and took the tip between her lips. The rich taste of his skin flooded her mouth. When she swept her tongue across him, he jerked in response.

"Stella..." he grated out, tangling his hands in her hair.

She took more of him, delighting in his salty flavor. Her tongue traced the veined hardness, as her hand squeezed the base in a suggestive rhythm.

He'd been big when she uncovered him. Under her brazen attentions, he grew even larger. How she loved knowing that she could arouse him like this.

A haze of delight enveloped her. She lost all connection to anything but the way that she tormented Gray.

When he shifted back, a soft mew of disappointment escaped her. He caught her head between his hands and angled her face up. With erotic languor, she traced the shape of her lips with her tongue.

Her eyes didn't waver from his. He needed to see that she wanted this.

"You don't have to." His voice emerged as rough as gravel.

His features were tense, and his pupils dilated so wide that the green was a thin ring around them. He was close to losing himself. After their tumultuous first union, she recognized the signs.

"I want to." Stella's voice was low and thick. "So much. Please don't deny me."

He closed his eyes and spoke as if he was in pain. "I shouldn't."

Her tone became more urgent. "I want to taste your seed, Gray. I want to take you inside me like this because…because I can't take you any other way." To confirm her eagerness, she tightened her grip and squeezed his entire length. She glanced down to see a drop of pearly liquid glistening on the tip.

Her passionate plea made his eyes flare, and a muscle danced in his lean cheek. "You give me too much."

It was a tacit acceptance. Smiling, she bent to lick the sensitive head. She took him again, sucking hard. With a muttered curse, Gray dug his fingers into her scalp. He moved her head, setting up a driving rhythm that stirred her.

She clasped his hard buttocks and felt him go taut, before he yielded to her on a long, guttural moan. He jerked again and flooded her mouth. She swallowed everything he gave her, and when he pulled free, they were both gasping.

"Dear God, you're superb," he growled and hauled Stella up to kiss her until she couldn't see straight.

They collapsed into a chair near the fire, with her curled up on his lap. His chest heaved as he regained his breath. She wriggled to gather her peignoir about her, then closed her eyes and rested against him, enjoying the gentle circles his hand made against her back.

"Shall we continue?" he murmured.

"Yes, please." She rose and stood back so he could follow her up. With a few urgent tugs, he released the belt of the peignoir and pushed it off. Her skin was so sensitive that the slide of her robe felt like a caress.

Now it was her turn to stand naked with a new lover. His face conveyed awe and an earthy appreciation that shouldn't sit together, but did so well that Stella forgot all her niggling dissatisfactions with her long, athletic body. Gray's riveted expression told her that he had no complaints about her being tall and lean rather than the rounded fashionable ideal.

"I was wrong. Superb doesn't do you justice." He stepped back to survey her. Admiration deepened his voice to a velvety rumble that made every hair on her skin rise in response. "Come to bed, sweetheart. Let me show you pleasure like you've never known."

Stella shook back her tumble of hair. "You've already done that."

Heavy lids descended over fierce eyes, making him look far too appealing. "We've only just started."

He caught her waist and swung her around until the back of her knees hit the bed. After a gentle push, she landed flat on the sheets. A huff of surprise emerged, then she drew him down to kneel over her. More kisses, more breathtaking caresses, more incoherent sighs of appreciation, as he learned the shape of her body.

After an extended interval of delight, Gray rolled to the side and leaned on one elbow. His glowing eyes ranged across her with a heated possessiveness that sparked needy throbbing in the pit of her stomach.

"It's my turn to return the favor," he murmured. He stroked her midriff, igniting heat wherever he touched.

"Oh..." Stella parted her legs to lure him to touch her where she ached.

The searching passion in Gray's kiss made her toes curl against the bed linens. Still kissing her, he began to explore the hollows of her body. Her gasp was full of wonder and encouragement, and she encircled his arm with one hand to anchor herself in a reeling world.

When his thumb found the secret nub, he brushed it over and over. A surge of female response drenched his fingers and made him purr with approval. He raised his head to watch her reaction to these intimate touches.

Pleasure spread inside Stella until she writhed against the sheets. As every muscle in her body convulsed in ecstasy, her nails dug into his arm. Then while she still quivered, he moved his fingers inside her. Before she'd recovered from her last climax, she set off once more on the feverish ascent to bliss. This time when she crossed the barrier, she flew apart in a thousand flaming embers.

With two of his fingers curling against her still-clenching inner walls, he kissed her. Voracious, open-mouthed passion that heightened her pleasure.

"Gray, you...you overwhelm me," she panted. "Let me catch my breath."

She released his arm and stretched out her fingers to relieve the stiffness. That last climax had ripped through every cell in her body like a whirlwind.

"You?" The lazy pleasure in his smile melted her heart into a sugary mess. "You're made of sturdier stuff than you think."

With a slowness that was a caress in itself, he slid free of her. Then her heart gave a great crash when he raised his fingers to his lips and licked them. Sensual appreciation lit his face as he took his time.

Stella lay shaking against the sheets as the emptiness inside her expanded to a huge, gaping space. Only Gray could answer this yearning.

Her legs sprawled across the bed. She swore that they'd turned into wet string. God help her if there was a fire and she needed to make a run for it. Except, she thought with sly humor, there was a fire. It burned like an inferno inside her, and every touch of Gray's hands stoked it higher.

He showed definite signs of recovery. She reached for him but he caught her hand and brought it to his lips for a quick kiss. "Let me pleasure you."

She frowned. "You have pleasured me."

"There's more."

Under her wondering gaze, he slid down in the bed and settled between her legs.

"You want to look at me?" Her voice vibrated with uncertainty.

"Oh, yes," he said as if he spoke a prayer.

After he'd tasted her on his fingers, what he did next shouldn't astonish her. But when he lifted her hips and placed his mouth on her sex, she cried out.

"Gray..."

Her hands fisted in the sheets as heat engulfed her. The heat of embarrassment, and the heat of arousal. She propped herself up on her elbows so she could see him.

With unhidden reluctance, he raised his head. "Don't you like this?"

She read craving in his burning eyes. "I...I don't know."

Satisfaction tinged his smile. "This is new to you?"

"It seems...rather strange."

Rather strange? It seemed like the outer edges of depravity.

"You did this for me."

"It's not quite the same."

"Perhaps not. But nice, for all that." His smile widened. "Will you let me show you?"

After a moment, she nodded. Speaking actual words was beyond her.

"Thank you."

Her heart somersaulting with nerves, she lay back and closed her eyes. She didn't think that she could bear to watch him do this extraordinary thing.

For a long time, nothing happened. She had a mortifying suspicion that he lingered to take in every private inch. She'd known that he'd use her body tonight, but she hadn't realized that things would become quite so intimate.

His grip on her hips tightened, and he tilted her higher. "Is this uncomfortable?"

"Do you count dying of embarrassment?"

A grunt of laughter was the response. "I mean is this hurting your back? If it does, I can position you another way."

It was her turn for a brief laugh. "Can you indeed?"

"Or I can save this variation until next time I kiss your quim."

Next time? She wasn't even sure that she'd survive this time. Even more embarrassing, sinful curiosity demanded to know how his mouth would feel on her sex.

"No, please, go ahead," she said with ironic politeness.

She opened dazed eyes and stared up at the elaborate plaster roundels on the ceiling. Another batch of sulky unicorns sneered down at her. No wonder. What happened in this bed was too brazen to believe.

Gray's mouth descended to her cleft. Her ability to see anything at all deserted her.

Molten pleasure streamed through her and made her judder, as his mouth explored the delicate folds. His tongue fluttered and tasted and enticed. Her grip on the sheets tightened until her hands hurt. Above her thundering pulse, she heard her rasping breath as Gray lit her world with vermilion.

With a tattered cry, she tipped over the edge into a fiery universe. She rode the spasms of pleasure, then realized Gray again stroked her with intent, even as she quaked and moaned.

It took a huge effort to lift her head. He appeared very pleased with himself. He also looked as if he struggled not to jump on top of her.

"I can't..."

"Of course you can." His smile held a definite tinge of self-satisfaction. "You liked it?"

She gave a wry laugh, although delight still radiated through her and speaking tested her limits. "You know I did."

"Excellent."

"But have a little mercy. I'm only human. "

His smile widened. "Deliciously human."

He dipped his head to kiss her between the legs, and her protest died unspoken as pleasure that had barely ebbed coiled anew.

By the time she drifted down to earth again, tears ran down her cheeks and her lungs hurt with the effort of filling them.

Gray watched her with an arrested expression. At least he wasn't looking at her sex, but she wasn't sure she liked the calculating light she read in his eyes.

He released her hips and wiped his mouth. The deliberate gesture made her shiver. She'd imagined that she knew what it was like for two ardent lovers to unite. It turned out that she was a complete novice.

With a powerful surge, he slid up her body to kiss her mouth. The salty taste on his lips was her. She shivered again. The act seemed so intimate.

And yet...

His hands slid down to stroke her swollen folds and despite her exhaustion, warmth stirred anew. This time, though, she stiffened and rolled away. "Gray, stop."

Supporting himself on one arm, he leaned over her. "What's wrong?"

She stared into his face and struggled to define what worried her. "You don't have to do this."

He frowned. "I want to. I love to please you."

She swallowed to moisten a dry throat that hurt after she'd cried out at her peak. When Gray said that he wanted to make her scream, he'd meant it. "You do please me."

"But?"

Stella feared what she was about to say might anger or even hurt him. Tonight she'd discovered quite how touchy his pride was. "I feel...I feel like you're trying to prove something."

His brows lowered further. "That we're perfect together."

"We are." She touched his cheek. The first moment of genuine sweetness since he'd set out to conquer her with rapture, she realized with a shock. "Because we are, you don't have to work so hard to convince me that you're the invincible rake, impervious to feeling."

Stella now realized just why she'd asked him to stop. It was because Gray used his sexual expertise to banish any recollection of his reluctant, harrowing confessions about his childhood.

"I don't know what you're talking about," he said, although he avoided her gaze and that telltale muscle jerked in his cheek, betraying his discomfort.

"Do you know what I liked best tonight?"

Displeasure tightened his lips, and he shifted away until they no longer touched. "Well, at least there's something."

She took an awful risk. Mustering her courage, she continued. "I liked it best when you pushed me up against the wall."

"I was a barbarian." Self-disgust edged his voice. "I did nothing to prepare you. I didn't even linger to make sure you found your pleasure."

"I did." She made herself continue. "I liked that you weren't thinking. I liked that I was your partner and not your toy."

Stella swallowed once more, hoping that what she said didn't destroy his interest in her. Because even after a few hours, she knew that she'd hate it if he denied her his sensual skills.

But then, she wasn't talking about his sensual skills. Those were never in doubt. She was talking about emotional connection. A connection that he found as troubling as she did.

Before he could protest, she rushed ahead. "Gray, knowing that life has left you with one or two scars doesn't stop me wanting and admiring you. The reverse. I want to hold a real man in my arms, a man with hopes and joys and sorrows."

Although his gaze was steady, she couldn't interpret his response. Was she insane to complain about a man willing to devote himself to her satisfaction with such single-minded dedication?

Stella dared to go on. "You said earlier tonight that I don't have to hide myself from you." She sucked in a shaky breath and forced herself to finish, whatever the risk. "I want you to understand that you don't have to hide yourself from me either."

CHAPTER THIRTEEN

*D*ear God, how could he resist her?

A great rift opened inside Halston as he stared down at Stella. She saw what nobody else did. She saw too much. He was vulnerable with her in a way he'd been vulnerable with no other lover.

Except that all his life, he'd been a stranger in the world. With Stella, he felt like he found a home.

Steady caramel eyes focused on him. In vain, he searched those golden depths for judgement or disdain or even triumph. All he found was acceptance. And desire.

She was right, damn it. He'd used that desire as a weapon against her. And he'd used the techniques that he'd learned through a lifetime of meaningless affairs. He had a painful presentiment that whatever else this affair proved to be, it wouldn't be meaningless.

He'd hated revealing his weakness. He'd hated hearing his self-pitying meanderings.

But her gaze was warm and admiring. He didn't need to pretend that he was a heartless rake. He didn't need to show her that all that mattered was how many climaxes he could give her.

He swallowed, then swallowed again to shift the unaccustomed lump of emotion in his throat. "Yet still you mean to leave me in a few days."

"We have so much." The glow faded from her eyes, and he glimpsed her turmoil. "Don't spoil it by worrying about what's to come."

She curled her hand behind his neck, drawing him down for a kiss unlike any he could remember in all his years of debauchery. It was a kiss that offered wordless acceptance. It was a kiss that questioned, demanding more than he knew he could give. It was a kiss that offered him everything in a way that not even that furious fuck against the wall had. Or that shattering moment when she took his cock into her mouth with such sweet willingness, that he ached to recall it.

The kiss burned away calculation and strategy, leaving only his need for this extraordinary woman.

Taking charge, he rolled over her. He was hard again. When he stroked her cleft, he discovered that she was ready, too. He shifted between her spread legs and drove forward. There was that same sleek welcome that he'd felt the first time.

Halston rested his weight on his elbows, so he could see that unforgettable face. He settled deeper and watched pleasure brighten her eyes. Eager hands caught his shoulders, as she lifted her hips.

He dipped his head to kiss her, then began to move in long, deliberate strokes that pushed her deep into the mattress. At the peak of every thrust, Stella caught her breath in an audible sigh that turned into the music of arousal. She closed her eyes and gripped his back, joining the possessive dance. Although he couldn't say who was the possessor and who the possessed. Another change from his usual amours.

He'd climaxed twice already. This time, he meant to give Stella a long ride.

The skin on her face tautened, as she succumbed to another climax. He thrust hard into her convulsing body. Her fingernails dug into his back. After tonight, he'd bear her mark.

Halston kissed her with all the primitive power that blazed between them and moved again until she shuddered and cried out. Then he took her across one final time in a gentle release that seemed to wash over her like the waves of a warm tropical sea.

"Oh, Gray, I had no idea." Stella still clenched around him.

Halston kissed her again and circled his hips, but this long, slow joining reached its end. He shifted once more before he drew free and pumped his seed onto her stomach. He shifted to the side and studied her as she lay next to him.

They'd barely spoken since he'd joined his body with hers. Now she opened tear-bright eyes and gave him a shaky smile. Exhaustion shadowed her striking features, and her mouth was bruised and swollen from his kisses.

It was unworthy to gloat, but Halston was delighted that he'd taken her to places she'd never been. "We've only just started."

This time, her smile held a trace of a grimace. "I might have hit my limit for the moment."

After their eventful night, she must be sore. More, she hadn't had a lover in years. He should have been gentler, curse him.

Halston brushed his index finger across the purple shadows beneath her eyes. "I've tired you out."

"Yes."

"I can wait until tomorrow night to do this again."

Familiar wry humor diluted her seriousness. "I'm not sure I'll be able to walk tomorrow." As if to remind them of time passing, the clock on the mantel chimed half past four. Her lips quirked. "Today."

"I'll help you down the staircase to the dining room, you poor old thing."

His small joke made a clumsy landing. Sorrow weighted her gaze. "Once the sun rises, we go back to being strangers."

"I hate that," he said, all urge to smile abandoning him as well.

It just seemed so bloody wrong that he had to hide his attraction to this wonderful woman as if it was a shameful secret. Halston wanted to shout her praises from the rooftops. He wanted to flaunt his pride in her. He wanted to walk beside her so that everyone knew that she belonged to him.

But daybreak rushed in upon them and with it, the demands and conventions of the world they lived in. It was a world of hypocrisy and glittering appearances that masked darker realities. But Halston had to bow to its power.

"I hate it, too," she confessed. She stroked his shoulders, claiming him in a way that she never could in the light of day.

As if to confirm the end of a night that had changed him forever, a lark started to sing from the trees outside. He'd spent weeks scheming to bring Stella Faulkner to his bed. Now he had, and he'd reveled in hours crammed with pleasure. More surprising, they were hours full of emotion and revelations, and a closeness he'd never felt with anyone else.

He and Stella had pursued sin with a wholehearted fervor that had shaken his world. They'd sin again tonight.

The pity of it was that right now, the real sin seemed to be that she must leave this bed and return to her room. It felt so wrong that they should be apart.

Halston collapsed at her side and rested his head on her shoulder. Her scent flooded his senses. Satisfied woman. A trace of sweat. A hint of the sandalwood soap that she must have used when she washed in his dressing room.

She smoothed his hair. Even that action conveyed deep weariness. It also betrayed a tenderness that he feared might become as addictive as the magic contained within her slender body.

Halston closed his eyes and battled the need to sleep. When he sucked in a deep breath, the air tasted like sex. She'd drained him to the dregs. He felt tired and satisfied, and heavy with lingering pleasure.

She must go soon. The maid would be in to tend the fire, which had burned down to embers while he'd dwelled in paradise.

"I should go." He heard aching regret in Stella's voice.

A thrush joined the lark, then a robin and a blackbird. As if Halston needed reminding of time's cruel progress.

"Not yet," he murmured, extending his neck to encourage her caresses.

When she dropped a kiss on top of his head, he responded with a low hiss of enjoyment. The deep, comforting peace extended for ten minutes, fifteen, before she shifted.

Halston bit back a futile protest. So far, he'd cared for her reputation. He wouldn't let her down now. But, oh, what agony it was to accept that the long, eventful night drew to a close.

He was too sapped to do much more than lie in her arms and dream about the night just passed. But that was sweeter than the most torrid encounter with any other woman.

Sweetness wasn't the usual currency that he traded in. It was strange to discover that after all their passion, it was sweetness that held him captive.

"I must go," she said again with even less conviction.

How Halston wished that he lived in a world where he could tell everyone to go hang themselves, while he basked in this delicious aftermath.

He sighed, and this time he was the one who moved, although only far enough to rise on his elbow. His eyes drank Stella in, as if he might never see her again. The hours before he had her to himself once again felt like a chasm. "Let me clean you up before you go."

"If you like."

His gaze swept over her. By God, she was a peach. He frowned and touched the chafing on her neck. "My beard caught you."

Her lips turned down in acknowledgement. "I'll have to wear a scarf."

With great reluctance, he left the bed and crossed to the dressing room. After a quick wash, he tugged on his red robe.

He returned to Stella with a bowl of water and a flannel. "The water's cold. Do you want me to try to warm it on the fire?"

She sat up, still naked. He liked her lack of shyness. Hell, he liked her.

"We don't have time," she said, stretching out against the rumpled sheets.

To his regret, those words didn't apply just to the heating of some water. He approached the bed and set the bowl on the bedside table.

"You don't have to do this," she said, eating him up with her eyes.

"I want to," he said. "Lie back and enjoy it."

She gave a short laugh. "Lucky me."

"No, lucky me." With a gentleness that paid tribute to her, he began to sponge her pale stomach. "Is the water too cold?"

"No." She closed her eyes and gave herself over to his ministrations.

Halston rinsed out the flannel and dipped it between her legs. Stella hid a wince.

Remorse pierced him. He lifted his hand. "I was too rough with you."

She opened her eyes and regarded him with such yearning that he cursed the hour and wished he could keep her here. "I loved every moment of what you did to me." She shot him a mocking glance. "Even when you set out to prove that you were in charge."

That hadn't come to anything, had it? If he'd hoped that a good fuck would loosen her hold on him, he'd been utterly misguided. Having Stella just made him want more.

He kissed the soft plain of her stomach. "I won't make that mistake again."

"See you don't," she murmured, softening the reprimand with a touch of her hand to his shoulder.

Too soon for his liking, he finished washing her and bent to retrieve her peignoir. "Here."

She stood and tugged it on, tying the belt. "Do you mind coming along the passage with me?"

"Not at all." He'd already lit a chamberstick. He was desperate to wring every second from these last minutes with her that he could.

He stepped forward and caught her hand. "Are you ready?"

She gave him another of those intent looks that made him burn, despite what he'd already done, despite knowing that she was in no fit state to take him again. "I don't want to go, mad as that sounds."

"That doesn't sound mad at all."

"It will feel like an eternity until I come to you tonight."

Halston grimaced. "I'm wishing every one of my esteemed guests to blazes."

"Give them lots to do today." He could tell that her smile took an effort. "Lots of busy, active things so they go to bed early."

His amusement was muffled against her lips, as he lost himself in a kiss that wasn't light at all, but a turbulent expression of longing for what he couldn't have. Stella kissed him back with the passion that he now knew was her essence. He hauled her closer and devoured her mouth to make up for the endless hours when he couldn't touch her.

After they drew apart, his head was swimming and his heart pounded. In a daze, Halston watched her cast a comprehensive glance around the room. It was as if she etched every detail on her mind. Then she took his hand and turned toward the secret doorway.

CHAPTER FOURTEEN

On the fourth night of the house party, Lord Halston held a small ball for his guests and neighbors. He'd booked an orchestra from London and had the great hall of his elegant house bedecked with garlands of flowers to welcome the arrival of spring. For once, the weather cooperated, so he set lights in the gardens, in case anyone wished to wander the paths outside.

"Isn't this just grand?" Imogen brought Stella a glass of champagne in the brief interval before the dancing started again. She looked charming in a leaf-green gown that would probably find its way to Stella in time. That pretty color would make her look bilious.

All night, Imogen had been a popular partner. Against Stella's expectations, so had she. Nobody here seemed determined to make her sit by the wall. She was used to taking part in a set, so managed to perform tolerably well. At the assemblies in Gloucester, she often danced, but the company at the county town wasn't so elevated.

"It is." She accepted the wine and took a sip. It was inevitable that the dry, refreshing taste made her think of drinking champagne with Halston in his chambers. She'd never expected their affair to involve so much conversation.

When she'd agreed to come to the earl's bed, she'd expected carnal pleasure. But she'd discovered a man not only of surpassing seductive gifts, but with a lively, curious mind. For years, Stella had starved for compatible company. How odd to find it in a dedicated debaucher. How odd and how dangerous.

Because those long, interesting discussions only deepened her hopeless infatuation with Grayson Maddox. She'd become so entangled in passion and fascination that she feared she'd never break free.

Over the last four days, Gray had offered her so much. But one thing that he hadn't offered her was a good night's sleep. Her attempt to hide a yawn drew Imogen's attention.

"Are you tired?"

Was she tired? She was exhausted and edgy with physical bliss and the strain of hiding her affair from sharp eyes. Those sharp eyes included her cousin's.

Stella felt as if these last few nights in Gray's arms had stripped off a layer of skin. Everything was more vivid than usual, and the world away from him turned into an unfamiliar place. Brighter. Louder. Harsher. More invasive.

At least now, though, her body had adjusted to her lover's attentions. After their first night together, every movement had been agony. Muscles she'd forgotten had protested at her wanton exertions.

"A little," she admitted. "I'll live."

Stella wasn't sure about that. She was so addicted to Halston's touch that she feared she'd wilt into oblivion once she went back to London.

The day after tomorrow.

She shoved away the horrid thought of how fast her time in Buckinghamshire rushed away. Since their first night, Gray hadn't mentioned the end of their affair either. But she'd noticed last night that his lovemaking held a desperate edge that was breathtakingly exciting. And a poignant reminder of how wretched life would be, once she left him.

"I've had problems sleeping, too." Imogen's voice dropped, although nobody paid them any attention. "I'm appalled to say it, but I think Lord Halston has rats. I swear I've heard things moving behind the wainscoting. It's such a magnificent house, I'm surprised."

Stella was glad that she wasn't drinking her champagne. Otherwise she was likely to snort it everywhere, the way she'd made a fool of herself with her tea that first night at Prestwick Place.

"I'm sure it's your imagination." Goodness, Gray hadn't exaggerated about how noise from the passage traveled. "Old houses always creak and groan."

Imogen's face set in stubborn lines. "No. Something is moving inside the walls. I wonder if I should mention it to Mr. Perrett."

"Who on earth is Mr. Perrett?"

"Halston's head gardener. He'll know what to do. We've been talking about how to keep rats out of compost heaps."

"Have you indeed?" Stella said faintly.

Imogen had seemed happy to spend her time with Lily, Elizabeth and Harriet. Stella had to admit that she'd been distracted, though, and hadn't been the most assiduous chaperone.

She'd assumed that when Imogen wasn't with her friends, she was pestering the outdoor staff. She wouldn't get into much bother talking about gardens.

Unless...

"How old is Mr. Perrett?"

Imogen cast her a confused glance. "You ask the strangest questions."

"Humor me."

"Oh, Papa's age at least."

Stella drew a relieved breath. In that case, she doubted that Imogen was developing an unsuitable *tendre*.

As if she had a right to criticize her cousin for unsuitable *tendres*. "Make sure you don't interrupt his work."

The music started again, and Lily Bilson's brother approached to claim his dance. "Lady Imogen, I believe this is our waltz," Ivor Bilson said, bowing.

He was a handsome young man with beautiful manners, but nothing about her cousin's demeanor hinted that she viewed him as anything more than her friend's older brother.

However preoccupied Stella had been with Gray, she remained convinced that Imogen had a beau. But as she glanced across the chattering throng, nobody raised her suspicions.

Stella had spent most of the evening doing her best to ignore Gray, which didn't mean that she wasn't aware of where he was and who he spoke to. For a fleeting moment, her wandering attention settled on him, while she combed the room to find a candidate for the man who had put that sparkle in Imogen's blue eyes.

It was impossible to miss Gray, even if he didn't make her ache with desire. He was back to playing the satanic earl, all in black and so much taller than most of the other people in the room. He was talking to Lady Tierney, who had just danced with him.

He'd kept up his habit of not singling out any particular female guest. So far tonight, he'd danced with all the debutantes and their mothers, and a couple of older ladies who must be the local *grandes dames*. With his lean grace, he appeared to advantage on the dance floor.

Where didn't he appear to advantage?

She was doomed. Even if she met a man who might want to marry her in the drab years ahead, how could anyone compete with Gray?

Imogen passed her half-empty glass to a hovering footman. "Stella, do you have a partner for this set?"

"No, I think I'll sit and catch my breath."

"I hope that's not the case," Gray said from just behind her. "I'd very much like to have this dance with you, Miss Faulkner."

For one dizzying instant, the crowded, noisy room receded, and Stella heard nothing but the furious drumming of her heart. When she returned to the present, Gray held her arm and regarded her with a quizzical smile.

The one minute when she lost sight of him because she was worried about her cousin had to be the one minute in all this busy night when he sneaked up on her. Her shaking hand crept to where her pulse thrummed so fast in her throat, surely it must be visible.

"How nice, Stella," Imogen said, showing no jealousy. Stella hoped that meant the girl hadn't set her cap at Gray. She took Stella's champagne glass from her and gave it to the same cooperative footman. "Lord Halston is a dream to dance with, and because you're so tall, you'll make a perfect match."

Imogen had no idea how well Stella and Halston matched. She nearly lost her balance again, as she had a sudden disorienting vision of lying naked under the earl while he thrust inside her. She hoped to the devil that she wasn't blushing.

Gray must share the thought, because those long black lashes veiled his green eyes and a muscle jerked in his cheek.

Stella struggled to regain her composure. She was well aware that where Gray went, attention followed. In truth, she wasn't just flustered. She was annoyed. He must know that what he asked was impossible.

"My lord, you do me too much honor," she said stiffly.

"Not at all."

"Stella would love to dance with you, my lord," Imogen said, placing her hand in Ivor's and letting him draw her away. She turned back to where Stella stood like a statue beside Gray. "She'll try and tell you it's not suitable because she's a mere companion, but don't listen to her."

"I won't," Gray said with a smile. He was better at subterfuge than Stella was. Anyone observing him would note a casual interest. But she could see his eyes, and his eyes were hungry.

"You can't do this," she said in a furious undertone, wanting to pull away from his hold but knowing that if she did, people would notice.

His expression didn't change. While the smile remained, neither his eyes nor his tone held any levity. Emotion roughened his voice. "I've danced with every woman in this room under the age of sixty so that now I can dance with the woman I want."

She couldn't help flashing him a look of longing. How could she not, when he said such wonderful things? "It's dangerous."

His eyes glittered down at her, sending messages that the polite interest on his face belied.

"If we stand here any longer, we'll attract much more attention than if you dance with me."

She glanced around. So far, nobody was looking at them, but he was right. So she gave up and did what might not be wise but was certainly what she wanted. "Very well. Don't make me look at you or everyone will know I'm besotted."

"Silly girl," he said with a teasing fondness that she feared she'd miss as much as she'd miss the touch of his hands and the power of his strong body.

"Because I'm besotted?"

"Because you think I'll let you deny me." He slipped his hand around her waist. His touch was familiar, as was her shiver of awareness when heat leaped from him to her.

"You won't always get your own way."

"I do when we want the same thing."

It was true, plague take him. "I'm glad it's a waltz," she said as he swept her onto the dance floor.

His smile took on a sly tinge. "So am I."

Her hand rested on his shoulder, and she gloried in his firm grip on her waist. Through their gloves, his touch was warm. A reminder of his hands on her during these last radiant nights. A promise of more radiance to come. "You arranged it."

"After all, I pay the piper." He swept her into a whirling turn, but she was already dizzy with a charged mixture of nerves and excitement. While it was risky to be so close to him in public, it was also delightful.

Imogen was right. He was a dream of a partner. As she twirled about the room, she felt like her feet had wings. Even better, the waltz gave them the illusion of privacy.

He went on. "By the way, I'm besotted, too."

Shock made her stumble and for a few fraught seconds, only Gray's strength kept her upright. "Oh."

Her inadequate response widened his smile. With deft skill, he guided her between the other dancers, somehow always preserving a bubble around them.

"Oh, indeed." He went on as if he hadn't just made a declaration that rocked her world to its foundations. "You're looking lovely tonight. In fact, you've looked lovely all week. I've been meaning to mention it. The other chaperones in London wouldn't recognize this gorgeous apparition as their demure companion."

"Thank you," she said, more warmth filling her. There was something terrifically gratifying in knowing that the man she wanted admired her appearance. Well, her clothed appearance anyway. Any niggling insecurities about whether he found her body unsatisfactory had faded during their first night together. He was too desperate to have her to suffer any complaints about her lack of curves. "Imogen insisted I act more like a guest and less like a servant."

"Good for Imogen."

For a sizzling second, she met his eyes then glanced away. "Stop looking at me like that. People will think you want to devour me."

He gave a wry laugh, although he took her warning and glanced over her shoulder to nod acknowledgement to a couple who danced past them. "I do."

She fought the urge to tangle her fingers in the black curls at his nape. "Later."

"Yes, later."

For a fashionable event, the ball had started early. In London, society gathered until well after midnight. If this party continued for the usual duration, it would be over by ten. Another deliberate choice, Stella now suspected.

For a few minutes, they lapsed into silence, enjoying their ease of movement. It was glorious to dance with Gray and yield to the demands of the music and the subtle press of his hand.

"I wish I could dance with you in London. You have no idea how often I wanted to fight my way through the serried ranks of dowagers to claim you as my partner."

Startled, she looked at him, then away. If she spent too long gazing into those brilliant green eyes, she didn't trust herself to conceal her attraction. "It would be lovely, but it would cause too much talk."

Here in the country, she could relax her strict control a little. The guest list was small, and Gray had avoided inviting the ton's worst gossips. In London, Stella would go back to being that prim, watchful, disregarded duenna. The thought was depressing.

Except Lord Halston hadn't disregarded her, had he?

"It would, but that didn't stop me wanting. That's when I resorted to the gazebo solution."

A choked laugh escaped. "Thanks to Imogen."

"Thanks to Imogen." He performed another swift turn and dared to bring her nearer.

Stella caught a drift of his scent, so evocative after hours of sensual exploration in his rooms. She drew it deep into her lungs, even as she forced herself to remember where they were.

"You're holding me too close," she said with audible reluctance.

"Damn it, Stella..." For one bristling moment, his grip tightened as if he considered dragging her upstairs. A thrill composed of fear and desire rippled through her. What a scandalous finale that would provide to the ball.

He eased his hold, and they returned to the distance that propriety demanded of waltzing couples. His features set in uncharacteristically stern lines.

Stella swallowed to loosen her tight throat and fixed a bland expression to her face. Her smile showed a lamentable tendency to slip. "Now you look like you want to take me away and spank me."

He didn't smile back. "Don't tempt me."

She had a sudden picture of herself draped across his knees and his hands on her bare buttocks. The idea shouldn't arouse her, but God save her, it did. When she shivered, she knew Gray noted her response.

The green eyes grew intent. "Does that interest you?"

She hoped that the heat rising in her face didn't show or that if it did, people would blame the close atmosphere in the room. "I don't know."

He bit back a groan and for a second, there wasn't a trace of artifice in his face. "Hell, Stella, there's so much more that I want to do with you. Why are you going back to London so soon?"

A hammer crashed down on her heart, and the happiness she felt in his arms disintegrated to leave ashes behind. "Because I must," she said in a dull voice.

She watched him bite back the urge to argue. It wasn't the time or place. His hand pressed on her waist and when he drew her nearer, she didn't have the heart to protest.

This time, the silence that fell between them didn't vibrate with unspoken promises and illicit attraction. This time, the silence was burdened with a looming separation that neither of them was ready to face.

After a while, she licked dry lips and ventured a comment to break the brooding atmosphere. "This waltz seems to be lasting a long time."

Gray, too, had regained his control, although she could feel his tension. "I told them to play all the repeats, then repeat the repeats."

"I'm glad."

He flashed her a surprised glance. "No complaints about the risks I'm taking?"

"No, no complaints," she said in a reedy voice, as the musicians began what she recognized as the coda to the much-elongated tune. She caught Imogen's eye across the room and plastered what she hoped was a carefree smile to her face.

"Will you join me on the terrace for some air?" Gray asked.

Although the temptation was powerful, she shook her head. "If you pay me any more attention, we'll become items of interest." She paused. "I'm sorry, Gray. I imagine affairs with your opera dancers are easier to manage."

At least that made him smile. "Yes, you're causing me a great deal of effort. You'd better make it up to me later, or I'll have something to say about it."

Her answering smile took more energy than it should. "I promise I will."

"I wish I could take you upstairs now," he said with sudden savagery, even while his expression remained neutral.

She didn't answer as the dance finished and he led her toward Imogen. What was there to say?

CHAPTER FIFTEEN

Stella arranged herself face down on the bed, with her head resting on her folded arms and her rump hoisted in the air. She was naked and felt rather silly. But three nights of blissful debauchery had taught her that if Gray suggested a variation – and it turned out that he knew an impressive number of ways to tup a willing lover – it was worthwhile cooperating.

"Hurry before I drown in embarrassment," she said in a muffled voice.

"I'm just enjoying the view," he said from behind her. She couldn't see him, but she could imagine the smile on his face. She heard it in his voice.

"You're a devil, Gray," she said without force.

He laughed. "I'm *your* devil."

Yes, he was. For this week, at least. Tonight, as he'd taken her to heaven over and over, she'd had to try increasingly hard to ignore the grim fact that after this, only one more night remained to them.

When they'd danced together, it had been difficult enough to remember that one waltz was all they'd ever have. After all these hours of rapture, time was her enemy.

No, she refused to ruin her remaining hours with Gray. She'd have years to weep and rage and yearn, once she got back to London.

The mattress sagged as Gray shifted. She gave a start as his hands caught her hips. Then melting tenderness seeped through her when he kissed the cheeks of her buttocks. Melting tenderness that came to an abrupt end when he bit her.

She cried out and pushed back in protest. "Ouch."

It was just a nip, and the sting tightened her inner muscles in a spasm of longing. Which was mad when he'd been inside her twice already tonight. One turbulent union on the sitting room floor when he couldn't last the few extra steps to the bedroom. A second time here in this bed, when he rocked inside her with such slow care that she felt as if time stopped.

If only time would stop.

No, she wouldn't think about that.

"Spread your legs for me." His gruff command betrayed his growing excitement.

Stella shifted to accommodate him. He kissed the small of her back. Who knew that was such a sensitive spot? But she'd come to realize that when desire was this powerful, everything Gray did was likely to set her off.

His hand traced her cleft until she shuddered in reaction. He caught her hips again and held her still while he pressed forward.

Her body had adjusted to accept his size, although she still thrilled at the snug fit. But this change in position tested her anew.

She released a low moan and edged back to take more. With a grunt of approval, he advanced to the end of his thrust. With a cry, she gripped him hard.

Every time she thought she'd scaled the last peak of pleasure, Gray showed her that whole mountain ranges extended ahead. This position, which had an inevitable touch of a stallion mounting a mare, reached parts of her that she hadn't even known were there.

"Are you all right?" His words emerged in jerky starts.

Her deep breath changed the pressure inside her. "I like this."

His laugh sounded hard-won, and the vibrations heightened her arousal. "I thought you might." He curved over her to fondle her breasts. "You might want to hold onto the baseboard."

She obeyed and angled her bottom higher. This time, the movement made her see stars. Then the stars burst into a conflagration, as he withdrew then plunged again with none of his initial gentleness. Each time his full length rammed inside her, he reached a secret place that sent volcanic sensation flooding through her. Within a miraculously short time, she was shaking and panting.

Gray continued until another, even more astonishing climax overcame her. She felt battered with pleasure. Lightning struck her from every direction. Her breath emerged in broken sobs, as her hands clung to the baseboard.

By the time he pulled free to lose himself in the sheets, every muscle was quivering. Her thighs gave up supporting her, and she collapsed face down on the bed beside him.

"I think I died that time," she said, her voice hoarse. She rolled over and draped a boneless arm over his chest.

"I said you'd like it," he said, sounding as exhausted as she did.

As her heartbeat slowed, Gray straightened the tangle of hair that spread around her. Through all their wild encounters, he'd kept his word and pulled free before his orgasm. Some nitwit part of Stella regretted that. It seemed such a lonely way for him to finish, when the rest of the journey was a union of equals.

But even at the height of her pleasure, she kept a faltering grip on prudence. A baby would be a disaster, even if in the few hours' sleep that she managed to snatch back in her own bed, she dreamed of children with Gray's green eyes and flashing smile.

Each time, she woke with tears on her face and an aching emptiness inside her.

Gray shifted closer and hauled her into his arms. She inhaled his scent, hoping to imprint it on her memory forever.

Stella pressed her back against his chest and rested her head on his upper arm. They lay together in sweet intimacy. Stella might even have dozed for a few seconds. It had been a long night, and she hadn't slept much these last four nights. She didn't want to miss even a minute of their time together.

She stirred to the brush of his lips on her neck and the sound of a blackbird trilling outside. Time hadn't stopped. It was almost morning.

"I hate that bird," she said in a drowsy murmur, shifting her head to give him access to her throat.

"So do I." He rose over her and kissed her lips with a languorous pleasure that acknowledged the joy they'd shared.

When Gray raised his head, Stella's arms curled around his waist. He settled between her legs and her knees rose on either side of him. "Do you want me to go outside and throw a rock at it?"

"No." She stroked his back. "I want you to stay right where you are."

He rubbed against her. Her eyes widened, as she stared into that remarkable face. "You can't possibly."

Self-mockery curved his lips, and his eyes glinted down at her with deepening interest. "I'm as surprised as you are."

He cut off her laugh with another kiss before he slid forward to fill her again. Her fingers ran up and down his back, feeling the rhythmic bunch and release of his muscles. A rhythm that echoed the glide of his body in hers.

This time, his possession was gentle, although she was soon shaking and gasping through an extended climax that dissolved every bone in her body into syrup.

"Let me finish you," she choked out, when his muscles hardened under her palms.

Gray groaned his cooperation and turned onto his back. She straddled his narrow hips and took his penis in her hands. After their nights together, she knew just how to please him.

He was so close that he soon spilled into her fist. She loved the way he gave himself up to her. Still holding him, she dipped to kiss the head of his rod. He made a weary sound deep in his throat and ruffled her hair. She sighed, and for a moment rested her cheek on his hard thigh, before she rose and went through to the dressing room to wash.

When she emerged, she wore the crumpled silk nightdress. She'd managed to launder it in secret.

Although how she'd managed to keep it away from Imogen's curious eyes, she had no idea.

Gray propped himself against the pillows. The sheet covered him to the waist, revealing that sculpted chest with its light dusting of black hair.

He was such a beautiful man. Stella was always aware of how handsome he was. But sometimes, like now, his male attractions stabbed her like a knife.

Her gaze fixed on the raised welt where the bullet had struck him. Every time that she saw the scar, her heart lurched. If his hysterical mistress had been a better shot, Stella would never have had these precious days with him. The idea of all his beauty and vitality consigned to the grave made her nauseous.

His eyes were somber. "You're going?"

Stella curled her hand around the bedpost to stop herself from reaching for him again. "I must."

The blackbird had woken up his avian friends. With every minute, the chirping rose. It was still dark, but the sun would soon rise. Over these last days, Stella felt as if her life only started once darkness fell. Everything in between just filled up the hours until she could be with Gray again.

"Let me come with you."

She shook her head. "You look like you haven't slept in a week."

"I haven't."

She waved toward the ruin of the bed. "Stay and catch a little sleep."

"I don't want to let you go, even for the few minutes it takes you to go back to your room."

Her heart, already so heavy with the weight of joy and sorrow, squeezed tight. Since their first day in the country, he hadn't mentioned setting her up as his mistress. Perhaps he'd lost interest in the idea. But every instinct, everything she knew of this man who had given her such joy, told her that he bided his time before he revisited the subject.

"Let me go, Gray." The request covered more than an announcement of her departure.

His expression told her that he didn't mean to accept anything but complete surrender. Stella turned away, too overwrought right now to start an argument. With unsteady hands, she lit a candle and released the catch to the secret door.

She was in a hurry to get away. She had a horrible feeling that she might cry. Once she started crying, when would she stop?

Fumbling, she shut the door behind her and made her way along the corridor. Was Imogen the only houseguest to hear "rats" in the fabric of the house? Despite everything, Stella muffled a laugh. Imogen had been so horrified at the idea.

By the time she reached the door to her room, Stella had settled down. She had one more night with Gray. She shouldn't bemoan the fact that she'd never lie in his arms again. Rather, she should remember how glorious these last nights had been. The affair might be short, but while it lasted, it gave her indescribable pleasure.

That thought was meant to bolster her determination to go on without Gray. It didn't. Her hands were clumsy as she opened the door and stepped into the darkened room.

There was a rustle from the shadowy bed and a soft voice broke the silence. "Stella?"

CHAPTER SIXTEEN

"*O*h, my dear Lord!" The violent tremble of Stella's hand put her candle out. She sagged back against the wall, as her heart crashed against her ribs. "Imogen, what in blazes are you doing here?"

One hand clutched her throat. Her bare throat. She'd given up wearing her threadbare peignoir, and she was clad only in the revealing nightdress. A nightdress that had cost ten times as much as the rest of her wardrobe combined. Never had she cursed so bitterly Imogen's assumption that she was free to wander in and out of Stella's room without permission.

"I couldn't sleep so I came in to see if you were awake, but you weren't here." Imogen sounded drowsy.

The fire provided enough light to reveal shapes but not much else. Stella heard her cousin fiddle with the tinderbox on the nightstand.

"Please don't light a candle," she said, even as she knew that she fought a losing battle. Once Imogen caught sight of her in this extravagant negligee and with her hair cascading around her shoulders, she'd know that Stella had been up to no good.

Except Imogen was no fool and must have already guessed that if her chaperone wasn't sleeping in her own bed, it was likely that she slept in someone else's.

Not that she and Gray had so far managed to do much sleeping.

Imogen ignored her, and flickering light bloomed. She raised the chamberstick to reveal Stella poised in guilty silence against the paneling. Even in the frail light, Stella saw her cousin's eyes round in amazement.

"Goodness me, Stella, where have you been?" Her gaze sharpened. As Stella had predicted, the active brain inside that pretty head kicked into motion. "And where on earth did you get that nightdress?"

"Imogen..." she began, as she frantically cast around for some innocent explanation for leaving her bedroom in the middle of the night that also covered why she was dressed like an expensive courtesan.

Imogen shifted to the edge of the bed and set her bare feet on the floor. "I didn't hear the door and it squeaks, so I should have. What's been going on? How did you get all the way over there without disturbing me?"

Her shiver had nothing to do with the cold. The passage had been chilly but here in her bedroom, a fire kept the air warm. "You were asleep."

"I was dozing, then I heard a click and I looked up and saw you. You appeared out of nowhere like a ghost."

Stella tried to make light of her cousin's suspicions. "I'm no ghost."

Imogen rose and approached, lifting the candle to reveal Stella in all her tousled, sexually satiated glory. Her eyes narrowed and when she spoke, her voice held a hard edge that told Stella it was too late to rely on self-serving lies. Not that she was coming up with even a shred of a reason for her appearance, other than the shameful truth.

The game was without doubt up.

"No. You're not a ghost. You're a woman returning at dawn from a lover's bed." Stella winced, but couldn't summon a denial. Imogen frowned as she contemplated the various possibilities. "Who is it? I can't see you with Ivor or any of his friends. Or Lord Lumsden, who is famously devoted to his wife. Not to mention that you wouldn't risk hurting Lady Lumsden. I know you like her. Lord Tierney is too old for you. So is Mr. Bilson." Her frown intensified. "That only leaves..."

Stella reached out but let her hand fall to her side before she touched her cousin. "Imogen, don't."

It was too late. Imogen's breath emerged in an explosive huff. She backed away and sank into one of the brocade chairs in front of the fire. With an unsteady hand, she set the chamberstick on a side table. "It's Lord Halston, isn't it?"

Stella swallowed, too upset to speak. She'd been in a state when she tore herself away from Gray. This unexpected confrontation with Imogen so soon afterward left her staggering.

Imogen didn't wait for confirmation. Why would she? Stella feared that the truth was written all over her face. She'd never been a good liar. Anyway Imogen knew her too well.

"I should have realized when I saw you dancing together." Displeasure darkened her expression. "Lord Halston has been pursuing you this whole time, hasn't he? The lilies were for you. And the note."

To her mortification, he hadn't had to pursue her too hard. "Yes," Stella said in a whisper, as her grip tightened on the chamberstick.

While she was in Gray's arms, she felt brave and free. This harrowing scene reminded her that the rest of the world would deride her as a round-heeled slut. Just another of Gray's many conquests. The thought made her feel sick, although she'd always recognized that reality.

"And the house party. He didn't ask us down to Prestwick Place because he's going to offer for me. Papa had it wrong. Halston asked us here, he asked everyone here, because it was the only way he could have you to himself. It's not about me. It was never about me. It was always about you."

Stella swallowed again and forced the words out of her aching throat. "I'm sorry."

A barbed silence fell, while Imogen studied her as if she'd never seen her before. After a while, Stella went on, her voice thick with regret for the pain that she must be causing Imogen. "I know you like him. I hate to think that we've hurt you."

She made her way to the other chair and sank down, her gaze never leaving her cousin's pale face. She lit her chamberstick from Imogen's and placed it on the table, too.

Imogen shook her head, as if Stella had said something inane. "I'm not hurt."

Stella waved that away. "You don't have to pretend."

"I'm not pretending." To her relief, Imogen gave her a small smile. "He's too old for me and too sophisticated and far too experienced."

Despite everything, Stella felt a tinge of amusement when she imagined Gray's reaction to that description, in particular the "too old" bit. "But you were so excited when he invited us to the country."

Imogen shrugged, looking less appalled by the minute, thank goodness. "Anyone would be excited. He's a leader of society. I was flattered when he singled me out. Anyway, I wanted to see the gardens. You know that."

"Oh, Imogen," Stella said, shaking her head. "So you hadn't set your heart on marrying Gray?"

Imogen hesitated before she answered, and Stella realized how the use of Gray's Christian name betrayed her intimacy with him. "No. But it was fun to be the girl who people said had captured the elusive earl's heart, and it stopped Papa pushing me at Lord Chippenham."

"Now, he really *is* too old for you."

Imogen gave a theatrical shudder. "He's too everything for me." Her eyes sharpened again. "So you've been a fallen woman since we came here four days ago? Or did it start in London?"

Little did her cousin know that she'd been a fallen woman for years. Stella's gesture conveyed embarrassment. "I shouldn't talk to you about this."

Imogen looked and sounded more like her old self. "I think you have to."

Stella sighed. "Or what? You'll tell your father?"

Temper flashed in Imogen's eyes. "No, of course I won't tell Papa. You know how he'd react. He'd throw you out to fend for yourself, which means I'd lose a friend and cousin I love. Give me a little credit."

"It might be better if you do tell him." Stella grimaced. "I'm not fit to be your chaperone."

Imogen's snort conveyed her disgust at that statement. "You're still you. You haven't murdered anyone. You've fallen for a rake's wiles. To be honest,

I can see the attraction. If Halston made any serious attempt to capture my interest, I couldn't resist him either."

Surprised, Stella regarded the cousin she'd always treated a little like an amusing child. Imogen's reaction to her fall from grace displayed a maturity that caught her unawares.

Somewhere during this season, Imogen had grown up. No, the change was even more recent than that. Stella couldn't see this girl playing the stupid trick with the note and the threatened elopement that had launched this whole series of events.

Imogen went on. "I suppose it all happened when I went to the wrong gazebo. Halston decided to chase you then. You were always so tight-lipped about what happened when you met him. I thought that was because you were angry with me."

"I was," Stella admitted. "But he said he'd noticed me before that."

"How could he help it? You try so hard to fade into the background, but you're not really a fading-into-the-background kind of woman. No wonder all those men who wanted to court you drove Papa to distraction."

The shock that gripped Stella was strong enough to overtake even her constant interest in Gray. "What men?"

Imogen looked surprised. "You know. Of course you know. There were at least half a dozen gentlemen who applied to Papa for permission to pay their addresses. You remember how Mr. Lamb hung around last year. And there was Mr. Cramer and Sir Anthony Padstow. I forget the others."

Outrage gathered inside Stella. "I had no idea."

"Papa told me that you'd said you had no wish to marry and that you asked him to send them away."

Stella made an impatient sound in her throat. "Does that sound like anything that I'd say to your father? Half the time, he can't summon the courtesy to call me by name, let alone take my instructions about dismissing a suitor."

Not just a suitor. Suitors.

It seemed that she'd had a chance to make a life and a home for herself, and her uncle had schemed to keep her as an unpaid dogsbody instead. Lady Lumsden's umbrage on her behalf came back to her.

Imogen considered Stella's response with a thoughtful frown. "Now you say that, it doesn't."

"Why didn't you tell me?" Stella asked.

"You never mentioned it, so I assumed you didn't want to talk about it."

"I didn't know."

"So I've discovered." She lifted her gaze. "But would you want to marry any of them?"

"I don't know." Stella spread her hands. "It might be preferable to living at Hamble Park as a despised charity case."

Imogen stiffened. "I never treat you like that."

She did, although from carelessness rather than spite. Imogen assumed that Stella existed for her convenience. While the girl was without doubt fond of her, she didn't allow Stella much agency.

But what was the use of saying anything? "You've always been very kind."

Painful knowledge descended, until Imogen looked so dismayed that Stella wanted to hug her. "Oh, no, I do treat you like that. I didn't even think. I'm so sorry. When you came to the house, Papa said you were to serve me and I was too selfish to realize how you must feel."

"You were only a little girl." Stella managed a smile. "You're always much nicer to me than my uncle is."

"That's not saying much, though, is it?" Imogen's distress didn't ease. "I treat you as though you exist for my purposes alone."

"It's not that bad. You don't need to wear sackcloth and ashes."

But Imogen still stewed on her sins. "I should have noticed that you haven't been yourself since we arrived. Since the Lumsden ball, in fact. I should have seen that Halston was no more interested in courting me than he was in sprouting wings and flying to St. Petersburg. I'm sure that's why he came to meet me in the Lumsdens' garden in the first place. He thought he could use me to get to you."

Stella didn't reply. What could she say? Imogen was right.

Imogen was still thinking. "He's gone to an awful lot of fuss over you. Yet you're not his usual style at all."

"Imogen Ridley, how do you know about his usual style? I know everyone says he's a rake, but I hoped that you remained innocent of the finer details."

Imogen's glance was unimpressed. "I know because people in London do nothing but gossip. And Lord Halston is always doing things that make people want to talk about him."

Stella had a queasy feeling that was true. It was just another confirmation that so far, she'd been lucky to escape notice as Halston's newest *inamorata*. Hiding an affair back in London would be impossible.

Imogen's expression grew solemn. "I'd never imagined that you'd fall under his spell, though. You've always been so sensible and self-assured. I suppose you must love him."

The frail net of illusion that had kept Stella's world in one piece disintegrated. Since that heartbreaking conversation on their first night together, she and Gray hadn't mentioned love. They'd certainly never mentioned love in connection with the voracious hunger that drew them together.

But of course she loved him. She'd fallen so fast and so headlong in love with him that now she feared she'd never break free.

After so long trapping the words inside her, it was almost a relief to say them aloud. Her voice was husky as she responded. "Yes, I love him."

"So are you going to stay with him?" Imogen's eyes were searching and full of an understanding that hadn't been there a month ago.

To Stella's surprise, she saw no condemnation. She'd broken every rule of their society, yet Imogen seemed to accept that she'd had no choice. Her cousin had become a stranger.

"No, the affair is over once we go back to Town." Her voice was leaden with sorrow – and determination. So much had changed since she first went to Gray's bed, yet in essentials, nothing had changed. She wasn't made to be a man's doxy.

Imogen made a distressed sound and rose to her feet. "Stella, you can't mean that."

"I have to mean it. He'd like the liaison to go on, but I'm not seeking a career as Lord Halston's mistress. Our association finishes the day after tomorrow."

Imogen fell to her knees in front of her and caught her hands. "But if you love him, how will you survive?"

Stella's fingers curled around her cousin's. Another change. It was more usual for Imogen to draw strength from her. "People don't die of a broken heart."

Imogen's expression didn't ease. "Not physically perhaps. Does he love you?"

"I doubt it. He's not someone who deals in love."

"Oh, Stella..."

Stella frowned, as she struggled not to break down. "Can we...can we talk about something else?"

Compassion filled Imogen's eyes as they rested on her face. Stella was sure that she failed to hide how leaving Gray was going to destroy her.

At least Imogen cooperated with Stella's request about changing the subject. "So tell me how you managed to appear like magic, when you didn't come through the door." She paused. "I can't picture you flitting along the corridors, wearing nothing but that very fetching nightie."

Stella, who despite her best efforts wasn't far off crying, gave a choked gasp of laughter. "Isn't it spectacular? Far and away the nicest piece of clothing I've ever owned. What a pity that nobody but you and Gray will get the chance to admire it."

"You look wonderful in it. That color is just right."

"Perhaps I should wear it to the Tierney ball."

The ball took place late next week and was one of the highlights of the season. Stella bit back a whimper as she realized that she'd spend the night sitting with the duennas and watching Imogen dazzle the company. Worse, she'd watch Gray from a distance with the knowledge that she'd never again lie in his arms.

How could she bear it? Yet she must.

"I'd love that," Imogen said. "The old tabbies would never call you dull again."

Except that dull was the effect she aimed for. Stella must go on doing her best to avoid notice or she'd attract her uncle's criticism. During these last few days, there had been so many joys. One of the greatest was that with Gray, she didn't have to pretend to be anyone but her real self.

She'd spent ten years feeling like a steel cage constricted her chest. At Prestwick Place, she could breathe free at last.

Enduring the restrictions of life in London once more would be insupportable.

"There's a secret passage that leads from this room to Gray's."

Imogen's eyes widened and for a moment, she returned to being the girl Stella thought she knew, a creature of sudden enthusiasms and vivid imagination. "How exciting. Show me."

"You must never tell anyone, promise me."

"I promise." Imogen was already on her feet and examining the paneling. "I can't see anything."

Stella rose and crossed to demonstrate the mechanism. When the door opened, Imogen stared down into the darkness with open-mouthed astonishment.

"So this is why Lord Halston gave you this luxurious room. It was nothing to do with being near me at all."

Stella closed the door, worried that the sound of their voices might travel. "It leads behind the bedrooms on this floor, then a staircase goes up to the earl's apartments."

"It's like a fairy tale."

"I'm no princess," she said with a hint of irritation.

Imogen smiled. "You can be Cinderella instead."

"Don't romanticize this, Imogen. I'm just one more of Lord Halston's women. He'll have forgotten me by next week."

Would he forget her so fast? Before their affair started, she'd expected nothing else. But sometimes looking deep into his eyes as his body claimed hers, she didn't know where she ended and he started. She caught sight of something that told her he, too, felt the bond that drew them together. "In this particular story, I won't be marrying the handsome prince."

Imogen turned and caught her hand. "He is handsome, though, isn't he? I vow the first time we danced together, I couldn't put two words together."

"Never," Stella said with mock amazement. Imogen had always been a chatterbox.

Imogen's gaze grew intent. Once that mightn't have worried Stella too much, but now she feared that her cousin saw the devastation beneath her thin veneer of composure.

"You know, you mightn't be Cinderella," Imogen said thoughtfully. "But I'll wager Mamma's pearls that you're behind the rumor that Prestwick Place has rats."

CHAPTER SEVENTEEN

*I*n the huge ceremonial bed where he'd been born, Halston cuddled a drowsy, naked Stella and gazed down into her face. Despite his current contentment, a twinge of guilt pricked him. All night, he'd used her without mercy. Violet shadows marked the delicate skin beneath her eyes. Her lips were bruised and full after a relentless storm of kisses.

How he'd miss those kisses. He'd never been a man particularly given to kissing, but if he was dying, he'd swear that a kiss from Stella could bring him back to life.

With a choked little murmur, she curled closer. Her arm stretched over his chest and one leg splayed across his. Even in sleep, she tried to get as near to him as she could.

He dropped a kiss on her disheveled head. Her leonine hair snaked around them in glorious disarray. A picture flashed through his mind of his fist making a rope of it, as he thrust into her from behind. The night had been replete with sexual pleasure. Every night with her had proven that the famous libertine hadn't known the meaning of ecstasy before he took this unlikely mistress.

That damned blackbird and its gang of ruffians had been caterwauling for a good hour. Fragile dawn light crept into the chamber, lending a gold tinge to Stella's warm olive skin. He'd never again admire a porcelain-white complexion.

How she'd hate succumbing to sleep. If he'd used her all night, she'd been just as desperate to cram a wealth of sensation into their last hours together.

They'd avoided mentioning that if the original arrangement held, this was indeed their final night. Since she'd appeared out of the passage – she hadn't waited for him to fetch her – they hadn't talked much at all. Although every touch, every kiss, every fuck had conveyed a universe of meaning.

With Stella, everything carried meaning. If she really intended to finish with him today, how could he retreat to his former shallow existence?

The world was a different place when he held Stella in his arms. Halston was far from ready to end a liaison that provided such unprecedented joy.

But what did Stella want? They hadn't discussed the future. Since she'd rejected his offer to become his mistress, he'd done his best to ensnare her in such pleasure that she couldn't face walking away.

Had he succeeded? The devil alone knew. That rakish sophisticate, the Earl of Halston, didn't have a clue how she'd respond when he offered her *carte blanche* once again.

Oh, she liked him all right. She wanted him. And by God, her situation with that skinflint bastard Lord Deerforth made Halston want to smash his fist into the pompous boor's self-satisfied face. An interval of luxury as Halston's *petite amie,* with a

secure income for the rest of her life, should appeal
to her if she had any sense. If he'd offered the same
arrangement to any of his previous mistresses,
they'd have leaped at the chance like the hungry
trout in his three famous lakes leaped to a well-tied
fly.

But Stella wasn't like his previous mistresses.
He'd come to realize that she wasn't like anyone else
at all.

Which was why he must convince her that
abandoning him was a pudding-headed decision,
unworthy of the intelligent woman he knew her to
be.

God help him.

A faint frown drew her tawny brows together,
and her grip on him tightened. She twisted her head
a few inches and placed a kiss over his heart. The
heart that beat with endless longing for her.

Her sleep had been troubled. Their parting
preyed on her mind, he guessed.

On a raspy sigh, she raised heavy eyelids over
misty golden eyes. The joy in her expression when
she saw him made him feel like a king.

Then dismay clouded her gaze. "The sun's come
up, Gray. I have to go. I'm surprised the maid hasn't
arrived to fix the fire."

"I told the staff that everyone wanted to sleep in
this morning. The maids will do the fires while my
guests have breakfast."

Stella sagged against him and touched his
cheek with a brief tenderness that reverberated
through him like a struck gong. "You're still thinking
of my reputation. Thank you."

He rose against the pillows and drew her up
with him. "I'm not thinking of your reputation, my
girl. I'm thinking that this way I get another couple
of hours with you."

"Silly me." Wry humor gleamed in her eyes. She rested her head on his shoulder and spoke with fond irony. "I mistook what a selfish libertine you are."

That made him kiss her, despite the sad truth that before he met Stella, selfish libertine had been an accurate description of the heartless Earl of Halston.

Her hand trailed down his body to his dick. He muffled a protest against her lips and caught her. Stopping her from touching him made every masculine impulse shriek.

She stiffened and drew away, her expression wary. "It's our last chance, Gray."

The plea in her eyes almost overturned his purpose. But he fought back his impulse to sin and stuck to his plan.

Halston studied the face that haunted his dreams and prayed with a fervor he hadn't mustered since he was a lonely child that he could convince Stella to take a chance on him. "It doesn't have to be."

Something that looked like terror flared in her eyes, turned them glassy. "Yes, it does," she said in a shaky voice.

Stella pushed away and scrambled out of the bed. When she glanced around the room, he realized that she was looking for the gold nightdress.

When she couldn't find it, she scooped his heavy velvet robe from the floor and put that on. It was so big, it swamped her, but any urge he felt to smile died when she drew herself up to her full height and glared at him.

She'd never looked more like a queen. Or more certain of her own mind. This wasn't a woman about to fling herself into her lover's arms and offer herself up to months of illicit bliss.

It seemed that the Almighty had ignored the sinner's prayer. Halston couldn't blame Him. He'd been a stranger to the Lord for too long to expect any special favors now.

With or without divine help, Halston wasn't giving up. He straightened against the headboard and met her glower with an uncompromising stare of his own. "Do you want to leave me?"

Bewilderment descended on her. He supposed that she'd expected to counter the practical arguments he'd already made for why she should become his mistress.

"That's not fair."

"Why?"

Her slender throat moved as she swallowed. One hand crept up to clutch the rich red fabric to her collarbone, always a sign of distress. Halston felt the sting of compunction, because he was the person upsetting her. But it wasn't enough to make him retreat.

This was too important.

He had to make her see that they were meant to stay together. He'd never had a lover to rival her. He never would. The prospect of sending her back to her stultifying existence as Imogen Ridley's dogsbody made him feel physically ill.

"You know I don't want to leave you."

"Well—"

She rushed on, in case he took that as a sign of weakening. "But what I want doesn't matter. It hasn't mattered since I came to England. It didn't matter much before that, if truth be told."

Temper had him rolling out of the bed and standing over her. "It's the only thing that should bloody matter. You have one life, Stella. Do you want to sacrifice it to people who don't give a rat's arse about you?"

She lifted her chin and flashed him a look that threatened to burn him to ash. "I don't live for my own pleasure with no care for who I hurt along the way. I'm not the noble Earl of Halston."

The words struck deep, drew blood. He'd reached for her, but now he pulled back. "You sound as if you despise me."

Her exquisite face seemed made of ice, even as she shook her head. "I could never despise you, Gray. But you're free in a way that few other people are."

His sigh verged toward a groan. He turned away, battling a premonition of impending defeat. He'd always admired her strength, but right now, he had a queasy feeling that her strength would help her prevail.

And they'd both pay the price.

"You could be free, too."

She shook her head. "No, I'd be the woman you pay to sleep with you. You know what that turns me into."

"The woman I desire above all others."

Her smile was the saddest thing that he'd ever seen. "A woman who is just like all the others."

"You wouldn't be." With an urgent gesture, he reached out to clasp her arm. She was trembling and not far from tears. "You aren't."

"I'm not like all the others because I said no." Her voice was tired in a way he'd never heard it. "Let's not part on an argument, Gray. These past five days have been so wonderful. The best of my entire life. Don't spoil them with a fight."

His heart flipped over as he surveyed her, taking in her bravery and her resolve and, yes, her misery. Because she didn't want this to be the end any more than he did. That made granting her heartfelt request even more difficult.

"I feel as if we've hardly begun."

Stella must have heard the reluctant concession in his voice, because he felt her tension ease. When she responded, she sounded a fraction less desolate. "Perhaps it's best for us to finish before I develop the urge to shoot you."

Her small attempt at a joke prompted a perfunctory smile. Their separation tore him to pieces. He didn't feel much like laughing. "If you say you'll stay, I'll damn well let you shoot me. I'll even load the bloody pistol."

Her pretense at control dissolved like sugar dropped into boiling water. "Oh, Gray..." she said on a broken sob and threw herself at him. Their lips met, and his arms closed hard around her shaking body.

A few rough tugs and the extravagant dressing gown crumpled to the floor. When he lifted Stella, she gave a choked cry but didn't stop kissing him. Frantic hands caught at him, then she cried out again when he dropped her onto the bed. Her long legs sprawled in coltish abandon across the disordered sheets.

When he came down over her, she grabbed him with greedy fervor, parting her thighs and clawing at his buttocks to draw him nearer.

"I'm crushing you," he managed to say somewhere during the whirlwind of kissing.

"I don't care," she growled and bumped her hips up in silent invitation.

During the last five days, he and Stella had been daring and experimental lovers, seeking delight in a hundred different ways. But as Halston slid forward and claimed her for this, the last time, it seemed right that he rose above her and met her dark caramel eyes. With every thrust, those eyes grew darker, then fluttered shut as she plummeted over into her climax.

He didn't move as she writhed and moaned around him. For a brief interval, pleasure had banished everything from his mind except how perfect they were together. Now as he ground his teeth and tensed every muscle against losing control, it was agony to know that he and Stella would never do this again.

It was bad enough to acknowledge that now. It would be worse when she was no longer here and he had to face up to the true devastation of losing her.

Halston meant to stay just where he was for as long as he could.

Eventually she calmed, staring at him through eyes that sparkled with tears. She'd cried on their first night. Then her tears had left him devastated. Tonight after these resplendent days, the thought of her crying made him feel like someone razored off his skin piece by piece.

"You've made me so happy." Her voice vibrated with emotion. "Thank you, Gray. Thank you for these days. I'll treasure the memory as long as I live."

He wanted to protest, to argue that if they were together, she wouldn't have to remember. But he couldn't find the heart when he recalled her stricken reaction after he'd asked her again to become his mistress.

"You've made me happy, too," he murmured and kissed her.

It wasn't a kiss of passion. It was a kiss of farewell. And he tasted goodbye on her lips.

Feeling as if he died in slow increments, he withdrew and lost himself upon the sheets.

CHAPTER EIGHTEEN

Within its first hour, the Tierney ball was pronounced a raging success. The orchestra that Lady Tierney had imported from Paris outplayed any band from London. The decorations were spectacular. The catering was lavish. So many people had accepted invitations that everyone complained about the party being a dreadful crush, the height of praise for a ton gathering.

Even the weather blessed Lady Tierney. For the beginning of May, it was warm and fine and in contrast to the Lumsden ball a couple of weeks ago, the well-lit terrace and garden proved popular with guests seeking a breath of air after the stifling heat inside.

Stella sat with the chaperones and leveled blind eyes on the whirling crowd of dancers. Around her, the endless tide of gossip that buoyed the ladies through event after event rose and fell. She paid it no heed.

All she knew was the ache in her heart. The pain had been with her ever since she left Gray's bed. A pain that all too often rose to a howl of anguish.

It had been so difficult to leave him, even though she knew that what he offered would end up destroying her. But each day since, her misery had worsened. She hadn't realized how missing him would turn every minute to dust. She hadn't realized how the compulsion to see him would cut at her like a knife. Nor how on the two occasions that she did see him, the sight would stab even deeper than his absence.

It was too cruel having him within touching distance, yet utterly, eternally out of reach.

He hadn't attended many events this week. Gossip had him staying at Prestwick Place for a few days after his guests left. When Stella had caught sight of him at the Bourton musicale three days ago, her reaction hadn't just been a massive wave of futile longing. She'd been appalled at how ill he looked.

While she'd never doubted that he'd prefer to continue their affair, she'd assumed that someone so used to women moving in and out of his life would recover from his disappointment in the blink of an eye. Seeing Gray haggard and desperately unhappy was a horrid shock.

Perhaps under other circumstances, she might be flattered to know that she'd made such an impression on him. But she couldn't summon any triumph. Instead she felt an excruciating sadness that he was no happier than she was. Nor was there any prospect of relief ahead for either of them. Because she loved him with such depth and devotion, his suffering only increased the burden of hers.

Gray was here tonight. He'd danced with Imogen and with Lily and with Lady Tierney. At the moment, she couldn't see him. She supposed that he and some willing lady strolled in the garden. Or he'd finished strolling and had retired to a private glade, designed for kissing. For more than kissing.

Her jealousy undermined her noble wish for his contentment. If some hussy dared to set her claws into Gray, Stella wanted to scratch the trollop's eyes out. He belonged to her.

Which was absurd, when they were apart and destined to stay that way. He might languish without her now, but she was realistic enough to understand that he'd soon find another mistress to divert him.

Lucky little bitch.

"Miss Faulkner?"

Her fantasies of eviscerating the next occupant of Gray's bed – and every occupant after that, for good measure – came to a sudden end. A footman hovered beside the uncomfortable gilt chair that was *de rigueur* for chaperones at London balls.

"Yes?"

"You're required in the small salon as a matter of urgency."

The words were worrying enough to pierce her brooding. She surged to her feet on a burst of concern. Her eyes sought out Imogen, but she couldn't see her.

"Where is that?" She'd visited this house when Imogen called on Elizabeth, but she didn't know her way beyond the drawing room.

"I'll take you there, miss," the man said.

Stella collected her reticule from where she'd placed it on the floor. Making her excuses, she threaded her way through the other chaperones and along the edge of the crowd. If Imogen had taken ill, a quick trip home and an early night might solve the problem.

The small salon was at the end of a long corridor, hung with inept watercolors that she suspected the ladies of the family had painted. The footman pushed open the door and stepped back with a bow.

As the door closed behind her, Stella rushed inside. "Imogen, are you all right?"

The room appeared to be empty. Puzzled, she turned around. When she saw the tall man resting his back against the door, her poor suffering heart contracted in painful longing.

"Gray..."

He didn't straighten, although he bent his dark head in a brief bow. "Good evening, Stella."

As confusion ebbed, anger replaced it. She'd said all she intended to say to him. That had been hard enough. Having to endure more arguments now, when the outcome could never change, verged on torture. He must know that.

Her reticule dropped from nerveless fingers. "What game are you playing?"

He didn't seem to hear. His eyes ranged over her with an urgency that made her blood pump with a force she hadn't felt since she'd left him. "By God, you look awful."

With a self-conscious gesture, she touched her hair. Thanks to Nancy, it was arranged in the curls that she'd sported at Prestwick Place, and she wore one of her own gowns. She couldn't bear a complete return to the prim creature that she'd been before the house party. That would be too much confirmation that her life promised to be an arid desert.

"Thank you very much," she snapped. "So do you."

By heaven, he did. At a distance, she'd noticed his tired and dispirited air. Now, from only a few feet away, she saw dark hollows around his lightless eyes and deep lines scored between his nose and mouth.

He looked at least ten years older than the lover who had given her such joy a mere week ago.

He shrugged, as if his appearance didn't matter. "Oh, you're still beautiful. You'll always be beautiful."

Stella doubted it. As bitterness and frustration took their toll, she'd turn into a vinegar-faced crone. But that wasn't the important issue right now.

She adopted a chilly tone. "Do you have something to say that I need to hear, or are you just playing with me, the way a cat plays with a mouse?"

A frown darkening his features, he straightened. "Do I look like I'm getting any enjoyment out of this?"

She fought against the urge to take him in her arms. "No."

"You've made me a complete wreck. I can't eat. I can't sleep. I can't think of anything but you." He shook his head, as if he couldn't believe what was happening to him. "When I see you now, I wonder if it's the same for you."

It was. She'd noticed tonight how loose this dress hung on her. If she didn't pull herself together, she'd soon be nothing but skin and bones.

But none of that mattered.

"Gray, we can't be seen together, or all the trouble we've taken will be for nothing. Let me go back to the ballroom."

He didn't shift away from the door. "I don't give a damn for scandal anymore."

"Well, I do."

Again he didn't seem to hear her. "I had to do something. I felt like I couldn't take another breath without seeing you."

"You've seen me several times this week. The Bourton musicale. Lady Freeman's ball."

"That's almost worse than not seeing you at all." He grimaced. "I feel like a dog chained to a post while someone parades a plate of sirloin a foot in front of him."

Plague take the rogue, she couldn't doubt that he meant it.

"Hardly complimentary," she said, although to her regret, she knew just what he meant.

"I don't set out to compliment you."

Her anger seeped away. Which was a pity, because it left crippling misery behind. "I'm sorry."

A savage light flared in his eyes. "Is that the best you can do?"

"Yes," she said on a breath of sound and retreated until she bumped into a chair behind her. One trembling hand fumbled back to grab the chair's carved back. She needed to hold onto something to stay upright.

Gray looked so hurt. She hated that. She hated even more that she was the cause. Avoiding notice had once seemed the most complicated element of this affair. How naïve she'd been.

"Don't you want to see me?"

She swallowed to ease a painfully tight throat. "Not if it just opens old wounds."

"My wounds haven't started to heal yet."

"If you keep doing things like this, they never will."

"Is that all you can give me?" He spread his hands. "After everything we were to each other?"

"What do you want?" Although she knew.

"Since you left me, I've been living in purgatory." That betraying muscle twitched in his cheek. This was a man at the limit of his resources. "I'm not in the habit of begging, but I'm here to beg you to come back, Stella."

Heaven help her, that was what she wanted, too. "Nothing has changed."

"Except now we both know what torture it is to be apart. Don't pretend you're not in hell as well. I won't believe you. You're a shadow of the woman who left me a week ago."

What could she say? He was right. "You have to let me go. This will destroy both of us."

"Not being together will destroy us," he said. "How can you bear it?"

She released the chair, and her hands formed fists at her sides. "Because I have to."

"No, you don't. You can come to me. We can have what we had at Prestwick Place. It will be even better, because we won't have to sneak around and the affair doesn't have to end until we're ready. Don't you want that?"

"Of course I want that," she admitted, her voice breaking with the tears that she fought not to shed. When she went back to the ballroom, it would be hard enough to hide her turmoil, without adding red eyes to the mix.

"Then stay."

"I can't."

"No scandal could be worse than this."

"That's easy for you to say. I'll bear the brunt of any gossip. You'll just go on your merry way."

He glared at her. "Do I look particularly merry to you? Your good name hasn't done you too many favors. Wouldn't you rather be happy and notorious with me than respectable and lonely?"

Oh, dear God, he tempted her. But her self-respect wouldn't let her become his doxy instead of his equal. That self-respect awoke a scrap of defiance. "I won't talk to you about this, when you block the door and stop me leaving. Is this how it would be, once I'm in your power? You'll bully me into getting your own way, every time my will clashes with yours? Pardon me if I don't leap at the chance to surrender my independence."

He paled at her accusation. Which she knew wasn't entirely fair. If she insisted on leaving with anything that sounded like firmness, he'd let her go.

"Your independence? When you grovel to that toad Deerforth for every morsel you eat? When you're at Imogen's beck and call? When you're so afraid of attracting notice that you can't say one word to a man you fancy? A fine freedom you rejoice in, madam."

Stella flinched under his attack, knowing much of what he said was just. She scrabbled to retrieve her anger, but it had vanished as if it had never been.

"Yes, that's all true." Her voice emerged laden with despair. "But none of that touches my soul. Being your whore would. It would tarnish everything between us. It would tarnish me."

She hurt him all over again. She could see that. The lines on his face etched even deeper. With a theatrical flourish, he stepped away from the door. "So go, then."

She should. Oh, how she should. But her feet remained glued to the floor.

Something told her that this was their last chance to be alone together. Despite the conflict and sorrow, she felt alive for the first time since she'd left him. How could she rush away from that, whatever the risk of discovery?

"Stella, have you changed your mind?" he asked, after the thorny silence stretched out to breaking point.

"I can't." She blinked back tears, although it turned into a losing battle. "Our arrangement was a few days at Prestwick Place, then we go our separate ways."

"Fuck the arrangement," he bit out. "I want more. I need more."

So did she, God help her. But she couldn't relent. She was wise enough to know that an extra day, an extra week, an extra year only promised an even more agonizing goodbye. And with every day, the chance of discovery grew.

"Gray, this has to be the end." At last the tears began to fall. "Damn you, you've made me cry."

He looked stricken. And heartbreakingly remorseful. "Oh, my darling..."

He strode across the room. Given his earlier behavior, she expected him to grab her, but his touch was gentle as he folded her into his arms.

That proved disastrous for her control. "How dare you make me cry?" she wailed, her fist hitting his chest. "Everything's been so vile without you, then you pull this trick and make it all worse."

"I know. I'm a beast and a brute."

"You are." She snaked her arms around his waist, fitting herself without thought into his body, as she'd done so often before. "How can I go back into that ballroom, looking like I've been bawling my eyes out?"

Gray's embrace tightened. She should feel confined, compelled. Instead she just felt warm and safe. Which was mad, when alone with him in this room, safe was the last thing she was.

"It's all right. I won't torment you anymore." He cupped the back of her head and pressed her face into his black superfine coat. His rich, spicy scent filled her senses and reminded her of the hundreds of previous times when she'd rested in his hold. How it broke her heart to think that the last time he touched her, it was to comfort not to seduce her.

After a long silence, he bundled her up in his arms and drew her onto a chaise longue in front of the unlit fire. Stella was too upset, too worn out, and too bereft to protest.

"I'll arrange for a footman to call your carriage," he said.

She regarded him through bleary eyes. "To take me back to Lorimer Square?"

"Or we can forget your carriage, and you can come home with me."

His voice was grave, and his eyes were steady. Stella saw such longing there that her heart crashed against her ribs. For one charged instant, she wondered if she could run off with Gray.

Was reputation more important than love? While becoming his temporary mistress meant that he'd send her away when he lost interest, would that be worse than these last few days without him?

If she said yes, she'd have more of Gray. More pleasure. More tenderness. More laughter.

Then she remembered Imogen. And she also recalled the careless way that Gray referred to his mistresses, like toys brought out for his amusement and discarded once a new toy came along. She felt sick to think that he might ever view her in the same light.

She had to remember that he wasn't a good man. He'd never pretended to be.

Although he'd been good to her.

As Lady Lumsden had said, he harbored the capacity to become a better man. But Stella was wise enough to know that only some major crisis would make him abandon a life of delightful self-indulgence. He'd have to change, and given how entertaining his existence was, why should he?

Right now, he grizzled and griped because the toy that he wanted was out of reach. But that didn't make her a toy in her own mind.

Because she loved him, the best thing she could do for either of them was let him go.

Stella pulled his head down until his lips met hers, knowing that she'd never kiss him again. She didn't rush the kiss, but infused it with every ounce of hopeless love she felt for this complicated, wonderful man.

When he raised his head, his expression was somber as she'd never seen it. "You mean to leave me."

"I'm sorry, Gray."

"I can't bear it."

She tried to smile, but she had a horrible feeling that she made a mess of it. "You'll forget me."

"Never."

Dear God, he sounded so convinced. How she wished that she could believe him. "Please find that footman and arrange my carriage. Although I hate to interrupt Imogen's night."

Gray must have accepted that the time when entreaties or arguments might win the day had passed. If such a time had ever existed.

"She can go home with the Lumsdens. They only live across the square."

Stella nodded, still clinging to him. It was past time to go, but she couldn't summon the will to leave. She was lucky that her uncle wasn't at the ball. He was attending some political dinner in Belgravia. He'd kick up a stink about Stella using the carriage for her own convenience. "Will you arrange to get a message to her?"

"Yes. I'll say you've taken ill. And I'll send a footman to escort you out the back way so you don't have to face that crowd."

That crowd with their nasty, prying eyes and clacking tongues.

"Thank you." She made herself stand. Forsaking his embrace felt like cutting off her hand with a blunt ax.

She blinked away more tears. She'd cried enough tonight, and not one single tear changed the stark reality. Her affair with Grayson Maddox was over.

He didn't rise when she did, but watched her with a hunger that made her ache. "You really mean to do this thing?"

She tried another smile, although she feared it was as ghastly as her last attempt. "I must."

"So I'm to have no more of you?"

She'd been wrong to think that he'd given up the fight. Couldn't he see that every word drove the knife further into her tattered heart?

Stella swallowed and told herself not to cry. "Only...only my very best wishes for your happiness, Gray. You'll always have those."

Those marked black eyebrows lowered with displeasure. "Even though what you're doing destroys any chance of happiness?"

Her gesture waved his question away. "Don't exaggerate."

"I'm not."

Studying him, she almost believed him. But she couldn't. Right now, he was suffering. No question. But he'd get over her, the next time a pretty face caught his eye.

When her heart would break all over again, to Hades with him.

Her shaking hands twined in her skirts. "Gray, if you have an ounce of respect or care for me, please go now."

He rose, his jaw set like granite, and gave her a brief bow. "I'll go, but you're making a mistake, Stella."

He sounded so certain. How could he sound so certain?

Stella picked up her reticule and turned away to stare into the fireplace. She couldn't look at him. Despite everything, she still feared that she might weaken.

"Goodbye, Gray," she whispered, and waited to hear the door close behind him.

Halston stood in the shadows by the Tierneys' garden gate and watched Lord Deerforth's carriage trundle away into the night. He'd never felt so wretched in all his life. Even in his desolate childhood, he couldn't remember feeling quite this low.

The irony of it all was that as an adult, he'd done his best to see that life caused him no inconvenience at all. His days were an endless round of pleasure.

His affair with Stella Faulkner was supposed to supply more of that same pleasure. The urgency of his desire had surprised him, but in all essentials, his latest dalliance would only be a more satisfying version of what he'd enjoyed so many times before.

Right from their very first meeting, since that wary, prickly, intriguing encounter in the Lumsdens' gazebo, things hadn't gone to plan. By God, if he'd shown an ounce of sense, he'd have taken to his heels then and there. And forgotten troublesome Miss Faulkner in the arms of another opera dancer or bored widow.

But Halston hadn't shown an ounce of sense. He'd already been too enmeshed in an attraction unlike any other. Every day since had only forged another link in the chain shackling him to this woman.

The awful truth was he was so lost in yearning that he didn't want to break free. He, whose name was synonymous with love them and leave them.

Halston didn't much like having the tables turned on him. After that scene tonight, he knew that despite her unhappiness, Stella had no intention of returning.

With most of the women he knew, their will was at the service of their appetites. Stella, he discovered, was made of sterner stuff. When she agreed to give him five days of her company, she'd meant precisely that. None of his blandishments – damn it, none of his anguish – would change her mind.

If he wasn't so blasted hurt, he might even admire her strength.

The sad truth was that he did admire her strength. He always had. Life had done its best to crush her, but she'd kept her integrity. Even more, she'd kept her heart. Stella Faulkner had no petty emotions. No jealousy. No self-pity. No bitterness.

She was the most remarkable person he knew. Not to mention the most passionate lover. He'd once imagined that he'd show her the meaning of pleasure. What a blind, arrogant ass he'd been.

She'd revealed a new world that beggared his previous experience. He'd fallen completely under her spell, before he'd realized that she lured him from the shallows where he was content to splash around and out into deep, dangerous water.

Now, devil take her, he was drowning, and she wouldn't even stretch out a hand to rescue him.

He shivered. It was cold here. He told himself that he should go back into the ballroom and look around for his next mistress. After all, the best cure for an unhappy love affair was sure to be another love affair.

Except that he was never unhappy at the end of a love affair. He was always the one looking to the future. That was why Francene had shot him. Not because he'd broken her heart. He doubted that she had a heart to break. But she had a surplus of pride, and Halston hadn't been careful enough to hide his boredom when pretending to regret the liaison's end.

Now he looked back and realized that he'd deserved that bullet. Hell, most of the women he knew should have shot him. He hadn't treated any of them with a shred of respect, however much jewelry he bought them.

The unacceptable truth was that when Stella told him it was over, it hurt much worse than a mere bullet. In his bleaker moments, he feared that she'd inflicted a mortal wound on a man who until now had believed himself unassailable.

Now he skulked around in the dark, feeling like a mongrel cur kicked into the gutter. This without question counted as one of those bleaker moments.

Of course, he could continue to pursue Stella, but he couldn't see her ever consenting to become his mistress, however much she might miss him. At least that was some small consolation from tonight. He now knew that she missed him almost as much as he missed her. Not that it did him a scrap of good.

Stella, like Francene, was overburdened with pride. That was the only thing the two women had in common.

Something in Halston recoiled from bringing Stella further distress. He loathed seeing her so torn. The damnable reality was that he'd rather cut off his own arm than cause her an ounce of grief.

So it was time to accept grim reality. He must let her go and revive the man that he'd once been. That should be possible. He'd been perfectly content before Stella came to his bed. He'd be perfectly content again.

In about a hundred years.

Maybe.

He blamed emotion for this disaster. How right he'd been to disdain all sentiment in his sexual arrangements. His emotions had focused on Stella from her first smart-mouthed response to his stale enticements.

Except nothing with Stella had felt stale. While he might claim that he'd been fine before she ruined his life, some tiny voice of honesty reminded him that he hadn't been. Not really. For months, he'd been bored and restless and out of sorts with himself. He only recognized that, now that he'd caught a glimpse of something more substantial.

Caught a glimpse, and now turned his back on it.

How it smarted that he had no right to escort Stella to her carriage when she was upset and unsteady on her feet. A footman had had that privilege, while Halston had to pretend that he had no special interest in the lady's welfare.

Whereas the lady's welfare was his dearest, his only concern.

It was deuced lucky that he was such a shallow man. The prospect of feeling like this for much longer was unendurable.

He'd forget Stella Faulkner, the way that he'd forgotten her predecessors. He just wished right now that the thought provided a shred of comfort. He'd get over feeling like it was wrong that he couldn't offer Stella support or comfort. He'd get over feeling like it was wrong that she went home without him.

Halston sighed from the depths of his black heart. In the house behind him, the ball continued. Lilting dance music had supplied a jarring accompaniment to his dark meditations out here in the cold.

He should go back inside and thaw out and ask some beauty to dance. If things went well, perhaps that beauty might favor him with more than a dance.

One last longing glance along the alley where Stella's carriage had bowled out of sight. Then he went to summon his own coach to go home.

Alone.

CHAPTER NINETEEN

A week later, Stella remained raw after that grueling encounter with Gray. She'd feared Imogen might make a fuss about her early departure from the Tierney ball, but the girl had been uncharacteristically reticent. And much less demanding than usual. She'd even taken to knocking and waiting for permission before she came into Stella's room.

Given that since she'd made a final break with her devilish lover, the mere act of breathing hurt, Stella was grateful. The signs of maturity she'd noticed in her cousin when they visited Prestwick Place were still in evidence.

Today, they were in the drawing room, spending a rare afternoon at home. There was another ball tonight. Stella's appetite for the season's entertainments, never robust, had waned even further since her return to London. Warmer weather meant late nights in a close, noisy atmosphere until she felt like screaming. Today, like most days, she battled a headache.

And weeks of hectic social activity extended ahead.

At least she was spared one ordeal. Since that fraught scene in the Tierneys' small salon, she hadn't seen Gray. She waited in agony to learn that he'd set up with a new mistress. But for once, the notorious Lord Halston did nothing to stir up talk. He remained in London, she gathered, but beyond that, she heard no news of him.

Speculation was rife on whether Halston's house party heralded a proposal to one of the young ladies he'd invited. But as he was yet to make his choice, if any, known, and his disappearance from ton festivities deprived the curious of further information, nobody had anything fresh to report.

The problem was that Gray's absence didn't stop Stella thinking of him and missing him. And crying herself to sleep in the early hours, when at last she could shut the door on the world and stop pretending that nothing important had happened at Lord Halston's beautiful country house.

Imogen lowered the lid on the pianoforte that she'd been tinkering on without any great enthusiasm. She drifted across to join Stella who sat on the chaise longue with Lord Byron's latest poem open in front of her. In reality, the words massed together into unreadability.

Stella had spent most of the last hour staring into space, wondering whether she should have cut off the chance of continuing her affair with Gray. She reached a point where she didn't much care about her good name or the future. In return for one more kiss from the man she loved, she'd give up every claim to virtue.

"Good book?" Imogen asked.

Stella shrugged. Byron's unhappy hero couldn't hold her attention when she was so busy yearning after her own wicked lover. "I don't know."

Imogen's blue eyes softened with compassion. "You miss Lord Halston."

Stella turned away on the pretext of putting the book on the table. "Let's not talk about it." The last thing she needed was for her uncle to come in and find her bawling.

"I'm sorry you're so sad," Imogen said.

Stella gave her eyes a surreptitious wipe and faced her cousin with what she hoped was a brighter demeanor. "I'll get over it."

Imogen's expression hinted that this attempt to make light of her misery failed. "Will you?"

She very much feared that she wouldn't get over it. But surely time would blunt the worst of her unhappiness. It was but a week since she'd seen Gray, a week before that that she'd shared her body with him for the last time. Give her a decade or two, and with a bit of luck, she'd be back to her old self.

Her gesture was apologetic. "I'm not much fun at the moment."

Imogen didn't smile. "You don't have to be fun all the time." She paused. "I've got something to talk to you about, but we've been so busy that I haven't had the chance."

Stella tried to summon some interest in what Imogen might say. Sorrow, she learned, was a supremely selfish emotion. Right now, it was a struggle to care about anything except her futile longing. Perhaps her cousin meant to confess her penchant for some young man.

"We're alone today. For the rest of the week, you're back to being the toast of the season."

Imogen didn't smile at that either. "I was talking to Eliot about you."

Horror flooded Stella. With a strangled cry, she lurched to her feet. "I can't believe you broke my confidence. I don't want anyone to know about Gray.

This is too bad, Imogen. I thought better of you. I really did."

"Don't be a henwit, Stella." Imogen glanced at the closed door and lowered her voice. "As if I'd say anything about that."

Stella sucked in a deep breath and tamped down her panic. The idea that she might suffer all this lonely anguish and still end up sparking a scandal was too much to endure. "I'm sorry. I'm on edge at the moment. Of course you didn't tell Eliot."

"Of course I didn't. So sit down and let me finish, before you fly up into the boughs again. You *are* on edge."

"At least your papa hasn't noticed." Feeling sheepish, Stella sank down beside Imogen. "I don't think I could take one of his scolds right now."

Imogen took Stella's hand. "You must hate being beholden to him."

"Your father has always been very good to me," Stella said, cringing at how insincere she sounded.

"No, he hasn't. He treats you like a servant, not like a niece. I've been thinking about your situation ever since the Lumsden ball."

"Have you?" Stella was surprised. She'd known Imogen was preoccupied with something. She hadn't imagined that it might be with her companion's circumstances.

"Yes. I should have thought long before this. But at Hamble Park, you didn't seem quite so oppressed. Or perhaps you were and I never noticed. Coming to London has made everything much clearer."

Stella pressed her cousin's hand. "You're just getting older and wiser."

Imogen released a puff of self-derisive laughter. "Not before time."

"I told you I don't mind serving you."

"But you shouldn't have to."

"I have no choice."

"That's what I talked to Eliot about. And he agrees with me, or at least he does, now that I've told him how Papa takes advantage of you."

Stella bit back a sigh. "Are you about to offer me a home again?"

"That offer still stands. But you'd still be taking charity from a relative. And living at someone else's behest."

"Are you going to marry me off to some worthy gentleman?" Stella tried to lighten the discussion, but still Imogen didn't smile.

"I would, if you weren't head over heels in love with Lord Halston. You deserve a chance at a husband and children and a home of your own. If I hadn't been so selfish, I'd have seen that long ago."

"Don't be too hard on yourself." Once perhaps Stella might have settled for a steady marriage that offered some small independence. Her uncle's dismissal of those previous suitors still rankled. But how could she wed some respectable lawyer or merchant or military man when her heart lay forever elsewhere?

Imogen studied her face. Stella had the odd feeling that the girl saw more than she ever had before. "Grandpapa set aside a large dowry for your mother. She was quite an heiress."

Stella's lips turned down in wry acknowledgement. "Until she ran away with an artist and found herself disinherited."

At last, Imogen smiled. "Well, Eliot and I are going to un-disinherit you. It turns out he'd already decided to settle some money on you if you married. Because I've explained your situation, he's going to give it to you now."

Stella's stomach lurched. An independent income? A chance to break free and decide her own future? Was it possible? "It's more charity."

Imogen's delicate jaw set with the stubbornness that Stella knew so well. "We knew you'd say that, but it's not charity. It's a restitution of your rights."

"Your father won't like it."

"No, he won't. But even if he cuts off Eliot's allowance, Eliot inherited a fortune from his godmother. He could set you up a hundred times without noting the lack."

It was true. Without factoring in the riches that came with the Deerforth title, Eliot was plump in the pocket.

"That's...that's very kind of him."

"Once I'm twenty-five and I come into my portion of Godmamma's money, I'll pay my share, too."

Her cousins' generosity staggered her. Stella blinked as she strove to imagine an existence where she chose where she went and what she did. Perhaps she could buy a cottage in the country. Or at the seaside. Perhaps she could go back to Italy. Or visit France. Ever since coming to England, she'd missed the Continent.

"It's too much to take in."

Imogen shot her a narrow-eyed look. "Don't go all proud and self-sacrificing and say you won't take it. Eliot and I both want to do this – and I owe you so much. I know Papa bullies you and I haven't always been the most considerate of cousins, but I think of you as a sister. While I have a say in her future, my sister shall never be a pauper."

Stella blinked away tears. She'd cried so much over the last fortnight that her eyes stung. But this time, she cried because Imogen and Eliot's gift moved her so deeply.

"You know," she said in a raspy voice, "I should tell you that I can't accept this wonderful offer. But I'm not going to. You're giving me the chance at a life of my own, and only a fool would say no. Thank you so much. I'm overwhelmed."

"Really?" Imogen regarded her wide-eyed. "I don't have to beg you to take the money?"

Stella shook her head. "No. I'm just grateful from the bottom of my heart. I must thank Eliot, too. Neither of you had to do this, and I'll never forget how you came to my rescue."

Imogen laughed. "You'll embarrass him. You know how he shies away from emotional demonstrations."

"He's just going to have to put up with it." Gray's loss was a seeping wound that Stella feared would never heal, but setting her own agenda for the future might offer some fragment of salvation.

"Thank you, thank you, thank you." She caught Imogen in a fervent hug.

When they drew apart, they were both teary. A soggy little giggle escaped Imogen, as she wiped her eyes. "I'm making a return on ten years of uncomplaining devotion. Will you please stay for the rest of the season? I'm not quite ready to send you off into your new life yet."

Stella fought back the urge to protest. After what Imogen had just done for her, it would be ungracious to complain about a few more weeks in London, no matter what pain it promised her.

"I'll stay. I imagine it will take a little while to make the financial arrangements anyway." While every minute of every day honed the agony of living without Gray. Her only hope of finding peace was going far away to some place where she'd never see or hear of the licentious earl. Thanks to Imogen and Eliot, she might soon make that a reality.

Imogen looked very pleased with herself. "Eliot plans to see his bankers over the next couple of days. Unless there's some hiccup, you'll be a woman of means by the end of next week."

A woman of means. The words settled in Stella's mind as if they belonged there. She'd always been poor, although in Naples that hadn't mattered so much until after her parents died. But Gray was right to call her proud. Her spirit died a little, every time her uncle treated her as a useless burden on his resources, even while he wrung as much work out of her as he could.

And she'd feared what would happen once Imogen married, as she was sure to do. Hamble Park with nobody but her overbearing uncle for company would be unendurable.

Now she didn't have to stay with Deerforth. She drew a breath that tasted of freedom. It wasn't the freedom that she'd known as Gray's brazen lover, but it was freedom all the same.

"I like the sound of that," she said, feeling a shred of genuine hope for the first time in years. When she laughed, she heard sheer relief in the sound. "I don't know how I'll ever be able to repay you."

Imogen went back to looking solemn. "It's actually me repaying you. I love Papa, but I loathe how he exploits you. While you haven't said anything, I know you loathe it, too. Yet you've never taken that out on me. That would have been so easy for you to do."

"You weren't at fault." Appalled, Stella regarded her cousin. "You must know that I..."

The door slammed open, and Lord Deerforth barged in. "Imogen, Lord Halston has sent in his card. He's here to ask for your hand. Go upstairs at once and make yourself presentable."

CHAPTER TWENTY

Halston here? To propose to Imogen?

Stella felt all the blood drain from her face. The room receded down a long, black tunnel. She couldn't breathe.

A sharp sting wrenched her back to the present, and she dragged air into her starved lungs. Dazed eyes glanced down to see bloodied crescent marks on her skin.

Imogen had dug her fingernails into Stella's hand to remind her that she couldn't break down. She was grateful. If she'd fainted at such news, even a man as blind to emotional undercurrents as her uncle would ask questions.

Imogen must have guessed that she was in control of herself, because she released her hand. "Papa, are you sure?"

Stella ignored the worried glance that Imogen cast her. She'd regained her composure, even if beneath her surface calmness, she felt like she was dying.

Oh, Gray...

She stamped down the memory of all they'd been to each other, because it turned out that everything had been a lie. Just as when he'd disclaimed any interest in her cousin, he'd lied.

The hurt cut too deep to comprehend yet. Too deep for anger. Too deep for tears, which was lucky, given her uncle was only a few feet away. Although she was grimly aware that when she contemplated Gray's last betrayal, her agony would make the misery of these past two weeks seem like a stroll in Hyde Park.

Lord Deerforth was in such a lather that he couldn't stand still. "Of course I'm sure, girl. Don't dawdle down here talking nonsense. Once his lordship has obtained my consent, he'll want to talk to you. You're to be looking your best and back in this drawing room in twenty minutes."

"Papa—" Imogen began, but her father spoke over her as he targeted Stella with a hostile glance.

"You, go up with Imogen and make sure she's ready."

Her uncle always avoided addressing her by name when he could. For once, Stella was too preoccupied to resent the clumsy slight.

"But I'm not—" Imogen began.

Again Deerforth ignored her. "For God's sake, I've spoken. I expect you to obey."

Marching forward, he hauled Imogen to her feet. A ruthless hand steered her toward the open door and down the corridor.

Stella rose and, feeling like lead weighted her feet, followed. What else could she do?

When they entered the large front hall, Gray was passing his hat to the butler. He was always dressed *comme il faut,* but today he was like a plate from a fashion magazine, with his crisp white linen and his dark blue coat that fitted him to the inch. Stella's heart gave an agonized thump, as she strove to discern some outer sign of the corruption in his soul. If a man who played this heinous trick on her could even own a soul.

It had been a game to describe him as satanic. She hadn't known how right she was.

As the butler left, Gray looked up. His gaze went straight to Stella.

She felt like someone hit her with a club. Her fists clenched so tight at her sides that the nails dug into her palms. After today, her hands would be in shreds.

Those green eyes had stared into hers when he was so deep inside her that she felt like she and Gray became one person. They still seemed to promise allegiance. What a fool she was. He was a rake. She'd always known that. If she'd stopped to think, she should have run a hundred miles before going to his bed.

Imogen dropped into a polite curtsy as Deerforth released her, trying not to look as though he'd had to drag his daughter here. Stella couldn't call up the will to curtsy. She was lucky that her uncle was so fixed on Gray, he didn't notice her rudeness.

"My dear Halston, I'm delighted to see you," he said with overly hearty good humor that had Gray wincing. How was it that Stella could read him with such ease, when it turned out she'd misjudged him so disastrously this whole time?

"Deerforth," he said with a coldness that surprised her. He'd have to curb his dislike for Imogen's father, if he intended to make her his bride. He made a brief bow. "Can you spare me a few minutes? I have something important I wish to discuss with you."

"Ho ho," Deerforth said with such bonhomie that this time Stella wanted to wince. "It's about this little minx, my daughter, I have no doubt. Dear Imogen wants to go upstairs and primp before you pay your addresses. But she'll be waiting in the drawing room, once you and I settle the details."

If Stella had been capable of laughter at that moment, she'd have laughed. Imogen and Gray's faces both froze in horror. Aghast, they stared at Deerforth.

"Papa—" Imogen started.

"My lord, you mistake me." Gray's voice turned even colder. "Your daughter is very charming, and I'm sure she'll make some fortunate fellow a wonderful wife. But that fortunate fellow isn't me. I'm here to request your niece's hand in marriage."

For the second time that day, Stella's head started to swim. Through the mists in her head, she felt Imogen's hand curl around her arm to keep her upright.

Thank heaven. Her legs threatened to fold beneath her. When she read about heroines in books collapsing in a heap from shock, it always seemed unrealistic. But at this moment, she felt just as ready to faint as any gormless maiden in a romantic story.

The smugness leached from Deerforth's face, leaving bafflement in its place. He goggled at Gray as if his words made no sense. "My niece?"

"Yes, your niece." Gray cast Stella another quick glance, but she was too shaken by the sudden switch from absolute devastation to burgeoning hope. She couldn't summon a response. "I'm going to ask Miss Faulkner to marry me. As you've been her guardian since her parents passed away and she lives in your house, I felt it only polite to inform you of my intentions."

Surprise cracked the jovial mask that Deerforth wore in public. He flushed bright red as his temper erupted. "What bloody twaddle is this? You've been courting my daughter since you were introduced at the Lumsden ball. You called. You sent flowers.

What about inviting her to that damned house party? You made your intentions clear then."

Gray retained his urbanity. The angrier Deerforth became, the more the power in the room seemed to flow toward Gray. "I'm sorry for any misunderstanding." He didn't sound at all sorry. "I've never courted your daughter. I've been courting your niece. The house party was designed to further my suit with Miss Faulkner. As she and Lady Imogen are so close, it was natural to include her in the invitation."

Stella saw her uncle struggle to make sense of what was happening. "Look here, Halston, this joke has gone far enough."

"This is no joke, sir." Gray didn't smile. In fact, Stella had returned to herself enough to see that he battled with anger of his own. "I'm here to propose to Miss Faulkner. As she's of age, obtaining your consent to the union is a mere formality. Miss Faulkner's acceptance is all I require."

Deerforth was too incensed to hide his reaction. A deep rumble of rage emerged as he whirled on Stella. His meaty fist bunched with unmistakable intent. "You sneaky little bitch."

"Papa, don't!" Imogen cried out, darting in front of Stella.

"Get out of the way, girl!" Deerforth snarled, shoving his daughter aside.

Stella recoiled and closed her eyes as she waited for the blow to land.

Nothing happened.

When she dared to look, Gray grasped Deerforth's wrist in an unrelenting hold. "My lord, if you lay one finger on Miss Faulkner, I'll ignore the fact that you're older than I am and not in fighting shape, and I'll beat you to a pulp."

Stella sucked in a relieved breath as she straightened. Now that her terror subsided, she felt the beginnings of elation. Gray was here to take her away and to make her his wife. She could hardly believe it.

Deerforth's bulk, usually so menacing, looked like weakness compared to Gray's whipcord strength. Nobody in this room could doubt how any scuffle would finish.

"Unhand me, sir," Deerforth snarled.

"Not until I have your word as a gentleman..." Gray snapped off the word with savage irony. "...that you will control yourself."

For a horrid moment, Stella wondered if Deerforth's rage would win out against wisdom. She had no doubt of the depth of her uncle's fury. Even worse, he was a man very sensitive of his dignity, and everyone in the hall knew that he'd made a complete fool of himself in making assumptions about Gray's purpose in calling.

Imogen edged toward Stella, as if she remained unsure of the outcome, too.

After a bristling silence, the madness receded from Deerforth's face, if not the anger. He jerked his hand out of Gray's hold and glared at Stella as though he hated her.

He'd always hated her, she realized with weary acceptance. Her mother had turned her back on her family and brought scandal to the Ridley name. Now that her mother was gone, Deerforth transferred all his bitter resentment to the only part of her mother that remained, her daughter.

"Get out of my house, you traitorous cow. I curse you and this cobbled-together match. Not that I need to wish you ill fortune. You're wedding a swine whose name is synonymous with lechery. He's a disgrace to his title, and if you imagine he'll change once a ring is on your finger, you're an even bigger fool than I thought."

Stella's eyes met Gray's, and she gave an imperceptible shake of her head. There was no point mentioning that until a few minutes ago, Deerforth had been beside himself with glee at the prospect of entrusting his only daughter to Gray's care.

"My lord, I'll take my leave," Gray said with a politeness that was an insult in itself. "You appear indisposed."

"Yes, go. To hell for all I care," Deerforth snarled. "And take your whore with you. Because I've no doubt she's already crawled into your bed. She's a harlot just like her mother."

Gray went white, and that muscle kicked in his cheek. Stella had no doubt that he was an inch away from making good on his threats. For her part, her uncle's insults had lost their power the moment that she realized she no longer needed to stay under his control.

"Lord Deerforth, I'd button my lip, if I were you," Gray snapped. "Or I'll be obliged to meet you on the field of honor. I'd regret starting my married life with putting a bullet into my wife's uncle, no matter how unworthy you are of that title."

Deerforth went back to goggling, although this time, there was fear as well as rage in his reaction. Gray was famous as a crack shot, while Stella had long ago recognized that her uncle was a coward. She stepped forward to place one hand on Gray's arm, to remind him that violence at this juncture would do more harm than good.

"There's nothing to be gained from staying." It was the first time she'd touched him in a week and despite this horrid scene, something troubled and uncertain inside her settled at the contact. "I'd count myself privileged to come with you, Gray."

"I'll help you pack, Stella," Imogen said.

Deerforth's eyes glittered with spite. "The slut came to me with nothing. By God, she'll leave me with nothing."

Stella saw that Imogen wanted to protest at this last unworthy act of vengeance. Again she shook her head.

"Goodbye, Imogen." She thought back to that terrifying moment when she'd waited for her uncle's fist to smash into her and how Imogen had placed herself in the way. "You make me proud to be your cousin."

"You'll have nothing more to do with this woman, Imogen." Deerforth's pomposity revived, now he realized that he'd escaped a duel with Gray. "As far as this family's concerned, she's dead."

Again, Stella sent Imogen a warning glance to stay silent. Then she looked up at Gray and found it in her to smile. Because however disagreeable this confrontation had been, one truth remained paramount. She was going to spend the rest of her life with the man she loved. "Gray, take me away and make me your wife."

When he smiled back, the glow in his eyes made her heart expand with love. He was the man for her. Whatever happened now, they'd always be together. She'd live in his house, she'd bear his children, she'd carry his name.

It was more than she'd ever dreamed of.

"With pleasure, my darling."

Ignoring a livid, wheezing Deerforth, Gray took her arm and escorted her from her uncle's house. She went with a light step that echoed the joy filling her heart.

Stella had wondered how she'd live without Gray. Now she didn't have to.

CHAPTER TWENTY-ONE

*H*alston handed Stella up into his stylish yellow curricle and nodded to the footman who held the high-spirited bays that were the envy of every horse-mad aristocrat in London. As Halston leaped into the seat, the man released the horses' heads. With a click of his tongue, the vehicle rolled away at a smart pace.

"I wish I'd brought a closed carriage," he said, smiling down at Stella who looked dazed, as though she wasn't sure what world she inhabited right now. Having said that, she curled her fingers around his arm and nestled her hip up against his in a most satisfactory fashion.

She glanced at him. Nor was she the only person glancing at him. As he bowled along the edge of Lorimer Square, heads turned in their direction. He didn't miss the curiosity in every face. As they passed the house where he'd met Stella in that chilly gazebo, he raised his whip to acknowledge Lord Lumsden's bow.

"I'm sorry I'm not dressed to be seen in public. I'm not even wearing a bonnet, for heaven's sake.

But you rather took us all by surprise when you arrived on the doorstep."

A grunt of laughter escaped. "I don't give a rat's arse what you're wearing, you delightful creature. But I can't kiss you out here on the street, and I have a burning desire to kiss you."

"Oh," she said on a squeak of pleasure and snuggled closer into his side. Her warmth seeped into him, when he hadn't been warm since she left his bed.

The garden in the middle of the square had burst into blossom in the last few weeks. He couldn't help feeling that his life was about to burgeon in a similar way, although he was yet to make his formal proposal.

They turned at the top of the square and passed the dark bulk of Fleetwood House with its overgrown grounds, also bright with flowers. "I want to kiss you, too," Stella murmured, smiling with such joy that it was almost as good as kissing her.

"Just as you should." He steered through heavier traffic, now they were out of the square. "But I'm at something of a loss. I imagined I'd see your uncle and gain his consent. Once I had that, I'd present my case to you, and I hoped to have a chance to kiss you then. I hadn't planned on an elopement."

Stella's laugh veered perilously close to a giddy giggle, although she was a woman who didn't in general giggle. A wry chuckle was more her style. A sign that she was beside herself. Halston hoped it was with happiness. Because he was beside himself, too, which after the last desolate weeks felt rather strange.

"So are we on our way to Scotland?" she asked with impressive calmness. "If we are, we'll need to stop somewhere to go shopping. I don't have as much as a spare handkerchief with me."

Halston was still smiling, just so damn glad to have her beside him once more. He felt like he'd suffered through an eon without her. "We can manage that."

"I don't even have your handkerchief, although I've slept with it under my pillow every night since you gave it to me."

Distracted, he shifted his eyes from the road. "You kept that?"

"I did. I think you should watch where you're going."

By the dickens, she had him in a complete spin. He pulled the horses back from near collision with a loaded dray. "I'm...I'm overwhelmed to know that you kept my handkerchief."

"Are you fit to drive to Gretna?"

"I hope so, although I wasn't thinking of taking you as far as that."

She studied him, her eyes the golden color they went when she was in the grip of deep emotion. "So where are you taking me?"

He paused and gave a startled laugh. "Devil if I know. I can't propose to you in an open carriage in the middle of Piccadilly. And I can't bear to wait to hold you in my arms."

"Hyde Park? It shouldn't be busy at this time of day."

Still too public. He shot her a questioning glance. "I can take you to Maddox House, at least until we work out where we go from here. It has the advantage of only being five minutes away."

He waited for her to say that would cause talk, although he had a suspicion that they'd already sparked a storm of gossip. Deerforth's bellows of outrage had been loud enough to reach Newcastle. His insults to Stella must have traveled to every corner of the house, including downstairs. The servants wouldn't keep such juicy tattle to themselves.

For himself, Halston didn't care, but Stella had always been so careful with her reputation. Although once she became the Countess of Halston, she'd have the cachet to weather any amount of gossip.

"That sounds perfect."

Startled, he turned to her. "Really?"

"Really." The glance she cast him under her gold-tipped lashes reminded him that it was far too long since he'd made love to her. "You're not alone in appreciating a little privacy."

"Let's go, then," he said, urging the horses to a faster pace along the busy street.

Stella paid no attention to the splendors of Gray's London house. All the way from Lorimer Square, his nearness had tantalized her. The tangy scent that had filled her dreams since she returned to London. The heat of his body crushed so close to hers on the narrow seat. Those strong, skillful hands that she burned to feel on her skin once again. All she cared about was finding a place where he could take her into his arms and transport her to the paradise that she'd thought lost forever.

A butler opened the door to them, as a groom drove the carriage away. Gray murmured instructions that she didn't hear over the blood thundering in her ears, before he led her down a corridor to a well-stocked library. She felt as if she floated a foot off the ground. Nothing seemed real, apart from the warm grip of his hand on hers.

He closed the door and prowled across the room to sweep her up for a fervent kiss that claimed her forever. She sighed approval for that idea against his lips and kissed him back, making her own demands.

By the time he came up for air, she was no longer the sad, frozen creature of these last weeks. She didn't even feel like the repressed companion that she'd played since leaving Italy. Instead, she felt like a woman who had found the place she belonged.

That place was at Gray's side.

"Stop looking at me like that, or I'll do something to shock the servants," he growled.

Her laugh was breathless. She still felt shaky and floaty and melty after that kiss. "Isn't that the idea?"

He groaned and closed his eyes. "Don't tempt me." He gestured to the sofa near the tall windows. "Sit down, please. I have something to say to you."

If he meant to ask her to marry him, he must know she'd consent. On the other hand, she'd love to hear his proposal and have a chance to say yes.

She stepped out of his arms and sank onto the sofa, her gaze never wavering from his beloved face. "I'm listening."

As she folded her hands in her lap, her heart danced. Since they'd parted, she'd been so wretched. She could hardly believe that she never had to leave him again.

Stella waited for Gray to sit beside her or perhaps fall to his knees. That would be too romantic for words.

To her puzzlement, he began to pace. It took her a few moments to realize that the worldly earl was eaten up with nerves. That pleased her, too. It showed that he didn't take her for granted.

After another few seconds, she decided to put him out of his misery. "I'm guessing you want to ask me to marry you. At least that's what you told my uncle. Or did that awful scene make you change your mind?"

"Don't be a nitwit, darling." He shot her a searing glare. "I'll never change my mind."

Some tiny niggle of uncertainty vanished, and she feared that her smile made her look completely besotted. Of course it did. She was completely besotted. "Then there's no need to worry about my answer. You must know it's going to be yes."

For a fleeting instant, incandescent joy lit his features before he frowned again. "That's capital. But I've got something else to tell you first."

Her hands tightened around each other. "That sounds like you're about to make a dreadful confession."

He stopped prowling across the carpet like a caged tiger and forked one hand through his glossy black hair, leaving him looking ruffled. Her devoted heart turned over at how beautiful he was. "I am."

This time, she didn't respond, despite the curiosity that gnawed at her.

He sucked in a ragged breath and stepped closer. "I've spent my life believing that love was nothing but manipulation and wishful thinking."

Love? The word thundered through her and made her go rigid.

He went on in the gruff voice that she'd learned betrayed his strongest feelings. "Then I met you, and everything I thought I knew turned out to be wrong. Those days at Prestwick Place were the happiest of my life. You make me happy, Stella. Since you left me, I haven't experienced a second of happiness. I might be a slow learner, but I get there in the end. I fell in love with you the moment I saw you, a thoroughbred trying to disappear into a crowd of cart horses. You with your stern expression and burning eyes and no time for a profligate wastrel like the Earl of Halston. Every day since then, I've come to love you more."

Gray paused as if waiting for her to say something, but she was too thunderstruck to utter a single word. He inhaled and squared his shoulders. "I wanted you. I still want you. I'll die wanting you. But you need to know that when I told you that I believed love was an illusion, I was a foul liar. Because I loved you then, and I love you now. If you become my wife, you need to know that you're marrying a man who worships the very ground you walk on."

Transfixed, Stella sat on the couch, striving to make sense of what he told her. It was all so far from anything that she'd ever imagined him saying.

He went on more calmly, although his tone remained urgent. "If we wed, it's forever. It's you and I, and only you and I, and whatever children the good Lord deigns to send us. I fear I'm going to be grumpy and possessive and mad for my wife, to the point where I make a spectacle of myself."

She swallowed, as she came to the astonished conclusion that he feared she mightn't love him back. When she'd been sick with love for him for as long, she now gathered, as he'd loved her.

She separated her hands and buried them in her dark blue skirts. "So you're saying," she began slowly, "that you love me, and you mean to be faithful, and that we're going to have a passionate marriage."

He made an incoherent sound deep in his throat. "Are you up for it?"

Silly man, that he even had to ask. She blinked away tears. She'd hoped that her crying days were finished, but it seemed that they weren't. "I'm sure I'll find a way to cope."

He held himself very straight, and the heat in his eyes threatened to set her alight. Overmastering emotion had him in its grip. At the Tierney ball, he'd looked at the edge of his control. He looked even more on edge now.

He regarded her down his long nose and when he spoke, his voice shook with the force of his feelings. "I love you, Stella."

He loved her...

"Well, that's altogether a good thing, Gray." She rose on wobbly legs. The tears she thought that she'd left behind thickened her voice. "Because I love you, too. More than you can ever know."

For a long moment, he regarded her as though he didn't believe her. Then he covered the gap between them in a single stride and kissed her as if he never meant to let her go.

A passionate interlude later, Stella drew away from Gray and regarded him with the adoration that she no longer needed to hide. They were sitting on the couch, entwined in each other's arms. "I had no idea you loved me."

"I was yours from the start." He frowned. "For weeks, I've only been able to think about you."

"Oh, I knew that," she said easily. "But I assumed that was a result of excessive masculine urges."

Genuine surprise rang in his laugh. "Did you indeed? I see I need to convince you that you've turned me into a romantic."

She kissed him again and shaped his jaw with one hand. "Don't change too much. I love the rogue in you. He's so exciting."

"I'll have to be a romantic rogue, then." To her regret, he drew away. "Now, I was in the middle of something important before your rude interruption."

She cast Gray a saucy look. "I'm not sure you got around to starting."

"That's enough out of you." With a rueful laugh, he stood. "I believe I was about to ask you to marry me."

"I'd forgotten about that," she said, her heart swelling until it threatened to explode out of her chest. Her voice lowered to throbbing sincerity. "All I ever wanted to hear, right from the start, was that you loved me."

When he smiled at her, the love that she'd never allowed herself to hope for shone in his eyes. "I'll always love you, and because that's the case, I want to make it official. If I'd been less distracted by how much I wanted you, I'd have realized weeks ago that the obvious solution to our dilemma was to put a ring on your finger."

It was Stella's turn to frown. "You know if we marry, it will cause talk. The ton won't consider me a suitable Countess of Halston."

"Bugger the ton."

That should have made her laugh, but she wanted Gray to understand that his choice of bride wouldn't receive universal acclaim. "You're a great catch, and great catches usually marry sweet little virgins of impeccable lineage and large fortune. I'm poor, and my family have disowned me, and as you very well know, I'm no virgin. Nor am I eighteen."

His snort dismissed her qualms. "What the devil would I do with a pretty little poppet who's sure to faint at the thought of bedding a man? A chit with no conversation and no fire and no worldly experience. I've made my choice, and it makes me happy. You're the one for me, Stella. You always have been. That makes you the most suitable Countess of Halston in the world. We can weather a bit of scandal. Once we're wed, I intend to hurry you back to Prestwick Place and take you to bed for the next twenty years anyway. Society will have forgotten about us by the time we emerge and come back to London."

She gave a shaky laugh. "Twenty years?"

"At least."

Then to her amazement and gratification, Gray fell to one knee before her. He took her trembling hand and stared at her with his heart in his eyes.

Shocked, she realized that he'd always stared at her with his heart in his eyes. She should never have taken his word for it when he described himself as incapable of love.

"My darling, will you make me the happiest man in the world and say you'll be my wife?"

Drat these annoying tears. Moisture prickled her eyes again, and her eager acceptance jammed in a throat that was tight with emotion. The best she could do was grip his fingers in hers and nod.

He smiled and kissed her with a tenderness that only made her more waterlogged.

By the time he raised his head, she'd located her voice, even if a thready version of it. "I'd be ecstatic to marry you, Gray. I love you."

That brought on more kissing, and she was breathless when she broke away at last. "What happens now?"

Gray was back beside her on the sofa. He drew a small green leather box decorated with gold tooling from his pocket. "Now I produce the ring."

Stella couldn't hide how impressed she was. "You're prepared."

His wry smile set deep creases in his cheeks and made him breathtakingly attractive. She told herself that if she kissed him again, they'd be here all day. And she very much wanted to feel Gray's ring on her finger.

"I am. I even have a special license in the top drawer of my desk. That's going to come in handy, now we have to marry in a hurry to avoid a scandal."

"You said you don't care about scandal."

"I don't. But you do. And as you said, the less trouble we're in, the better things will turn out for Imogen. I've become very fond of Imogen. I was very fond of her indeed, when she tried to protect you from Deerforth." As Gray clicked the box open, he glanced up at her. "This isn't the time to talk about your cousin. This is the time to concentrate on us. We can marry tomorrow, if you like."

Stella's head was whirling and not just from his intoxicating kisses. She'd woken this morning, convinced that only sorrow awaited. Now before the week was out, she was going to marry the man she loved. No wonder she felt giddy. "I like."

"Until then, I need to send you to a hotel. I'll get one of the maids up from downstairs to go with you."

Disappointment flooded her. "I can't stay here?"

"I want to do things right." His laugh held a self-mocking note. "As it is, we shouldn't be alone together for too long. There's one compensation. After the ceremony, I'll have you to myself, and nobody will raise an eyebrow."

Stella realized that somewhere since the Lumsden ball, the romantic had definitely overtaken the rogue. When he looked at her as he looked at her now, she didn't mind a bit.

Gray went on. "I'm beginning to wish I'd cultivated some respectable connections. What we need is an older lady of impeccable reputation to take you in, until I make you my bride. I'd assumed you'd stay with Deerforth until we married, but his theatrics render that impossible."

Stella frowned in thought. "You know, Lady Lumsden said that if ever I needed somewhere to go, she'd give me a home. She and Mamma were great friends. Perhaps she'd be willing to lend her consequence to the wedding. It would silence some of the talk."

"That's a good idea. I'll write her a note and ask if I can take you over there." He paused. "But first I have something important to do." He withdrew the ring from the box and caught her hand. "I want the world to know you're mine, Stella. Forever."

By the time he slid a spectacular sapphire onto her finger, they were both shaking.

"Forever," she echoed, as he bent to kiss the ring that symbolized a lifetime of happiness to come.

EPILOGUE

Three days later

Halston shouldered his way into his apartments at Prestwick Place. In his arms, his bride of twelve hours clung to him with pleasing eagerness.

After lingering to kiss Stella, he set her on her feet. He was glad to see that his instructions had been carried out to the letter. Every flat surface supported a vase of flowers, with lilies predominating, and a bottle of champagne cooled on the sideboard.

She glanced around in wonder. "It's just like the first time."

He smiled, glad that she remembered. "The third happiest day of my life."

She shot him an unimpressed look. "Tact should put it further up the list, even if you're not being altogether honest."

He laughed, in part because he was just so bloody topsy-turvy with elation. "Today is the second happiest day of my life."

"Better."

"And the happiest day of my life was the day you told me you love me." He watched her face soften into one of her adoring smiles, and he caught her around the waist as he stepped closer.

"I love it when you say such sentimental things."

His smile broadened. "That's good, because I'll warrant that there's a lifetime of them ahead."

More kisses and feverish caresses and sighs of pleasure, before her thick hair tumbled around her face. He caught her head in his hands and surveyed her, hardly able to believe that she was his at last. "Did I tell you that you were a vision today?"

After that rain of kisses, she looked dazzled. "You may tell me again."

Her gown came from Madame Lisette, Lady Lumsden's London modiste. The rich purple silk was the perfect complement to Stella's leonine beauty.

Lady Lumsden had proven a great support through these hectic days since Stella had accepted his proposal. Halston wanted to get married the day after he stole Stella away from Deerforth's house, until Lady Lumsden had protested that his bride couldn't walk up the aisle, wearing one of Imogen's castoffs. Thanks to Deerforth's spite, Stella didn't own anything else either, not even a hairbrush.

To Halston's surprise, while Lady Lumsden had offered to pay for everything, the savior of the hour ended up being Eliot Ridley, Viscount Colville. Imogen got word to him about the stormy scene that resulted in Stella's banishment from the family. He immediately offered to buy Stella's new wardrobe, including her wedding dress, and had supplied her with a generous dowry as well. Despite Halston telling him that he'd take Stella in her petticoat and still consider himself the luckiest man in England.

This morning, Eliot had walked up the aisle with Stella, so she'd even had a member of her family at her wedding. Halston was sorry that Imogen couldn't be there, but as the scandal had spread, Deerforth had packed her off back to Gloucestershire. It seemed that he'd boasted a little too often and a little too loudly that his daughter would be the next Countess of Halston.

Halston had never had much to do with Viscount Colville. Eliot had always seemed too much the proper gentleman to associate with a dissolute libertine like him. Now he looked forward to establishing a friendship with his cousin by marriage.

With reluctance, Gray released Stella. "You should feel right at home."

The humor he loved lit her caramel eyes. "At least today I came through the door and not via the mistresses' corridor."

He laughed. "We'll have to call it something else, now that you're my wife."

"The rathole?"

He laughed again. Stella had told him about Imogen's horror at the idea of vermin infesting Prestwick Place. "The path to love?"

"Oh, Gray," she said and melted into his arms again. By the time he came back to earth, his coat and neckcloth lay crumpled on the floor and the back of that fiendishly becoming gown gaped open.

"Would you like some champagne? Or perhaps you're hungry?"

"After that good dinner on the road? How could I be?"

The wedding had taken place this morning in the church where the Lumsdens worshipped in Mayfair. Which also happened to be the congregation that Stella had joined in London.

The vicar had been cooperative about arranging a quick ceremony. A small number of guests attended. The Lumsdens and their children. Eliot. A couple of Halston's oldest friends and their wives.

After the wedding, Lady Lumsden had hosted a gathering at her house in Lorrimer Square. For Stella and Halston, that location had a special and very private significance. After all, it was where they'd met.

Over the last few days, while Stella was occupied with seamstresses and shopping, Halston had put some thought into where to take her for their wedding night. Maddox House was a possibility, as was a hotel, or perhaps somewhere beside the sea. In the end, the most obvious choice was Prestwick Place, where they'd found such joy and where they'd fallen in love with each other.

So they'd traveled down to Buckinghamshire in a much more luxurious closed carriage than that ramshackle horror where he first kissed her.

"Are you tired?"

More wry amusement. "Gray, it's more than a fortnight since we shared a bed. I don't want wine. I don't want food. I don't want to discuss the weather. I just want you."

It was his turn to stare at her, lost in enchantment. "Stella, I love you."

"And I love you. Very much. Let's do something about it."

She didn't need to ask him twice. With rough hands, he hauled his shirt over his head. Then he sat and ripped off his shoes, so he could remove his trousers. Only when he was naked did he realize that his bride hadn't shifted from the middle of the room.

"What the devil game are you playing, my love?"

With a delicious gurgle of laughter, she made a helpless gesture. "I'm congratulating myself on what a fine figure of a man I married." She strolled around him, studying him with a concentration that made Halston's skin tighten with a heady mixture of arousal and self-consciousness. "I wonder if I can arrange for Canova to carve a statue of you for the great hall."

"Naked?"

"That's when you appear at your best."

He gulped to moisten a dry throat. His growing excitement was clear for Stella to see. "It might turn our visitors off their afternoon tea."

She trailed her hand down his spine to squeeze his buttocks. "It might incite the ladies of the neighborhood to kidnap you."

The bold caress was too much for his fragile restraint. Because she wasn't alone in finding these past weeks excruciating. His love wasn't based on physical desire alone, but carnal pleasure was an important part of it.

"I'd fight free and come back to you, my darling," he said in a hoarse voice.

She released an excited gasp, as Halston swung her high into his arms. He carried her across to the huge bed, where he'd discovered what magic he and Stella could conjure together.

After he set her against the covers, he descended to kiss every part of her that he could reach. He shoved aside her dress, nipped at the top of her breasts, scraped his teeth over the sensitive nerves of her neck, until she was panting and digging her fingers into his shoulders.

He shoved up her skirts and petticoats and ripped at the frail cambric drawers beneath. When his hand cupped her mound, they both sighed in relief. He could smell her excitement and when he stroked her between the legs, he discovered slick heat.

Stella kissed him hard and pulled away to meet his eyes. Hers had deepened to the color of peaty whisky.

"Don't wait." Her voice rasped with need. "I want you now."

"My beloved wife…" he sighed, as he slid forward to join his body to hers.

She gave a piercing cry and spasmed into immediate climax. He gripped her hips and angled her so he penetrated further. Like Stella, he was too desperate to make this a leisurely loving.

They'd have a chance to linger and tease later. Hell, they had a lifetime ahead to explore the outer boundaries of bliss. Right now, Halston just needed this most profound and irresistible expression of his commitment to his wife.

He thrust once, twice. Then while she was still in the throes of ecstasy, he lost himself on a long groan. For the first time, his seed flooded Stella's womb.

As the shudders receded, he slumped exhausted against her. Halston came back from that incandescent pleasure to find her touching his back. Each glide of her hands claimed him as hers.

He didn't mind. He was hers. He was hers until the day he died.

"Am I squashing you?" he forced out of a throat constricted with overwhelming love.

When he and Stella came together, it was never just a matter of fleshly satisfaction. He should have known that he was in hot water from their first time together. But this furious, intimate, explosive union just now had been so soaked in poignant emotion, it surpassed even those earlier rapturous encounters.

Stella was his wife, his countess. She'd bear his children. They'd grow old together. What they'd just done contained a profundity that he'd never experienced before.

Her hands continued to drift across his skin. "No, I like it."

Halston lay still a little longer, then rolled to the side, rising on one elbow to survey his bride. "For pity's sake, I was in such a hurry that I didn't even undress you."

She smiled up at him. "You can do that next time." Suddenly she stretched out on the mattress and laughed up at the ceiling. Her voice rang with such happiness that he couldn't help smiling. "In fact, I'm the Countess of Halston, and I order you to undress me. No dillydallying about it, my good man."

He laughed, too. How he loved her spirit. Hell, how he just loved her.

"That would be my great pleasure, my lady." Hope for a glorious future with his precious wife flooded Halston's heart, as he reached to undo the last fastenings on her splendid wedding dress.

ABOUT THE AUTHOR

Australian Anna Campbell has written 11 multi award-winning historical romances for Avon HarperCollins and Grand Central Publishing. As an independently published author, she's released more than 30 bestselling stories. Right now, she is working on a new series called Scoundrels of Mayfair, set amidst the glamour and sensuality of Regency London. Anna has won numerous awards for her stories, including RT Book Reviews Reviewers Choice, the Booksellers Best, the Golden Quill (three times), the Heart of Excellence (twice), the Write Touch, the Aspen Gold (twice), and the Australian Romance Readers' favorite historical romance (five times).

Anna loves to hear from her readers. You can find her at:

Website: www.annacampbell.com

facebook.com/AnnaCampbellFans

twitter.comAnnaCampbellOz

bookbub.com/authors/anna-campbell

One Wicked Wish:
A Scandal in Mayfair Book 1

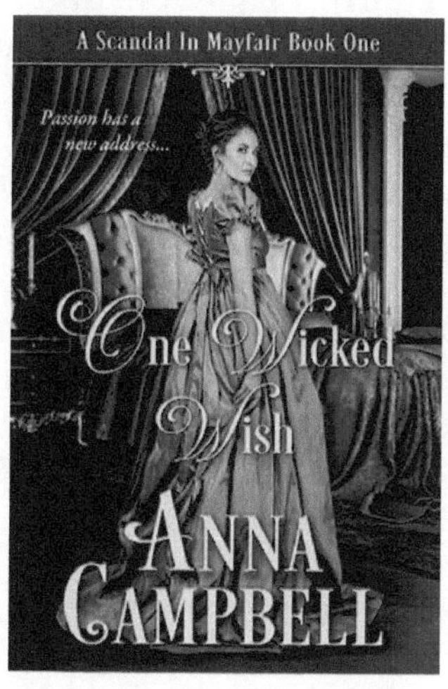

Her secret lover...

Stella Faulkner has been a despised poor relation in her odious uncle's house since she was forced to flee Italy ahead of Napoleon's invasion. In return for a roof over her head, she acts as her cousin's unpaid governess and companion. Stella knows that if she shows the slightest trace of her disgraced mother's wildness, she'll be cast out to face destitution. But after ten years of thankless servitude, Stella encounters a dashing libertine who turns her world to flame. Handsome Lord Halston is irresistible, but every kiss, every caress carries the risk of discovery, and with discovery, disaster.

The rake beguiled…

Grayson Maddox, Earl of Halston, glories in his reputation for charm, seduction, and ruthlessness. His mistresses know that the profligate lord offers them pleasure and luxury, but when he says goodbye, the affair is over. To Halston, love is a sentimental myth and fidelity a trap. One night at a glittering ball, he sees a beautiful woman trying to fade into the crowd of dowdy chaperones and every instinct clamors to make this mysterious lady his. But all bets are off when Stella Faulkner promises to become the lover he'll never forget.

Forbidden passion.

Halston and Stella start a sizzling affair under the cover of a respectable house party at his country estate. But once this interval of heady delight comes to an end, what will become of the humble governess and the wicked earl? Must they return to being strangers as they originally arranged, or will five days of intoxicating sin turn into forever?

Two Secret Sins:
A Scandal in Mayfair Book 2

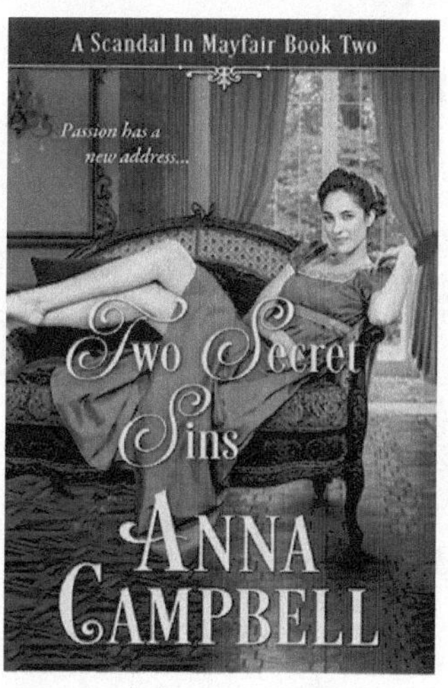

The Saint and the Sinner!

Eliot Ridley, Viscount Colville, is a man of immaculate character with lifelong ambitions to make his mark in parliament. Lady Verena Gerard is a headstrong, independent widow with a string of lovers in her scandalous past. Two people with absolutely nothing in common, apart from the irresistible desire that draws them into an explosive, secret affair.

Now Eliot is so determined to claim the reckless beauty as his own that he's ready to throw away his stainless reputation and his political hopes. What choice does Verena have when he proposes but to end the liaison? Taking a notorious woman as his wife will taint Eliot and his family, not to mention that after the brutal misery of her first marriage, she's vowed never to wed again.

Never say never.

In the glamorous, sophisticated world Eliot and Verena inhabit, wickedness thrives behind closed doors and the only unforgivable sin is falling in love. Will the handsome viscount defy society and Verena's fears to win the bride he wants? Or will Eliot and his wild lady part to follow their separate destinies and forever spurn the forbidden longing in their hearts?

Three Times Tempted:
A Scandal in Mayfair Book 3

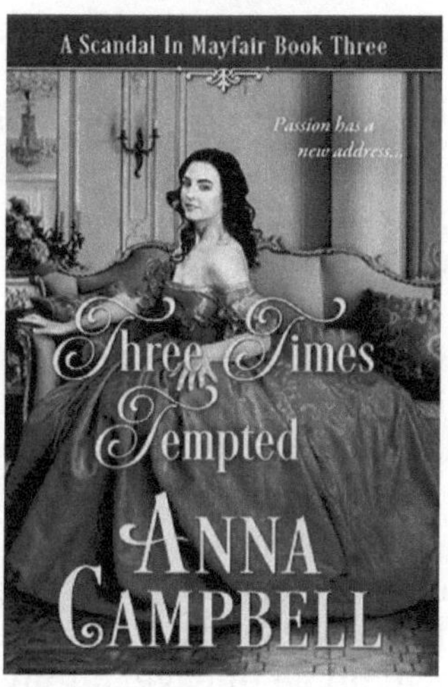

A secret rebel...

Beautiful, spirited Lady Imogen Ridley is the toast of London's glamorous season. Her blue-blooded admirers would be shocked to know that beneath her glittering veneer, she loathes society's shallow snobberies. All she wants is to return to her gardening projects in the country.

Her reckless attempt to spark a scandal that will result in a quick trip home goes awry when she meets a handsome stranger in a dark gazebo. A string of forbidden trysts follow that fateful encounter, as immediate attraction soon turns to blazing passion. But Imogen has been promised to another, and her father is powerful and ruthless. He won't tolerate any challenge to his ambitions for his daughter.

A man from a different world…

American Caleb Black finds himself at odds with England's hidebound rules. Despite his wealth and brilliance as a landscape designer, he's considered little better than a servant in status-obsessed Mayfair. So when he sets his sights on marrying the Earl of Deerforth's lovely daughter, he knows he's asking for trouble.

And trouble is exactly what he gets. Caleb needs to call on all his cleverness and determination to court his exquisite lady, let alone engineer a chance to make her his. With every secret meeting, every stolen caress, desire burns hotter, while danger and disgrace loom ever closer. Will this impossible love affair shatter the towering barriers of class and pedigree? Or will noble lineage, family duty, and centuries of tradition forever separate this man of the people from his aristocratic beloved?

Four Christmas Kisses:
A Scandal in Mayfair Book 4

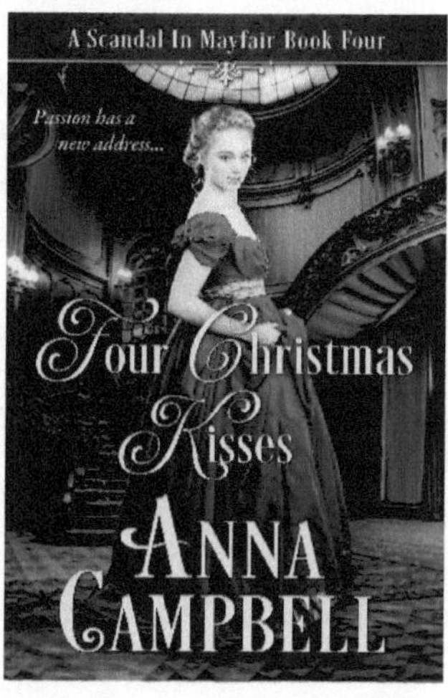

A mysterious guest at Christmas.

Spirited Anthea Bryars already has enough
problems to deal with when a few days before
Christmas, she stumbles across an unconscious
stranger in the woods. She and her half-sisters will
be homeless after New Year, now that Lord Denton
has inherited Yardley Hall and given the family
their marching orders. The last thing Anthea needs
is a handsome, smart-mouthed distraction who
makes her long for forbidden pleasures.

Secrets and passion...

After rakish Christopher Trant, Earl of Denton,
tumbles from his horse in a snowstorm, his rescuer
is the loveliest woman he's ever seen. But waking
up the next morning, he's horrified to discover that
at Yardley Hall, he's universally hated as Wicked

Cousin Christopher. He'd left London assuming the remote manor house was empty, but it turns out it's occupied by three unknown cousins and an alluring lady called Anthea. To play for time, he pretends that his injuries have stolen his memory. But one small lie leads to others, until he's so tangled in desire and deception, he doesn't know where to turn.

A season of goodwill?

Will the revelation of Christopher's identity destroy all his chances to win Anthea? Or might the magic of Christmas unite these two unlikely lovers and conjure up a bright new future for the whole family? Could four Christmas kisses mean goodbye or happy forever after.